The
ANTIQUE STORE DETECTIVE
and the
Deadly Inheritance

BOOKS BY CLARE CHASE

Bella Winter Mystery series

The Antique Store Detective

The Antique Store Detective and the May Day Murder

Tara Thorpe Mystery series

Murder on the Marshes

Death on the River

Death Comes to Call

Murder in the Fens

Eve Mallow Mystery series

Mystery on Hidden Lane

Mystery at Apple Tree Cottage

Mystery at Seagrave Hall

Mystery at the Old Mill

Mystery at the Abbey Hotel

Mystery at the Church

Mystery at Magpie Lodge

Mystery at Lovelace Manor

Mystery at Southwood School

Mystery at Farfield Castle

Mystery at Saltwater Cottages

Mystery on Meadowsweet Grove

CLARE CHASE

The ANTIQUE STORE DETECTIVE and the Deadly Inheritance

bookouture

Published by Bookouture in 2025

An imprint of Storyfire Ltd.
Carmelite House
50 Victoria Embankment
London EC4Y 0DZ

www.bookouture.com

The authorised representative in the EEA is Hachette Ireland
8 Castlecourt Centre
Dublin 15 D15 XTP3
Ireland
(email: info@hbgi.ie)

ISBN: 978-1-83618-369-3
eBook ISBN: 978-1-83618-368-6

For Mum and Dad, with much love

1

THE LAST HOURS OF CLEMMIE CROWE

It was a hot morning in July, and Bella Winter was on a clandestine mission, crossing Hope Eaton from her home by the River Kite to the western fringes of the town. Her outing was so secret, she hadn't even admitted what she was up to to John. Her second in command at her antiques shop, Vintage Winter, wouldn't approve.

She made her winding way up Boatman's Walk, past worn red-brick walls festooned with sweet-scented honeysuckle, anticipation mounting. She'd been curious about the contents of High Seat House ever since she'd met its matriarch, Althea Powell. Now, she'd see it all, albeit under slightly questionable circumstances.

She branched off right, up narrow St Giles's Steps, past Old Garden roses that billowed over the boundary walls of the whitewashed cottages clinging to the hillside. Moments later, she was in High Town, dashing past the imposing sandstone church and the ancient moot hall on the high street before weaving through back lanes lined with quaint half-timbered houses, until she reached the start of open countryside.

As she neared her destination, she skirted a field, the soft summer air full of birdsong and the smell of hay.

She approached High Seat from the south side, as instructed by Althea. It had most of the immediate land to itself, but there was one neighbour and Bella didn't want to be seen. The substantial red-brick house rose up in front of her, three storeys high. She had to sneak past dark, mullioned windows to reach the back door. It was quite a place. Not smart – it could do with some TLC – but historic.

Bella texted Althea to announce her arrival, and her hostess opened the door, her bright eyes twinkling. 'The coast is clear. Bernard can't reconcile himself to selling the family possessions yet, but I have a feeling you're right – he might agree once he sees what we could make.'

Bella only hoped there was something really valuable, after suggesting she assess the house contents in secret. She'd need an impressive result to win Althea's husband over.

Bella had guessed money was tight, the first time she'd met Althea. She'd been browsing Vintage Winter for 'something delightful yet cheap' as a birthday present. Bella had revelled in her frankness and was able to help, which created a bond. By Althea's third visit, she was wishing aloud that her husband would agree to sell some heirlooms to raise funds. It was during a chance meeting in the Castle Gardens that Bella suggested tempting him in by quietly finding out what he could make.

The underhand approach felt entirely justified when Bernard wouldn't countenance downsizing to ease the situation. Bella found his impracticality irritating, though she'd never met him. It was sad, of course, but if the writing was on the wall, you had to face facts.

Althea stood back to let her in. 'Come on through!' She seemed excited at the adventure they were having. Bella knew she was seventy or so, but she looked at least ten years younger.

They walked through the large farmhouse kitchen, wicker

baskets and drying herbs hanging from hooks on its beams, then along a corridor.

'That's Bernard,' Althea said, nodding to a decent portrait in a handsome gilt frame decorated with acanthus leaves and flowers. The frame itself would fetch a couple of hundred. Nineteenth century, Bella decided.

'It was painted fifteen years ago, but he hasn't changed much,' Althea said.

Bella married what she knew of him so far (his refusal to face facts) with how he looked. He had a rather charming smile, and appealing, craggy features, with a moustache that made him look soldierly. He held himself formally, but then people usually did for that sort of portrait. She wouldn't hold it against him without more information.

'That was just ten years after we married. He was my second venture on that front. My first husband was a faithless stinker, so Bernard's devotion was like spring coming after winter. He wrote me poems for a year when we were courting. Can you imagine?' Althea laughed, but her smile was fond. 'He still composes one on my birthday.'

'How romantic.' Bella wondered what it would be like to be worshipped, but suspected she'd find it annoying and claustrophobic.

'We talk about anything and everything,' Althea went on. 'Books, politics, late into the night.' But then she sighed. 'The financial situation is off-limits though. It always leads to a row.'

Bella was pleased she might be part of the solution.

This trip to High Seat was only a preliminary visit. Althea wanted to show Bella which rooms to prioritise when searching for saleable items and to ensure she knew the layout. That way, she could make herself scarce if Bernard or anyone else came home unexpectedly while she was at her illicit work.

As they ascended the sweeping staircase, Bella appreciated High Seat's shady, draughty interior. It was perfect for summer, but it must be terrible in winter; the radiators were nowhere near enough to heat the vast space. It made Bella think lovingly of her cosy flat in seventeenth-century Southwell Hall.

On High Seat's landing, Althea laid a hand on a grandfather clock, her expression fond, but Bella shook her head in response to her questioning look.

'It's delightful, but I'm afraid the market's rather flat for that sort of longcase clock.' It was pretty, with attractive marquetry, but there were imperfections, and its dial was painted tin, not brass. If it had been well looked after, and made by one of the collectable London or Welsh firms, it could have been a different matter. But the clock, just like the French mahogany bookcase to its right, looked aggressively well loved. That was fair enough in Bella's book. Why have nice things if you weren't going to use them? Much of her income came from selling pieces at the cheaper end of the market. But the state of the furniture wouldn't help save the Powell finances.

After a guided tour of High Seat's three floors, Bella wondered if there'd be any hidden treasures amongst the scuffed walnut card tables and battered dressing-room screens. But she still felt the usual prick of excitement. The apparently slim chances were enough to hook her.

Althea offered Bella coffee.

'And we must talk soon on the phone,' she said, as they sat down with their drinks, 'to work out when to sneak you in to start the valuations in earnest.' She closed her eyes for a moment. 'I mustn't neglect other things though. The Lammas Day feast is almost upon us. It's held in the one field we still own.'

Bella had attended the event herself, long ago when her father still lived in Hope Eaton.

Althea shook her head. 'Most of our farmland was sold off years ago. Another sore point. Still, maybe you'll find something marvellous and rescue the Powell fortunes. It's such a strain. The family's fighting like cats over how to generate income.'

She was distancing herself from the fray, Bella noted. Of course, she'd married into the clan late, inheriting two stepsons, so it made sense.

'You've seen Bernard's portrait, out in the hall,' Althea said. 'And here are his children.'

She indicated two photographs in matching Victorian frames, decorated with scrolls and latticework. Worth around a hundred and fifty each. Bella couldn't quite switch off the running totals in her head.

Althea sighed. 'Bernard insisted on having formal shots done last summer, though neither of them were keen. They think he's old fashioned.'

Bella guessed the stepsons were in their late thirties, and both were dark haired, but that was where the similarities ended. One looked serious, pinched and worried, the other smug, a smile playing on his lips. A man used to winning, Bella imagined.

'My husband has assets on top of this place,' Althea was saying, 'but they mustn't be sold. That's my red line.' She shook her head. 'They're cottages and premises – people's homes and livelihoods. But selling High Seat is a no-go for Bernard. He'd rather die than let that happen.'

Bella had a feeling she meant it literally.

'He wants to leave it to my stepsons.' Althea waved at the photos. 'Though they'd never settle here together. There's enough room for two families, but there would be fireworks.'

They were certainly in a fix. The whole thing sounded dysfunctional, but Bella liked a challenge. She planned to make friends with Bernard. If she could get him to trust her, Althea might convince him to sell some antiques. Even if there was no stand-out item, the income from lower-value pieces would add up.

She leaned forward. 'Can I lend a hand with the Lammas Day feast?' That ought to build bridges with Bernard. It was a whole-town affair, but he and Althea were still seen as the hosts, as in days of yore.

Althea beamed. 'Now that's an offer I won't refuse.'

With a sense of purpose, Bella excused herself to visit the cloakroom. Attempting to talk some sense into Bernard was appealing, and she'd get to socialise with the townsfolk too.

She was crossing the kitchen when her hostess's miniature schnauzer, Eustace, bounced in through the cat-cum-dog flap. He knocked over a wine bottle by the recycling bin, scampered towards her and deposited a grubby-looking tennis ball at her feet. That looked practically antique, though *definitely* not saleable.

She bent to fuss him, righted the bottle, then walked on to the loo, which was in a lobby by the back door.

As she returned, approaching the door to the sitting room, she heard a one-sided conversation. Althea must be on the phone.

'My dear Clemmie! I wish I'd never persuaded you to have it. It's only ever made you feel awful.'

Bella's chest contracted. Pain, sympathy and sorrow. She knew Clemmie, assuming it was the same one, and she was having the worst time of it right now. Bella re-entered the room and Althea smiled, motioning with her hand that she was winding up the conversation.

'My best friend from childhood days, Clemmie,' she said, after she'd rung off. 'She lived opposite me until she was fourteen. To think that she's a year younger than I am, yet so very ill. And now the tonic I recommended isn't agreeing with her. She's been taking it ever since she was staying here, before she transferred to Hope Eaton Hospice.' There were tears in Althea's bright eyes. 'I think she's been too scared to stop, in case it was helping. Nothing will save her, I'm afraid. The doctors have given her days. I can't bear to see her so ill. It's like having my heart ripped out, each time I visit. It hardly matters now, but I'm going to ask the hospice to suggest a different preparation. It might at least give her hope, even if it's false. That's not wrong, is it?'

Bella shook her head. She'd clutch at the same straws. 'I really don't think so.' She could feel tears pricking her own eyes.

'I'm so sorry,' Althea said. 'I didn't mean to upset you. You know her too?'

Bella bit her lip hard. 'A little.' She thought of Clemmie in happier times. The delight she'd taken in the Victorian glass vase a friend had bought her from Vintage Winter. The way she'd come to visit Bella, to say how much she'd appreciated the certificate that went with it, explaining its history. And their periodic chats afterwards. She was always so warm and friendly. Later on, she'd come into the shop looking pale and thin. Reading between the lines, Bella had gathered she was ill, and that it was serious. Her heart had sunk; she'd thought of nothing else that day. Bella remembered Clemmie's words now. 'A difficult diagnosis focuses the mind, that's the thing. There are problems I ought to have tackled years ago. Time might be running out.'

Bella had asked if she could help. She'd yearned to ease her worries, and she'd been curious too. But Clemmie had thanked her and shaken her head. 'No. It's something only I can do. I just need to work out the best way.'

Bella had never found out what she was talking about. She wondered if Althea knew. She turned to her. 'I like Clemmie very much, but it's she and my colleague, John Jenks, who are really close.' John knew everyone in Hope Eaton, and Clemmie more than most, as she'd volunteered at the museum where he used to work. But even John hadn't known what Clemmie's worry was, when she'd asked him.

. . .

Later that day, Bella was walking towards Hope Eaton Hospice, next to John, ready to visit Clemmie Crowe. John was a private person who'd only opened up gradually, but the rewards had been immense. After months of working together, she felt as close to him as he was likely to let her get. Yet she still didn't know what to do for him now, when it counted. It was an uncomfortable feeling, finding she was powerless against this emotional trial.

The closest relatable experience she had was when her father – Hope Eaton's local copper – had died unexpectedly, twelve years earlier. For John, it was a close friend, and everyone knew what was coming. It was less of a shock, but horribly drawn out. And John wasn't like Bella, who'd abandoned her stiff upper lip to a storm of emotion after her dad's funeral. She'd never seen him be anything less than self-contained.

She wondered for the umpteenth time if she was doing the right thing, coming with him to visit Clemmie. John's partner Gareth was working, and Bella had thought he might like company, but she knew he'd loathe to lose control in front of her. Perhaps she was heaping on the pressure by being there. And though she wanted to see Clemmie, she didn't know her like John did, so her claim to this precious bit of time felt shaky. He might prefer to see her in private. But it felt odd not to do something concrete to support him. There was nothing worse than inaction, combined with that feeling of helplessness.

When they reached the hospice, a squat modern building on the east side of the River Kite, down in the valley, Bella paused. 'Are you sure you wouldn't rather see her alone?' It might be his last chance.

John shook his head. 'If she knows we're there, she'll be glad I've got company. She's thoughtful like that.'

Bella was satisfied with the answer. She was adept at spotting lies and bluffs, thanks to being the oldest of four sisters and an antiques dealer to boot. John was looking down at his polished shoes, but that would be to hide his emotion.

They went inside and Bella fished in her bag for the crackle-glaze vase she'd bought at a sale with Clemmie in mind. John had flowers to go in it.

As they entered her room, they found she was asleep, but there were a couple of chairs where they could sit quietly.

But before Bella got that far, her attention was caught by a large paper carrier bag on top of a cupboard. Smart-looking and French: La Boutique Lafayette. She peered inside and saw it contained some vintage worry beads – substantial and rather beautiful, made from amber with a golden tassel on the end. Perhaps someone had brought them as a present, but Bella guessed Clemmie was past the stage when they might bring comfort.

Once seated, Bella focused on Clemmie's thin, elfin face and chin-length grey hair, her skin tight across delicate high cheekbones. Her eyelids flickered, as though she was dreaming.

Then suddenly, she stirred. Her eyelashes fluttered and her voice slurred slightly as she peered at John, who sat nearest her bed.

'Oh, you're here.' She squinted, as though she was having trouble focusing. 'Thank you. Thank you for coming. I didn't like to ask, only it's important. Something I should have dealt with before. It relates to the Powells.' Then she blinked again, and peered momentarily at Bella. 'Who's that with you, Adam?'

John's sad, pained eyes met Bella's. 'She's never not recognised me before,' he murmured. 'It's me, Clemmie, John.' He leaned in close. 'Were you expecting someone else?'

Bella saw her swallow, then she closed her eyes. When she opened them again, she took John's hand and squeezed it. 'John. Of course, I'm so sorry. I was confused.'

'And I've got Bella with me,' John added.

Bella felt even more uncomfortable, but Clemmie managed a faint smile and touched her hand too. Just a light pressure. She looked so thin, her skin like tissue paper. It brought tears to Bella's eyes, which was all wrong. Of the three of them, she was the one who should be strong. She was glad John had taken the chair nearest to Clemmie. She could hopefully keep her reaction to herself. She clenched her fists tight, so her nails dug into her palms. It worked, and she pulled herself together.

'Each of the Powells has been in this afternoon.' Clemmie's voice was thin as a thread. 'Even Rory.' She looked surprised. 'Though it's Althea who's most like family to me, and we're not even blood relations.' Bella knew there was a link between Clemmie and the Powells. She'd heard mutters about an extra-marital affair.

There was a long pause. 'Althea's always looked out for me,' Clemmie went on at last. She shook her head. 'She was brave when I was weak, daring when I toed the line.' She stopped for a moment, then began again. 'She was willing to risk everything for me, even when I wished she wouldn't.' Bella wondered what she meant, but she couldn't interrupt when each word sounded like a struggle. Clemmie took John's hand again. 'It's people like you and Althea who've kept me going over the years.'

At last, the effort of speaking seemed too much and Clemmie closed her eyes, pillows banked behind her head.

John leaned forward and asked in a whisper if they should go, but Clemmie shook her head slowly. 'Please stay. Unless it's a bother.'

So he talked quietly about old times and Bella sat and listened. It was touching yet heartbreaking to watch happy emotions flit across Clemmie's lined face. Gradually, her breathing became a little deeper and Bella and John's eyes met.

'Asleep?' Bella mouthed.

John nodded. He put his flowers in the vase Bella had

brought, picked it up, and whispered, 'I'll ask one of the staff for some water.'

But before they'd left the room, Clemmie started awake again. Her eyes were pained and she seemed to reach out for something, her hand clutching at thin air.

The need to offer comfort felt urgent. John had lunged for the button to call a nurse, but Bella sensed she wanted something to hold, and her mind leaped to the worry beads. She moved towards the French bag, her gaze still on Clemmie. 'Let me get you—'

But a look of anguish shot across Clemmie's exhausted features. 'No!'

Her tone made Bella spring back. Perhaps Clemmie had misunderstood her, but the last thing she wanted was to cause more distress.

One of the carers came. Bella knew her – she was Paula Richards, Althea Powell's niece. They'd been into Vintage Winter together once. The contrast between her strong, healthy limbs and Clemmie's weak ones was stark. Paula was tanned, as though she spent her free time outdoors, her sun-streaked hair swept up into a French pleat.

'There, there, Clemmie, don't fret.' She stroked the woman's hand with great tenderness, then glanced from Bella to John. 'What happened?'

'I think she fell asleep.' John's voice was unsteady. 'Maybe she had a bad dream. We might have overtired her. Please could we have some water for the flowers?'

'Of course.'

'I need more tonic.' Clemmie's voice was barely audible.

Paula nodded. 'That's an idea. Althea suggested you might like something different. I asked my colleagues, and I've found one that comes recommended.'

As she disappeared, there was a glimmer of hope in Clemmie's eyes. A moment later, Paula returned with the flowers and the tonic. She set the vase down, then broke the bottle's seal and poured Clemmie a measure.

As Paula held it to her lips, John caught Bella's eye and they rose to leave.

Bella had only been back at her flat in Southwell Hall for ten minutes when John texted to let her know the hospice had phoned. Clemmie Crowe was dead.

2

A DISTURBING POSSIBILITY

Bella wanted to ring John to tell him how sorry she was, then rush round and give him a hug. But he wasn't a huggy person and she knew he'd want time alone. He'd probably be doing something distracting and mechanical like cleaning his and Gareth's cottage. She texted him back instead, saying she wished he wasn't going through the mill and please to tell her if she could do anything.

She suggested he should take the following day off work, too. She knew he wouldn't, though. It wasn't his way, and she sympathised. After her dad died, she'd battened down her feelings at first too. Carried on, made all the arrangements. Sold his flat – the same flat she now occupied, though there'd been two owners in between. It was only later that she'd bawled her eyes out. But did John ever get to the bawling stage? She couldn't imagine it.

When Bella entered Vintage Winter on Tuesday, she found John looking as though he hadn't slept. 'I'll make coffee.' It was unheard of for John not to have prepared some and he jumped, as though she'd caught him out.

'You are allowed to grieve, John.'

'You sound like my mum.'

Bella always had mixed feelings when people compared her with Jeannie. Salt of the earth, and all that, but Bella hoped she was a bit more subtle than the pub landlady.

Minutes later, Bella handed John his drink, strong with just a trace of milk as he liked it.

He thanked her. 'I wish Clemmie had had a happier life.'

'Remind me of her story?' It might do him good to talk. 'Althea was her best friend, but it was Bernard and his sons who were related to Clemmie?'

John nodded. 'Clemmie was some kind of cousin – the result of an affair. Her Powell dad left his wife for Clemmie's mum, but they each of them died soon after. His heart gave out and the mum got meningitis.'

'Good grief, how awful.'

John nodded. 'After that, her half-sister Myra – her dad's legitimate daughter – gave her a home. Only she died young too, after a tyre blowout on the motorway one Christmas.'

'Sweet Agnes, poor Clemmie.'

John bit his lip. 'It must have been traumatic, but Myra treated her badly, according to town gossip.'

John always knew the word on the street. He didn't chatter himself, but he was an excellent and sympathetic listener. Of course, having a pub landlady as a mother helped too. Jeannie made it her mission to know her clientele's business in case they needed 'steering'.

Bella imagined Clemmie's half-sister, Myra, landed with the product of her father's affair – not a recipe for harmony. She topped up John's coffee. 'Myra resented her?'

He nodded. 'I think so. Their dad had left funds for Clemmie's upbringing, and word has it that Myra took her in for the cash. She regarded it as her right, despite getting almost all her father's money direct.'

She sounded deeply unpleasant. Resenting her dad's affair was only natural, but none of it had been Clemmie's fault. 'There must have been lawyers, making sure she spent the money on Clemmie?'

John's eyes were hollow. 'A tame, Powell-family lawyer who was under Myra's thumb. Myra went through the motions, but she treated the terms of the will very loosely. And she made Clemmie's life a misery.'

Bella wished Myra was still around, so she could tell her what she thought of her.

John pushed his glasses up his nose, picked up a cloth and began to polish the base of a vintage lamp. 'Myra died on Christmas Eve when Clemmie was fourteen years old. She was travelling to meet an exciting new lover. A wealthy French play-boy, apparently, who showered her with gifts. She'd left Clemmie with a childminder for Christmas – that was where her dad's money went. On that and "entertainments" she claimed were for them both.' John was polishing harder and harder as he spoke. It was just as well the lamp was nice and solid.

'What happened after she died?'

'Clemmie finally ended up with a kindly guardian.'

Bella breathed a sigh of relief. 'Thank goodness. So things got better for her?'

John paused briefly with his polishing, his head on one side. 'Yes, while she was a child, before the maintenance money ran out. But after that, things were difficult. She worked as a nursery nurse until she retired, but the pay was terrible and her guardian was hard up, with nothing to leave her. If it hadn't been for Althea's staunch friend-ship, I don't know where she'd have ended up. Althea wanted to see Clemmie secure after the awful time she'd had. When she married Bernard, she pushed him to let her a cottage for mates' rates. Mum thinks she can be a bit patronising, but I see her as Hope Eaton's answer to Robin Hood.'

'I gather the Powells have a portfolio of properties.'

'Yes, all belonging to Bernard. Several cottages and the Steps' premises, too.'

'Really? That's a bit close to home.' It was the café run by John's brother, Leo. 'Though Althea's told me she's determined not to sell.'

John looked anxious now. 'Only it's not really up to her, is it? And from what I hear, Bernard might crack and let them go.'

'What makes you think that?'

He sighed. 'I bumped into one of the staff at the Nest.' It was the estate agents on the high street. 'He was after gossip about Leo's plans for the café. Apparently, Bernard and his son Rory have had the premises valued, along with some of the other properties.'

'Oh no. Did you ask Leo about it?'

'Rory told him it was for insurance purposes, but I'm not so sure.'

After Bella's conversations with Althea, she wasn't either. Perhaps it was time to confess how much she knew about the Powells' money worries, along with the scheme for Bella to secretly value High Seat's contents.

She told him, then mentally ducked.

'You're valuing pieces belonging to Bernard Powell without his knowledge? Bella, just think of the reputational risk! He'd be furious if he found out, and it's not ethical.'

'I know. But he sounds as stubborn as a mule, and I want to help Althea. You don't need to worry. I've got no intention of getting caught. And now I know about the threat to the Steps, it's essential to help them raise money another way. You can't deny that.'

John said nothing.

. . .

Later that day, Althea called her. '*My niece Paula said you and John were with Clemmie just before she died. I know I'm being maudlin, but I wondered how it was for her at the end. I wish I'd been there. I was with her earlier in the afternoon. If only—*' She gulped back a sob.

Poor, poor woman. It was such a rotten situation to be in. 'Look, I'm free after work. Would you like me to come and tell you about it?'

Althea sighed. 'I would. Thank you.'

Althea's eyes were red when she answered the door. Bella always found other people's emotion contagious. She couldn't help imagining what they were feeling and feeling it too. She handed over the flowers she'd brought before she could manage to say anything.

'Thank you.' Althea's voice cracked as they went inside. 'It's just so sad. Clemmie was a good friend, and her life wasn't easy. Myra, her late half-sister, had lots of money – all inherited from her and Clemmie's dad – but it was only his tiny ring-fenced allowance that went to Clemmie after Myra's death. It was so unjust.' She shook her head. 'Myra had done nothing to earn her fortune, but her will ignored Clemmie completely. And Clemmie could never quite... Well, never mind. It's too late now.'

Bella managed to express her sympathy at last, though her eyes were still pricking. Stupid, not to be able to switch it off.

'Please,' Althea said, leading her to the kitchen, 'come through and have a drink.'

Anything alcoholic would be disastrous. Bella opted for a pineapple juice and soda instead. Althea put ice and mint leaves in it and helped herself to a gin and tonic.

'Clemmie said how much you meant to her,' Bella said. 'She was very sleepy at the end.'

Althea took a tissue from her pocket and dabbed her eyes. 'She was peaceful?'

Bella hesitated a moment too long. *Bother.* She'd have to tell the truth now. 'Almost entirely. She mistook John for someone else at first, but she didn't seem too upset by it.' Bella remembered her calling him Adam. Clemmie had wanted to discuss the Powells with this unknown man, but it felt wrong to mention that. Whatever the topic, it had died with Clemmie. Telling Althea would leave her with questions that could never be answered – a recipe for anxiety. Bella was curious though, naturally.

Althea was looking at her, a query in her eyes. 'There was something else?'

Bella shouldn't have paused. 'At one point she woke suddenly and thrust out her hand, as though she was grasping for something. I wanted to comfort her, and I'd noticed some worry beads in a bag on the side, so I moved to fetch them, but I abandoned the idea when she got anxious.'

Althea's eyes filled with tears. 'She asked me to fetch the beads from her house; I only took them in yesterday.'

'The upset didn't last. She was happy to try the new tonic the hospice had found.' At least that was a positive note. 'I think you were right – it did give her hope.'

Althea nodded. 'That's something. Thank you. And for the flowers too.'

John's brother's café flitted through Bella's mind as she got up to leave, but it would be unforgiveable to ask about Bernard's plans at a time like this.

Clemmie had requested a private funeral and cremation – John said she hadn't wanted to 'drag' everyone along. Her lack of self-confidence made Bella even sadder, but Althea had hired John's parents' inn, the Blue Boar, on Thursday, to bring her friends and relatives together for an informal send-off.

Bella had continued to worry over the Steps in the interim, though work had been a good distraction. As well as the in-person customers, Bella had fulfilled online orders – pleasing, but exhausting. She could do with more help, but she wouldn't risk hiring someone until she was certain it would be sustainable. On Wednesday evening, she'd longed to veg out on the sofa before falling into bed, but it was no-go. She'd agreed to go on a date with Robert Mead, a fellow antiques dealer she'd met in Shrewsbury a while back. She'd been pleased when they'd bumped into each other again recently.

They'd been to watch a weird arthouse film with no discernible plot. Robert had seemed to get more out of it than she had, but perhaps it was just tiredness that made her unreceptive. Robert himself was nice – and no one could deny they had lots in common. That was the important thing. She was mulling his suggestion of a second date as Clemmie's nearest and dearest gathered in the bar, but the robust tones of John's mum Jeannie snapped her back to the here and now.

'I can't help being glad that they're doing it this way,' Jeannie said. 'Funerals are such depressing things. I rarely enjoy them.'

John's brother Leo snorted, but turned it into a cough when his mother glanced beadily at him.

In truth, Bella was relieved too, though her father's funeral had offered a strange sort of comfort. There'd been no formality. People had gathered at his graveside and shared personal memories, to the backdrop of birds swooping overhead and the wind in the trees. It had made Bella feel close to him, as though he was out there somewhere, borne on the breeze.

The old coaching inn and its timber-framed courtyard were bathed in sunlight, its hanging baskets crammed with nasturtiums and lobelia. The doors were propped open to welcome the townsfolk. It was all so pretty, and Bella found it achingly sad that Clemmie wasn't there to appreciate it.

Althea stood near the richly polished front bar, gleaming brasses and glinting glasses behind her. As Bella approached, she handed her one of the short biographical pamphlets she held, which paid tribute to Clemmie. Her sweet-natured face was on the front, with her birth and death dates: 7 June 1955 to 21 July 2025. RIP. Seventy was no age, these days.

The gathering began quietly, but as people began to relax, the noise of conversation rose. People tucked into the refreshments – delectable mini pastries, courtesy of John's partner and his team in the Blue Boar's kitchen. Althea had done Clemmie proud.

'I must make sure everyone eats something.' Jeannie swooped around the room with platefuls of the sumptuous food. As ever, she reminded Bella of a mother hen, corralling her chicks. She'd regard Clemmie's death as a shock to the system and sustaining snacks as essential for everyone's well-being.

Bella got chatting to a sandy-haired young man with a boy-scout air who'd met Clemmie through the allotment society.

'She reminded me of my nan,' he said. 'One of the first things she did when she got ill was to tell the society she didn't need her plot any more, so someone else could make use of it. Who thinks of that when they've just had terrible news? Heart of gold.' He sighed and shook his head. 'I'd been meaning to go and see her, but I felt a bit awkward. You know.' He blushed deeply. 'It was only when she asked me to come that I finally got my act together, and then I was too late. By the time I got there she'd already died.'

He looked as though he wanted absolution, so Bella did her best. 'It's always hard to know whether to push yourself forward when it's someone you don't know well...'

She let the sentence hang, and he nodded sadly.

Bella's attention was caught next by a familiar face. Althea's smug-looking stepson who she'd seen in the silver-framed photograph at High Seat. He had the air of a truculent teenager, despite being a grown man. Late thirties, Bella guessed. He might have been good looking if he weren't so sulky, slouching by the bar, hands in pockets and a pout on his lips. It was as though he didn't want to be there, but someone had made him.

John's mouth was a thin line. 'That's Althea's stepson, Rory. I hear he's cross because he expected something in Clemmie's will. She cut him out without telling him, apparently.'

Bella was surprised. 'I didn't think she'd have anything to leave. And they were only distant relatives, weren't they?'

John sighed. 'It wasn't much: two hundred and fifty pounds each to him, his brother and Althea's niece, Paula Richards. The Powells were her closest relations.'

Rory didn't look as though he'd taken the snub well. 'I wonder what he did to upset her.' It must have been significant to warrant altering her will. It might have cost her almost as much as the bequest was worth to do it.

In the background, Althea was talking to a man and a woman who looked around seventy or so, just like her. Bella guessed they might be twins. Their iron-grey hair stuck up in exactly the same way. After a minute's earwigging, Bella realised they were the children of the childminder who was looking after Clemmie when her half-sister, Myra, had been killed on the motorway.

'I always wished she'd come to live with us,' one of them said. 'But things were difficult after Dad walked out. At least she was with us over Christmas after the news came through. Poor Clemmie.'

'She wouldn't leave her room,' the other one said. 'And you know as well as I do that Myra didn't deserve to be mourned like that. I remember Mum saying she'd taken up with a new man.' He rolled his eyes. 'She didn't realise I was listening, but

I got the gist. Myra had even less time for Clemmie than before. But for all that, Clemmie sat in her room with the curtains closed and cried and cried. All through Christmas Day too.'

'I wish I could have come to her,' Althea said, 'but my mum told me it was too soon.'

'It would have been. It was four days before she finally came downstairs. I remember how pleased she was to see you when you did come, though. Goodness, it's over fifty-five years ago now, but I remember it like it was yesterday.'

There was much shaking of heads.

'Even when she went to her new guardian, she never got her confidence back. I suppose that's what being with Myra until she was fourteen did to her.'

The group drifted apart, and sulky Rory Powell wove past with Althea's niece Paula, all bronzed and blonde, at his heels. After a moment, she slipped her hand into his and Althea flinched. No wonder. Bella wouldn't like her relations being involved with him either, though he looked the type her youngest sister might go for.

Bella was just making her way back to John when she passed the guilt-ridden sandy-haired allotment man she'd chatted to earlier. He was sighing. 'Well, I'd better get back to work. DS Dixon will be wondering where I've got to.'

Bella pulled up short. 'Sorry, did I hear you mention DS Dixon? You work with him?' Bella had dealt with him over a couple of cases involving violent death.

The sandy-haired man frowned. 'I'm a trainee on his team. Just transferred from uniform.'

Bella introduced herself and he responded in kind.

'Adam Davies.' He shook her hand, standing up straight, chest out.

The name sent a flicker of recognition through her. Adam. The Adam Clemmie had mistaken John for? It had to be, surely.

He'd said he was due to go and see her, but she'd died before he got there. It would explain why he'd been on Clemmie's mind.

The thought lodged as the conversation moved on.

'So you know DS Dixon?' Adam said.

'Yes, Barry and I have had dealings before.' She probably shouldn't call him by his first name, but it was hard to think of him formally. In her eyes he was an overgrown schoolboy-cum-beleaguered dad. She'd even given him childcare advice, having done a lot of the work bringing up her younger siblings. 'Please tell him Bella Winter sends her best wishes.' She had the urge to keep him talking. She wanted to think more about his connection with Clemmie, but she had to let him go.

It was as she and John walked back to Vintage Winter, along Hope Eaton's high street with its ancient timber-framed shops, that she got the chance to analyse her thoughts. By the time they entered St Giles's Close, and passed the old sandstone church, bathed in sunshine, tiny shards of worry were needling her.

Clemmie had been shy and retiring. She'd never had much confidence, from everything Bella had heard. When John had asked her if they should leave, the day she died, she'd said she'd like them to stay – but only if it wasn't a bother. Even on her deathbed, she hadn't wanted to put them out.

They entered the communal antiques centre. As Bella unlocked Vintage Winter, to be hit by the familiar smell of old wood and polish, her thoughts ran on.

Despite Clemmie's diffident character, she'd summoned Adam Davies. And assuming he was the same Adam who Clemmie had mistaken John for, she'd wanted to talk to him about the Powells.

Clemmie and Adam knew each other from the allotment society but she doubted it was to do with that. So what had Clemmie wanted to discuss with him? It must have been important, for her to summon him in such an un-Clemmie like way.

John put some coffee on and Bella tried to push the thought to the back of her mind. They'd never know the answer now. But as she wrote out labels for new stock and served customers, the question wouldn't leave her. On the day she'd died, Clemmie had been expecting a visit from a policeman. She'd plucked up the courage to ask him to come. And she'd just cut one of the Powells out of her will...

3

THE BEGINNINGS OF A PLAN

It was around an hour later, when John set to work polishing a beautiful crystal orb chandelier, that Bella finally decided she'd have to say something. It would eat away at her if she didn't. She'd been telling herself that it would be fruitless to pursue it, but a second inner voice – which sounded distinctly like her dad – was pushing back. If only she'd asked Clemmie about Adam before it was too late.

Then further regrets crept in. She remembered Clemmie's words from months back, when she'd realised she was ill. 'It focuses the mind, that's the thing. There are problems I ought to have tackled years ago. Time might be running out.' When she'd asked Adam Davies to visit, had she been tackling the problems she'd talked about? If Bella had pushed a little more, offered an extra cup of tea, might Clemmie have confided in her? Bella could have helped her. If she knew something damning about the Powells, it was no wonder she was loth to deal with it. She'd have been worried about the effect it might have on Althea.

Bella perched on the refectory table they used as a cash desk and shared her concerns with John. From his lack of reply, she could tell he thought she was getting carried away.

'Summoning him about something official is the only thing that makes sense.'

His frown deepened. 'So why not call the station?'

'If you were ill and anxious, wouldn't you rather talk to someone you knew?'

He pushed his glasses up his nose. 'I'd choose someone I *didn't* know. It would make it less awkward.'

She should have predicted that. 'I wish we'd asked her about it. It's a crying shame Adam Davies didn't see her before the end.'

'He couldn't know the timing was crucial. The doctors said Clemmie could have lasted another few days.'

Try as she might, Bella couldn't help wondering if the hour of her death was down to something more than her illness. If she was intent on passing on information about the Powells, it was awfully convenient, from their point of view.

The niggle over Clemmie and Adam Davies continued to bat around Bella's brain for the rest of the afternoon. By closing time, she'd decided to talk to him again. It might be enough to allay her fears.

She didn't have his address, but it was summer, and he'd seemed the keen sort. She could guess where he'd be after work. That evening, she went to loiter by the allotments on Yew Tree Lane, down in Low Town next to the river, with the hills rising above them. She was surrounded by birdsong and there was something appealing about the calm way the gardeners did their work.

She got chatting to a friendly woman who assured her Adam Davies would be along. 'He uses it to destress.'

He turned up half an hour later and she gave him a wave. 'I thought I'd come and have a look. I've got a garden – I'm in one of the ground-floor flats at Southwell Hall – but it's small. Nowhere near enough room to grow veg.'

Adam looked as though he doubted she'd be up for the digging and mud involved. She should have changed into trousers perhaps, though maybe her fifties cigarette pants wouldn't have helped. 'There's a heck of a waiting list, I'm afraid.'

Just as well. Imagine if he'd told her she could take one right away. Her fondness for the Shropshire countryside was growing by the day, but if she wanted to commune with it, she'd stroll or sit on a bench. 'Not to worry. It was just a thought.' She closed her eyes for a moment. 'I keep thinking about Clemmie. I was sitting with her just before she died; I think she was anticipating your visit. She mistook my friend John for you at first. Were you surprised when she asked you to call on her? Only she always seemed like a reticent person.'

Adam pursed his lips. 'It did feel out of the blue. She left a message on my answerphone, and I wondered about it before I called her back.'

'She didn't say why she wanted to see you?' Thoughts of the Powells floated in Bella's head.

He shrugged. 'No.'

Bella's hope for easy answers faded.

'I must admit, I was curious,' Adam went on, 'but I couldn't ask. She might have thought I resented the invitation.' He shook his head, just as he'd done at the pub. 'I should have gone sooner, only I couldn't think what I'd say to her.'

He was clearly the sort who wanted to help, but he was very young. He'd probably always remember letting her down and be wincing about it years later. 'You'd already told her about your job? That you were moving to CID?'

He frowned. 'Yes, I had.'

The shards of doubt got bigger.

'I wish I'd made it,' Adam went on. 'I would have, if I hadn't had bike problems.'

'What happened?'

'Flat tyre. There was a nail in it. I suppose I must have ridden over it and the tyre went down slowly. Took me an hour to mend and by then...' He shrugged his shoulders sadly.

The story only added to the uneasiness she felt. She made an excuse to get his number, telling him she was planning a do for the townsfolk at Vintage Winter. As anticipated, he was too polite to say he wasn't interested. She had a hunch she might want to talk to him again.

The moment she left the allotments, she called John. 'When's Clemmie's cremation? And where?'

'*Monday afternoon, I think.*' He gave her the details before asking why she wanted to know. Only someone like John would display such restraint.

Time was of the essence if she wanted to do anything about her fears.

Bella abandoned the idea of calling DS Barry Dixon. It was getting late and besides, she couldn't expect him to act without more to go on. She sat on her sofa at home instead, wondering how to make a stronger case. In lieu of a post-mortem on poor Clemmie, Adam Davies's bike felt like the best chance of supporting physical evidence.

It was nine by the time she called Adam, prepared to do some heavy-duty persuading, but in the end, it wasn't necessary. Her questions at the allotments had got him worried. He was already going down the route she'd been going to suggest. So far, what he'd found had worried him further.

By the time she woke the following morning, he'd sent her a text confirming her worst fears.

. . .

She was outside the police station at eight in the morning, where she'd arranged to meet Adam Davies. In fact, it was Barry Dixon she saw first. He cringed slightly when she hailed him, as though he could hide by making himself smaller.

'I was waiting for Adam.'

Relief flooded his face.

'We wanted to talk to you together.'

He deflated again. 'It'll have to be quick. All hell's let loose in the last week. Whoever heard of someone joyriding a tractor? And on top of that, I've had no sleep. The twins have got chickenpox.'

'I feel your pain.' Bella remembered nursing her three younger half-sisters when they'd gone down with it. She could still conjure the smell of calamine lotion.

He looked at her, a spark of hope in his eyes. 'What would you recommend to keep them entertained? They're not well enough for nursery but they seem remarkably boisterous, considering.'

She suggested treasure hunts and indoor assault courses – quickly arranged with little effort – and hoped he'd remember how helpful she'd been.

At that moment, Adam Davies arrived, appearing next to Dixon and standing to attention, chest out, looking very young. Keen but anxious.

'Sir!'

Dixon sighed. 'Come on, then.'

They followed him into an interview room and Adam let her speak first, to explain the background.

When she'd finished, Dixon looked at her blearily. 'You think someone killed this Clemmie person to stop her telling Adam something about the Powell family, and punctured his tyre to delay his visit?' He shook his head, then turned to his new recruit. 'And you agree?'

Bella had a feeling the detective sergeant felt betrayed.

'After speaking to Ms Winter last night, I got worried. It was out of character for Clemmie Crowe to ask to see me. I should have thought of it at the time.'

But Bella could see why he hadn't. He'd been too busy feeling guilty, focusing on himself, not on her. She'd been there – it was human nature.

'On the back of that,' Adam went on, 'I had a look at my bike. I found there was a small patch on one of the wheel rims that wasn't as dirty as I'd have expected. So I asked Mel from SOCO to pop in first thing to dust for prints.' He shrugged. 'None at all on that one bit of rim and less dirt there than anywhere else. Mel reckons it was wiped. I repaired the puncture of course, but I can't have touched that bit. I remember where the nail went in – close to the tyre valve. The clean patch was just where someone would have had to grip the wheel to force the nail in.'

Some new officers might have looked excited by the turn of events, but Adam Davies looked shocked, upset and earnest. Bella's mind was half focused on him, and half on the miserable thought of having to tell John about the evidence they'd found.

Bella leaned forward to make sure Barry was taking notice. 'Her death was expected. If she was killed, there was every chance no one would ask questions. I realise this isn't proof, but I'm worried someone might get away with murder if it's not investigated. Clemmie's cremation's on Monday, so it's pressing.'

Dixon sighed and glanced at his mobile, where a message had flashed up. 'Another stolen tractor found. The farming liaison committee's up in arms.' He took a deep breath when Bella refused to look sympathetic. 'There must have been plenty of staff at the hospice to make sure your friend was safe.'

But they hadn't had eyes on her all the time. 'She could have been poisoned.' *Sweet Agnes, even she and John could have managed it.* They'd been quite alone with her.

'She was still eating and drinking?'

'She took some tonic while I was there.' Bella didn't admit it had come from a sealed bottle even though he'd find out quickly enough. She needed to argue her case.

At last, Dixon took out his notepad.

'Clemmie said "I need *more* tonic", so one of the staff, Paula, poured her some from a new bottle. But it mightn't have been her first lot that day. Perhaps something she'd been given earlier was doctored. And Clemmie said each of the Powells had been in to see her.' Then Bella thought of Clemmie's upset over the worry beads. 'She seemed to panic for no reason while I was there, and she thought my friend John was Adam. Maybe she was confused because someone had drugged her.' She could tell Barry thought she'd strayed into the realms of fantasy now, but she'd been focused on it longer than he had.

Adam Davies looked tactfully non-committal, but she knew that was just over the details. He believed someone had tampered with his bike, and that Clemmie had had something important to say.

'If someone targeted her like you're suggesting, they must have known Adam was going to visit,' Dixon said sceptically.

'Any staff or visitors at the hospice could have found that out.' She turned to Adam. 'I expect Clemmie rang you in private, but you mentioned she'd left a message, so you had to ring back. Anyone could have learned about that call.'

Adam hesitated. 'That's true.'

He looked anxiously at Dixon, who slumped at his desk for a moment. A second later he roused himself. 'All right. Tell me where the cremation is.'

Bella gave him the details she'd got from John.

'I'll organise a request to delay.' He added it to a very long list on the notepad in front of him, but Bella was relieved to see him put an asterisk next to it. He turned to Adam. 'Request a warrant, please. And call the hospice to arrange a meeting.'

.   .   .

At work, Bella broke the news of Adam's discovery to John.

'I'm sorry. It's not conclusive, of course.'

But in her heart of hearts, Bella felt that it was, and John's look was bleak.

She spent the day trying to distract him, while feeling constantly empty herself. If only she'd got Clemmie to confide in her when she'd had the chance. She might have taken a weight off her mind long ago, and possibly saved her from an unnatural death too. Though that was jumping the gun. There was no proof.

She kept wondering if Barry Dixon had been granted permission to postpone Clemmie's cremation, and what a post-mortem might reveal. She could probably find out if she called her godfather, Tony. He'd known her policeman father through work, and though he'd retired from CID, he still had fingers in many pies. Someone had put him on a committee of retirees, checking everyone stuck to protocol, which was a laugh. Tony had never played by the book, though he was always well-inten-tioned. The key point was that he still had access to notes on the latest cases as well as station gossip. She could get him to monitor progress and bend Dixon's ear if necessary.

The moment she got home, she pulled out her phone and was making for the sofa, ready to put her feet up and call, when a yowl from her bedroom made her jump.

She ought to be used to it by now, but how had her next-door neighbour Matt's cat, Cuthbert, got in again? He was always slinking inside when she wasn't looking. Sighing, she went to investigate and found he'd got shut in her wardrobe. He gave a sharp, indignant meow as she let him out.

'Well, if you will keep sneaking into my home...' After checking he was all right, she examined the hems of her vintage dresses. She wouldn't put it past Cuthbert to use them for entertainment. Thankfully, they were undamaged. She picked the cat up, to immediate, contented purring. *Honestly...* A moment later, she deposited him in the shared hallway outside her front door.

'Off you go. Matt will be wondering where you are.' She could hear he was in, playing something surprisingly intricate and beautiful on the guitar. As usual, she marvelled at him being John's youngest brother. They were very different in character.

She'd wondered previously if it was Matt's revolving door of girlfriends which put Cuthbert off staying on home territory. She'd understand if the cat preferred a more serene atmosphere. But lately, things had quietened down next door. It was almost as though Matt might be growing up, though Bella doubted it. A leopard didn't change its spots. Either way, Cuthbert remained a frequent visitor. It was a secret source of triumph that he seemed to favour her.

She shut her door, went back to her sofa and called Tony.

He let out a long whistle when she'd explained everything.

'*So Barry's contacting the coroner, is he?*' He gave a low, rumbly chuckle. '*Nice one. You're a chip off the old block. Though I sometimes think you use your mum's chutzpah to get the same results as your dad.*'

This was deeply annoying. 'I am a separate individual, you know.' In particular, she was nothing like her mum. 'Besides, it was largely down to Adam Davies.'

'*All right,*' Tony chuckled again. '*Keep your hair on.*'

It was just as well he wasn't in the room.

His tone turned serious. '*So the Powells are suspects, if you're right about this poor woman.*'

'Yes. If Clemmie was killed to stop her talking, I'd guess someone connected with High Seat House is guilty. Clemmie said each of the Powells visited her, the afternoon she died. I'll have my eye on Althea Powell's niece Paula, too. She works at the hospice, and I think she and Althea's horrible stepson Rory are involved. Althea doesn't look happy about it. The Powells and Paula each had access to Clemmie that day.'

Tony was crunching. Crisps, at a guess – he had a habit of snacking when chewing over a case. Two pleasures combined, she supposed. '*Interesting.*'

'If the post-mortem flags anything, then Dixon will investigate, naturally.'

Tony grunted. '*Yeah, but you've got one foot in the door already. Makes sense for you to have a nosy.*'

She'd known he'd say that, and was secretly pleased. He was right, she did have an advantage, and last time she'd investigated a crime she'd come up trumps. She couldn't help being proud about it. On top of that, she felt responsible. If she'd picked up on the significance of the visit Clemmie was expecting from Adam, or pushed harder when she'd fretted, months back, things might be very different.

Of course, Tony would be dying for her to get involved. He loved nosing into other people's cases, especially now he was retired, and in his eyes, Bella was simply reprising her father's role. Douglas Winter had been the local copper, with an in-depth understanding of the town.

Bella still felt slightly disgruntled that Tony didn't advise her to butt out for her own safety. It was in a godfather's job description. But she'd have ignored him if he had, naturally. Her career had given her useful skills, from reading people, to in-depth research and spotting clues. Deep down, the prospect of investigating lit a flame of excitement.

'*So what's next?*' Tony asked, munching some more.

'I want to know if one of the Powell family is hiding something, and if so, what. It must be something Clemmie only decided to act on just before she died, but given a conversation we had a while back, I suspect it had been preying on her mind for a bit.

'So far, Rory Powell feels most worrying.' She pictured the two images she had of him, by turns smug and petulant. 'Clemmie cut him out of her will and though the amount was small, I guess he'd done something she couldn't tolerate. But I'm curious about the others, too. Althea said Clemmie stayed at High Seat before she went into the hospice. She could have uncovered something about any of them.'

'*You'll want to visit the house too, then. Any thoughts on how to get access?*'

'That's already in the bag. I've made friends with Althea, and got myself involved in some secret valuations.' She explained the illicit arrangement to Tony. 'If I find something really valuable, she'll tell Bernard and imply I stumbled across it by accident when I visited. It might convince him to bring me in on a more official basis.' That would be perfect; she could snoop to her heart's content. 'And I've offered to help them organise Hope Eaton's Lammas Day feast, too, so that should help.'

Tony grunted. '*All right. Don't do anything I wouldn't.*'

Bella tried to imagine what that might be, and failed. 'And you'll let me know, once you have the verdict on Clemmie's death?'

'*You can count on it.*'

The moment she'd hung up, she clicked to call Althea to arrange her next secret visit to High Seat.

4

———————

HIGH EMOTIONS AT HIGH SEAT

The following morning, Bella called John to explain what she'd agreed with Althea.

'She's going to let me in in secret again this morning, once Bernard's gone out for his daily stroll. Their elder son Gregory's visiting a friend for the day so he'll be out of the way too and it turns out sour-puss Rory doesn't live there. He's in and out though, by the sound of it. Being on the spot should help me find out more.'

'*I can't believe you're really going to risk valuing someone's property without their knowledge.*' John's voice had risen in pitch to high-anxiety level.

'Don't worry, I'll be careful. And if he comes back unexpectedly, I'll think of something.'

She heard John groan.

'It'll be fine, honestly. I want to help Althea, and I need to find out more about the whole family.'

She suspected her new antiques-dealer love interest, Robert, would disapprove too. She'd made sure not to mention it when they'd spoken the night before to arrange a second date.

'*Shouldn't you wait until you know it was definitely murder?*' John persisted.

'Even if it wasn't, she tried to contact Adam Davies about the Powells before she died. There was *something* bothering her.' Bella was already gripped with a desire to know the truth. She couldn't work out John's lack of curiosity. It was unnatural.

But the sadness in his sigh distracted her from the thought.

'Are you all right?'

It took him a moment to reply. '*To be honest, I was wondering why she didn't confide in me.*'

The thought had crossed Bella's mind too; she'd suspected it would upset him. 'You know how upstanding she was. I'm sure she'd have loved to tell you, but it probably felt akin to sharing gossip, even if it was serious. She'd have wanted to go straight to the police.'

John answered slowly. '*I suppose.*'

'Do you mind opening the shop while I head to High Seat?'

'*Of course not,*' he said at last. '*But please, please be careful.*'

Half an hour later, Althea showed Bella to one of the huge untidy rooms she'd scanned briefly on her previous visit, crammed full of knick-knacks and shabby furniture.

'Shout if you need anything,' Althea said. 'Gregory's not due back until late this afternoon, and Bernard's normally gone for hours. He stops for a round of golf after his walk. Another thing we can't afford, but he uses it to keep up with his friends. As for Rory, he only visits when his father's here.' She sounded tired. 'He and I aren't close. I'll bring you a cup of coffee in a moment.' She left Bella to it.

Bella scanned the room, her attention lighting on a pair of mid-seventeenth century Dutch Heemskerk candlesticks. They might be worth the best part of a thousand pounds, but when she looked more closely, she found someone had scratched the surfaces when removing the wax. The resulting damage would send the value plummeting. Nearby pieces, from an old snuff box with a wonky lid, to a bent antique paperknife, did nothing to raise her spirits.

But even if the individual valuations were modest, the total would gradually mount up. She took out her camera and a notebook, so she could catalogue everything as she went and tot up the potential profits. She'd make a proper start, then see if she could get Althea chatting about her younger stepson. The reason behind her and Rory's lack of closeness might be telling. Althea might know or guess why Clemmie had approached Adam Davies too, but Bella didn't want to wade in with hobnail boots. Althea might not care for Rory, but she seemed protective of her husband, and who knew what secrets any of them were keeping? If Bella went too far, Althea might decide she was trouble.

Soon after Althea had delivered her drink, Bella found a very pleasing three-panelled photo frame – French, from around 1900, framed in gilded bronze and – oh heaven! – in very good condition. It might fetch three thousand. More, if the Powells were lucky. She'd just recorded it in her notebook when she sensed a change in the air. She went still, hairs on the back of her neck rising. A moment later, her phone vibrated.

A text from Althea.

Bernard back unexpectedly with Rory in tow. Sorry! They're headed to Bernard's study, next door to where you are. But if you keep quiet they shouldn't hear you.

She'd ended with the fingers-crossed emoji. Bella imagined John's reaction if she was caught. She should have told Althea to say she was there on Lammas Day business if anyone asked. She'd been too excited to think of it. Fingers crossed indeed.

She considered easing the door shut, but it was too risky.

Instead, she tiptoed across the floor and tucked herself into a tiny side room. It was just a large alcove really, but if anyone came in, they shouldn't see her.

It was only as she steadied her breathing that she realised being next door to Bernard and Rory might be an advantage. She could hear their voices and if she strained, it was possible to make out the words. The fact sent her pulse quickening again.

'Well, I'll see what I can do, dear boy.' That had to be Bernard talking to Rory. He sounded placatory and on the back foot. 'But things are tight, you see.'

'Poor old dad. I do sympathise. But they're not so tight that you can't afford the odd indulgences, like I said.' Bella pictured Rory's pouty face as he spoke. Althea's younger stepson sounded smooth and cynical.

'Well, but I'm having to borrow to afford that. Truly.' Bernard's tone was pleading. She imagined him wringing his hands.

'Borrow, really?' Rory managed to lace his sympathy with a note of disbelief. 'Well, I'm very sorry to come round with the begging bowl, Pa, but you know how things are. That deal I told you about with Foxy hasn't come to fruition yet, and like I said, the oven's packed up at home. I've been living off cold meals for weeks.'

Bring out the violins.

'I'm expecting more money in soon,' Rory went on, 'so long as that other matter I'm brokering comes off. But at the moment, I'm stuck.'

Bella wondered how many times he'd played the same tune. He sounded unpleasantly practised.

If Rory was constantly borrowing, it was no wonder the Powells were in a financial mess. And it sounded as though Bernard had been splashing out, too, from Rory's passive-aggressive comments. Was that just on golf-club fees, or was there something more? She wondered how much Althea knew about the situation. She seemed too sharp not to have an idea.

'I know, I know.' Bernard sounded troubled. Didn't he realise he was being played? Bella had the urge to call through the wall and point it out. It was hard to feel sympathetic when it was so obvious.

'It was wrong of me,' Rory said, sounding accusing rather than repentant, 'but for a second when I saw you spending like that, it felt like favouritism.'

Perhaps Bernard had been subbing Rory's brother Gregory too.

Downstairs, the house phone rang, loud and insistent. Rory and Bernard paused their chat but began again when the ringing stopped.

'No, it wasn't wrong of you.' Infuriatingly, Bernard sounded keen to meet him halfway. 'I can see why you feel like that, but there are reasons. And you know what those are, my boy. If only you'd felt able to do what was right.'

That was significant. Some kind of wrongdoing on Rory's part, and Bernard knew about it. Not that it was necessarily the same thing Clemmie had wanted to report to the police.

'And make everyone miserable?' Rory said, in an I'm-so-reasonable voice. 'Would that have really been the proper thing to do?'

There was a pause. 'No, perhaps not. You're right. Here, look. This is all I can manage at present.'

What a pushover. If Bella had caved in that easily with her sisters, chaos would have ensued.

'Forty?' Rory was saying, sighing in turn. 'Won't buy much these days, Pa. We need to release some capital and fast. The estate agent's report was encouraging. We could start by selling the café. Come on, what's your objection? It's not even anyone's home.'

How dare he? It was John's brother's livelihood, and a Hope Eaton institution.

'How about we—'

Rory was interrupted by a furious cry from the ground floor: Althea yelling at him and Bernard. This was met with a volley of barking from Eustace, followed by Althea's footsteps, thumping up the stairs.

'Bernard and Rory, how dare you? Is this where you're hiding? Out, now!' She must be outside on the landing.

Bella heard a door creak open.

'I might have known you'd be in there together. I've had enough of you turning your father's head, Rory, plotting and scheming. Not giving a fig for anyone else.' Bella had no trouble hearing Althea's words.

'What's wrong, Althea?' Rory sounded quietly amused, which was desperately annoying. Whatever the trouble was, he clearly didn't care two hoots.

'Adele Lewis from the grocers has just called to ask me how much Clemmie's cottage is going for.'

Bella remembered John saying it was a Powell property, let to Clemmie at mate's rates.

'Well, she is dead, Althea.' Rory's words came out with a light laugh. 'She's hardly going to need it now. And in case you hadn't noticed, we're very short of money.'

'Rory, please!' Bernard's pleading was worrying. Who was in charge?

'But it went on sale *before* she died.' Althea's voice was shaking with anger. 'That's what Adele Lewis says. She heard on the grapevine three weeks ago! Am I to understand that you were attempting to sell it from under poor Clemmie before she was even dead?'

'Uh-oh, Pa, looks like we've been rumbled.'

'What would Gregory say?' Althea thundered. 'This is your

older brother's inheritance as well as yours. At least the rental properties bring in an income.'

'But Gregory would sell this place, wouldn't he?' Rory said nastily. 'Is that what you want? Because Dad can't bear that, can you, Dad? And I'm on Dad's side.'

Bella was quite sure Rory was on no one's side but his own.

'That's not the point.' Althea was still yelling at the top of her lungs. 'The *point* is that you were selling a cottage with a sitting tenant.'

'She signed a waiver to say it was all right,' Rory said lazily. 'She knew she'd never be going home.'

How could he be so callous? Bella longed to enter the fray and tell him what she thought of him.

'You mean to say you went to visit her *in the hospice*, and told her as she lay dying that you wanted to evict her?' Althea was spluttering now. Bella felt for her. 'And then you got her to sign away her rights to make your life easier? She must have felt you couldn't wait for her to give up the ghost. I ask again, how could you? And Clemmie, your own cousin.'

'Hardly!' Rory was shouting now too. 'She was the illegitimate child of a home-wrecker who destroyed a marriage.'

'As though you care about that! Either way, Clemmie was a dying woman, and you took advantage of her. And all because you can't keep your spending under control.' She turned to her husband, her fury tinged with sorrow now. 'And you can't say no to him!'

Perhaps this was what Clemmie had meant about Althea's bravery, and her willingness to risk everything for her. She was clearly fiercely loyal, even if it meant a monumental row with her family. Bella could see exactly where Althea was coming from.

'You're making a mountain out of a molehill.' The lack of guilt in Rory's tone made Bella quiver. She was sure he was deliberately winding Althea up.

'And what do you say, Bernard?' Althea's voice had turned dangerously quiet.

'My dear, you're right.' He sounded pathetically nervous. A man who wanted to have his cake and eat it. 'Your stepmother's a better person than we are, my boy. It's true we're up against it but we shouldn't have taken advantage. And it's not as though we had long to wait, as it turns...' He left his sentence unfinished. Very wise.

'It was morally wrong.' Althea said. 'And those rentals must not be sold. The cottages are people's homes, the Steps is someone's business. My own niece is one of our tenants,' she went on. 'Would you throw her out?'

'On the contrary, I'd invite her in.' The way Rory spoke told Bella he was leering. 'I can't imagine I'll have long to wait before she starts staying over at my place. Perhaps she'll move in with me, eventually.'

Bella had a nasty feeling Rory might be using Paula simply to get at Althea.

Althea didn't reply, so Bella was left to imagine her expression. 'Bernard, I want your word that you won't even consider selling any of the other properties. Think what everyone would say if you evicted your tenants. The Lammas Day feast is fast approaching. How would you face them all?'

Bella knew he and Althea were thought of as the king and queen of the annual celebration, though it was a whole-town affair.

'We might be running out of money,' Althea went on, 'but standards must be maintained. Yes?' She waited, then added. 'Are we in agreement, Bernard?'

At last, Bella heard a mumbled, 'Yes, my dear.' But in the pit of her stomach, anxiety was squirming, laced with fury at Rory. The future of the Steps and all those homes was hanging by a thread. Althea held a lot of sway, but when she wasn't watching, Rory was slowly but surely pushing his dad to the brink. Poor

Leo and his lovely café weren't safe and the other tenants weren't either. Bella would move heaven and earth to safeguard what they had.

The discussion seemed to be over, but she stayed where she was. If she moved, they might hear the floor creak.

She was still standing there, five minutes later, when she heard the door of the room she was in open. Her heart beat faster. It could be any of them; she didn't dare peek. If it was Althea, she was bound to explore further and find her. Bella waited, heart in mouth, for the jump scare.

But no one came to look in the alcove and after another minute, she heard the door close again.

It was ten minutes after that that Althea came in, her miniature schnauzer hot on her heels. 'They've gone again. I suppose you heard all that?' She still looked livid and Eustace shook himself, as though similarly affected.

Bella nodded.

'They mustn't sell off the rental properties.'

Now was Bella's chance. She mentioned John's conversation with the estate agent who'd valued the Steps. 'I got the impression they'd been asked to look at all the Powell holdings.'

Althea went puce. 'Thank you for letting me know. I will not have it! The properties *must* stay in the family, let out at affordable rents. As for the idea of my niece moving in with Rory...' Althea took a deep, shuddering breath. 'They've only just started seeing each other. He's simply pushing my buttons, but all the same, the thought is horrendous. It's essential she maintains her independence. I sometimes wonder if Rory's trying to goad me into leaving Bernard and washing my hands of the Powells completely.

'Well, I may not have the legal right to stop the sales, but I intend to fight – both for the properties and Bernard. He knows right from wrong and he still loves me, as I do him. I just need to make sure I'm around when Rory's pouring poison into his ear. They'll sell the Powell properties over my dead body.'

5

———————

MINING FOR GOSSIP

Bella decided not to tell John how close she'd come to being found out when she returned to Vintage Winter at lunchtime. She'd agreed with Althea to use the Lammas Day feast as an excuse in future. It wouldn't happen again. But she filled him in on everything else.

'Rory's clearly a nasty piece of work, and Bernard's weak. Althea's a positive influence – Bernard's moral guardian – but when her back's turned, Rory gets the upper hand. The more I think about it, the odder it seems that he visited Clemmie at the hospice. He called her the daughter of a home-wrecker, and she'd cut him out of her will.' He hadn't been there out of fondness, that was for sure.

'Tell me exactly what they said.' John took out his meticulously prepared packed lunch with its bulgur wheat salad, hunk of cheese and home-baked roll.

Bella dug out the salami-filled baguette she'd bought from Leo at the Steps and filled him in, between mouthfuls.

John shrank in on himself, like a full-body wince, when she revealed Rory was pushing to sell the Steps. 'So all the business about a valuation for insurance was rubbish then. Have you told Leo?'

Bella shook her head. 'I'm hoping we can put paid to Rory's influence before we need to. We might neutralise it completely, if he's guilty of something serious. At least Althea knows he's pushing his dad to sell. She's determined to stop it.'

John paused for a moment, then nodded. 'I can't believe Rory and Bernard tried to sell Clemmie's house from under her too.' John being John, he looked devastated rather than angry.

Bella was still fuming. 'I know. And if he's capable of that, who knows what else he might do.'

John took another forkful of salad. 'Have you met Gregory, the other brother?'

Bella grasped her baguette, rescuing a bit of salami that was making a bid for freedom. 'No. He'd gone out for the day when I arrived.'

'I bumped into him after closing yesterday when I nipped over to see Tom.' John was related to half of Hope Eaton, and his cousin Tom was the town's solicitor. 'You know Gregory works for him? He's a legal secretary.'

'No, I didn't know. What are you thinking?'

He sighed. 'It's probably nothing, but I was paying special attention after your visit to the police. He's got one of those privacy screens on his computer, but he still clicked out of what he was working on when I came in. He leaned over his notepad so I couldn't see it, too.'

'I suppose his work must be confidential.'

John frowned. 'I know, but there was something about the way he looked. I would have said he's poles apart from Rory, but he seemed guilty and flustered.'

Another suspect to add to the list. 'Right, thanks. We must find out more about him.' She looked at her watch. 'Tony's taking his time, letting me know about the post-mortem.'

'They only agreed to it yesterday.'

It felt like forever. 'You'd hope they'd rush it through.' She popped Tony a text to make sure he was on the case.

John's worried eyes met hers from behind his glasses. 'What will you do next?'

'Find out more about Althea's niece, Paula Richards. She and Rory started dating recently, so she might know what he's up to. They could even be in league, if she's in the throes of passion. New relationships can be intense.' Not a good thought. 'She works at the hospice. If she gave Clemmie extra tonic, Clemmie wouldn't have questioned it. The question is, where to go for gossip.' She met John's eyes. 'You must know someone with a link to the hospice.'

He gave a heavy sigh. 'One of mum's flock, Gilbert Rowntree, might be your best bet.'

Jeannie regarded the clientele at the Blue Boar as a sheep dog might regard its sheep. She watched over them in a well-intentioned but distinctly bossy way.

'She noticed he liked a good gossip,' John said, 'and decided he was lonely.'

'She took him under her wing?'

He nodded. 'Turns out he's got loads of friends, he just really enjoys speculation – the juicier the better. He volunteers as a hospice visitor, so he's bound to be in the know. Mum says he's addicted to shortbread, if that's any help.'

'I'll take him some.'

'But how will you introduce yourself?'

Bella turned to get her bag. 'I'll say I'm considering volunteering too, and ask him what it's like. Could you ring him and let him know to expect me?'

He looked uncomfortable. 'He's bound to realise I'm spinning him a line. I'm not good at lying.'

'One of the many reasons I love you.' She smiled sweetly as he squirmed. She'd known it would tease him, but the comment was genuine. He was like the brother she'd never had. 'Where can I find him?'

John shook his head and provided the address.

Bella bought some shortbread from the less heinously expensive delicatessen, then crossed town and made her way to Gilbert Rowntree's address. She found a small, snug cottage at the end of Market Street, the tiny front garden stuffed with lavender, the vanilla front door adorned with a fox-head knocker. *Lovely.* She could definitely sell that, if it was on offer.

The door opened the second she'd knocked.

'Mr Rowntree? I'm Bella.'

He was positively beaming. 'Gilbert, please!' He shook her hand warmly, his wispy grey hair bobbing as he nodded at her. 'Come in, come in! Young John just called to say you were on your way.'

As she handed over the shortbread his smile became wider still. 'I can see my reputation precedes me. So, you're thinking of volunteering at the hospice? Good, good. Let's have tea. You can't eat shortbread without it.'

She followed him through to a tiny galley kitchen where he put a kettle on a gas hob.

Bella thanked him, offered help and was declined. 'How long have you been a visitor at the hospice?' she asked.

'Oh, a long time! My wife and I used to go together until she passed.' He put a hand to his chest.

'I'm so sorry for your loss.' She left a decent pause and then went on. 'I thought of volunteering because I visited Clemmie Crowe at the hospice, just before she died.'

He shook his head. 'Tragic.'

'I know her best friend too, Althea.'

He nodded. 'She visited poor Clemmie regularly. I felt for her, having to watch her friend suffer so gravely.' He sighed.

'She had tears in her eyes, each time she left. A stoical friend and a brave woman.'

'That's Althea all over,' Bella agreed. 'And you must know Paula Richards, her niece, as well. I guess it was a comfort to Althea to have her there, looking after Clemmie. Paula seems very dedicated.' In reality, Bella had no idea about her work ethic, so she watched Gilbert's reaction. If he disagreed, he'd probably show it.

He smiled as the kettle came to the boil. 'She does, but it's interesting you should mention her. If you do come to visit, I'd love a second opinion.'

He poured water into the pot and set it next to some cups on the tray.

'Really? That sounds interesting.'

His eyes twinkled as he glanced at her over his shoulder. 'Bring the shortbreads through and I'll tell you more. Purely between ourselves, you understand. I wouldn't want her or Althea to think I've been gossiping.'

Perish the thought...

In his front room, a small boy was playing with a trainset, a *Bluey* rucksack on his back.

'Say hello, Thomas!' Gilbert said, to the child's back. The child ignored him but Gilbert's smile didn't dim. 'My grandson. He comes with me to the hospice sometimes. It livens things up.'

Bella watched as Thomas took a train off the track and put it in his rucksack.

Gilbert chuckled. 'He loves *Bluey*. He and that rucksack are never parted. Now, where were we?'

They sat down on chintz sofas and Gilbert poured their teas. 'So, entre nous, I saw Paula accept two fifty-pound notes from a young man called Rufus Hartford. Son of an exceptionally well-heeled patient.'

'How odd.'

'Well, exactly.' He handed her a cup. 'Do have a shortbread, too.'

She took one.

'Of course, if she'd taken money from his mother, it would have been a sacking offence, but her son's not vulnerable – anything but. All the same, it's mysterious, don't you think?'

It felt wrong to encourage him, but she couldn't stop now. 'Yes, very.'

'I hear one of the staff told the manager, but she said he was probably paying Paula back for something she'd bought for his mum. The woman who ratted on her is always complaining about something. When the management didn't rise to the bait, she accused them of turning a blind eye to avoid a scandal.'

'I suppose there could be an innocent explanation.'

'Possibly.' Gilbert laughed. 'But that would be quite boring, so let's hope not. One thing I can say is, I'm certain Paula wanted to keep the payment secret. Rufus wasn't guarded when he handed the money over, but she flushed and turned away quickly.'

He was incorrigible. 'You think she caught you watching?'

He drew himself up. 'Certainly not! But Rory Powell had just turned up. He and Paula have got a thing going, you know. Perhaps she didn't want him to see her take a hundred pounds from another man.'

'Quite possibly.' Apart from anything else, Bella bet he'd have asked to borrow it if he'd seen it. She'd been wondering if Paula and Rory might be in cahoots, but perhaps Paula had her own fish to fry. If so, Clemmie could have picked up on it, given she was on the spot. It was clear she wanted to talk to Adam Davies about the Powells, but Paula's actions might affect them too.

Bella decided to steer the conversation onto Paula's relationship with Rory and the change in Clemmie's will. It would be useful to find out when she'd updated it and

Gilbert was the sort to have found out. 'I don't imagine Althea knows about Rufus Hartford – she'd be concerned. She's already worried about Paula's budding relationship with Rory.'

Gilbert's eyes widened. 'I'm not surprised.'

'I gather it's early days, but are they madly in love, do you think?'

'I don't imagine that boy loves anyone but himself.'

It matched Bella's impression.

'That said, he's been popping in to see her. Perhaps he does it to irk Althea, if she doesn't approve.'

'Figures.' Without that kind of ulterior motive, Rory was the sort to target someone wealthier. But as well as annoying Althea, seeing Paula gave him a reason to be at the hospice. Was it possible he'd taken up with her to provide that excuse? Bella still thought it was odd that he'd visited Clemmie. She mentioned it to Gilbert.

'Oh yes, I noticed him go in and wondered too. All the Powells visited on the afternoon poor Clemmie died. Rory at around three, though he didn't stay long, Gregory at half past or thereabouts, then Bernard on his way home from some meeting or other, followed by Althea. And then you and John of course – though we weren't introduced.' He twinkled at her. 'I'm very glad to make your acquaintance now!'

'You too.' Bella gave him her best smile. He really was coming up with the goods. 'I wonder what Paula sees in Rory.'

Gilbert's brow crinkled. 'A very good question. They strike me as an odd couple, and I know about true love. My wife and I were inseparable.' He glanced fondly at a photograph on the mantelpiece as his grandson made chuffing noises and pushed a train round the track.

Bella leaned forward. 'Speaking of Rory, I hear Clemmie cut him out of her will!'

Gilbert looked very excited now. *Honestly…* 'Absolutely

right, and quite late on too! We saw Tom Butler go in, just a week before she died.'

Bingo. 'I wonder what made her do it.'

His eyes glowed. 'We all do too.'

Damn. He didn't have the answer, clearly.

'And then there's Gregory. He's another dark horse.' He pushed the plate of shortbreads towards her and took another himself, with a look of glee. 'You know Gregory? Rory's elder brother?'

'I saw him at the celebration of Clemmie's life, at the Blue Boar.'

Gilbert nodded. 'Well, I overheard him talking to Clemmie a few days before she died. I just happened to be passing and the rooms aren't totally soundproof.'

Bella was starting to wonder if she should report him, though the intel was second to none. 'Yes?'

Gilbert paused dramatically. 'I heard Gregory say, "I didn't know you knew. You won't tell anyone, will you? Dad wouldn't understand if he found out." And I must say, he looked *very* anxious when he left afterwards. Up until then, I'd never believed people actually wrung their hands.' He grinned as his grandson put some shortbread into his rucksack. 'I think you'll fit in admirably at the hospice. We'll have so much to discuss!'

Bella reported back to John when she returned to Vintage Winter. 'Thank you for the excellent tip-off. He's absolutely shameless! But the gossip was invaluable. It sounds as though the whole team live for it. I wondered if I should warn the management, but they'd probably lose every volunteer.'

John groaned. 'I can imagine.'

'I might try to find some way to discourage him.'

'You think you stand a chance?' John looked dubious. 'Mum's already tried.'

Bella could imagine Jeannie going about it with gusto, but Bella's methods would be different. More subtle. John ought to realise that.

'What does it mean for Clemmie's death?' he said, before she could voice the thought.

'It's significant that Paula and Gregory have secrets. Clemmie had discovered his, and possibly hers too. I need to know why this man Rufus slipped Paula money. And what Gregory's hiding as well. But whatever they're up to, I won't lose focus on Rory. There's sure to be dirt to dig on him.' It was possible Clemmie had cut him out of her will for making her sign away her house, but she bet there'd be more too. He was just that sort.

John nodded. 'Good.'

'I'm going to visit the Blue Boar after we close and ask your mum what she knows about him. I think if I—'

Her mobile rang. Tony.

'*Seems you were right.*' His voice reverberated down the line. '*Clemmie Crowe died of an overdose of sleeping pills. Can't prove how they were administered or even guess at a time, aside from it being that afternoon. Barry agrees it was probably slipped into an extra dose of tonic. She hadn't consumed anything else.*'

Bella had guessed it was coming, but her legs felt wobbly when faced with the reality. A second later, she was tearful. Partly in sorrow and anger for Clemmie, partly at the need to tell John. She knew how deep the news would cut.

She tried to focus on practicalities and shared what she'd heard from Gilbert Rowntree. 'I'll pass it all on to Barry, especially after what you've just told me.'

She watched John's expression change. He must have guessed Tony's news, and her heart went out to him.

'*I'd get more information first,*' Tony said, in answer to her suggestion. '*The Gilbert stuff is just gossip, and if Barry wades in, it could put the frighteners on Gregory and Paula. Whereas if you watch quietly, you're in with a chance of finding out more. That's when you should tell him.'*

'You have worryingly little faith in your former colleagues.'

He chuckled. *'Nah, it's just logic. You're on the spot, almost unseen, so you'll glean more. And for you, it's personal, isn't it? Makes a world of difference.'*

He was right, it was vitally important to her, because of the chances she'd missed, and what Clemmie had meant to John. But it was more than that too. She had the skills for it and she wanted to get stuck in. She hoped her dad might be out there somewhere, cheering her on.

'What about a meet-up this evening for a proper chat?' Tony added.

'Good idea. The Blue Boar after work?' Persuading Tony wasn't too difficult. Despite his unaccountable love of the Mitre in Shrewsbury, with its beer-infused swirly carpets and lack of style, he had a soft spot for Jeannie and her mini kingdom.

They agreed a time, then she rang off and watched the pain in John's eyes. It filled her with a rush of adrenaline. She was determined to get Clemmie justice. Then the rush turned heady. She wanted to win too, defeat the monster who'd committed such a horrible crime against someone so defenceless. She could do this.

She could see John was still adjusting to the news as the shop bell jangled and a customer walked in.

Only it wasn't a customer. It was John's former boss and Bella's arch enemy, Sienna Hearst. And she was looking worryingly happy about something.

6

A NEW THREAT

John had loved Sienna's aunt, old Mrs Hearst, and had worked happily for her for years, but Sienna was a very different character. Within days of her taking over the Hearst House Museum following the old lady's death, John had decided it was time to change jobs. Bella had been looking for a second in command and had rejoiced when she'd convinced him to join her. She'd already known what a gem he was after visiting the museum with her dad, years back. The place had been fun, and he and old Mrs Hearst were two of the best things about it. Since Sienna had arrived, it had changed character entirely.

Sienna eyed Bella icily. She hadn't forgiven her for 'poaching' John and had been looking for ways to pay her back ever since.

She looked over Bella's stock with a sneer. 'I'm on my way to the other antiques outlets – some of them have such vision – but I thought I'd look in. I've heard on the grapevine that the Steps might be up for sale soon. I wanted to let you know that I'm thinking of buying.'

Bella felt a hollow in the pit of her chest. The thought of John's brother losing the place to someone like Sienna was unspeakably awful. She'd love to think Sienna was bluffing, but she bet she could afford it. She dripped expensive jewellery and designer clothes, and she'd sold a house before moving into her aunt's place. She probably had plenty of capital.

'Establishing an eatery with more finesse would be an excellent addition to my business interests.' She smiled. 'It'll open people's eyes to what they've been missing. I'm sure we'll pull some customers away from the Blue Boar too.'

It was a direct attack on the Jenks's livelihoods.

John's knuckles were white on the vase he'd been dusting.

Bella stepped closer to him. 'I think you'll find it never comes up for sale. The Powell family haven't decided to let it go.'

Sienna smiled again. 'Really? I thought it was a done deal. In any case, I'm planning to put in a very generous cash offer. I imagine that might tip the balance.' She turned to leave.

Bella couldn't believe it. She knew Sienna was too stingy to do it purely from spite, but her relish at the idea of turfing Leo out was transparent. And all down to John coming to work for her.

As soon as she was gone, Bella turned to him. 'I won't let her do this, John. It's Rory driving the sale. Althea will fight him tooth and nail, and in the meantime, I'm going to find something on him that'll stick. Come along to the Blue Boar later. Tony might know something useful.'

John bit his lip. 'We're going to have to tell Leo and Carys about this now.' Carys was Leo's wife. 'And Mum.'

Horrible but true. 'I know.'

While John called to break the news to Leo, Bella composed a text to Barry Dixon. Clemmie had cut Rory out of her will, for heaven's sake. She'd known something about the Powells and, most probably, him. He had to be a prime suspect for the murder.

. . .

Later that day, Bella and John made their way to the Blue Room, the inn's snug, where they always met Tony for official business. Bella loved it – its dark blue walls, leather sofas and the soft light from the standard lamp left her feeling cosy and cocooned. There was a long, low mahogany table, a roaring fire in winter, paintings on the walls, and a delightfully full bookcase.

Tony had texted to say he was on his way and they left him the armchair at the head of the table, while they occupied the sofas.

Inevitably, Jeannie came to join them the moment she saw them skulking.

She flumped down next to John. 'What's all this?'

'Tony's on his way to provide a full update,' Bella replied, 'but I'm afraid we've got bad news. Clemmie Crowe was killed with an overdose.'

Jeannie shot up, her face full of indignation, and knocked John's drink. He grabbed it with a well-practised move before he lost the lot. 'Who did it? I demand to know! This is an outrage.'

John rose to take Jeannie's arm and Bella stood too. 'We'll find out. She knew something damning about someone, most probably from the Powell family. She planned to report it to a member of Barry Dixon's team, but didn't manage in time.'

John nodded. 'We won't let it rest, Mum.'

Jeannie carried on standing for another half minute, but at last she sighed and dropped into her seat again, narrowly missing John's glass a second time. It was no wonder his reactions were so quick.

'And it may not be relevant to Clemmie's murder, but I'm afraid we've got other news too, also relating to the Powells.' Bella filled Jeannie in on the threat to the Steps, and Sienna's intention to buy.

Jeannie thumped the table. 'Well, if that isn't the frozen limit! The woman is a monster.'

Bella grimaced. She was at the root of all this, and Jeannie must know it. 'I'm sorry. If John hadn't come to work for me, she wouldn't have it in for the entire Jenks clan.'

'Nonsense!' Jeannie's voice carried at the best of times and customers peered at them through the internal windows.

John looked put out. 'You might credit me with some agency. I *wanted* to come and work for you. You could say I'm to blame.'

'Don't be ridiculous, John.' Jeannie was still puce in the face. 'It's the Hearst woman who's responsible. I shall bar her from the inn.'

Bella had never seen her drink there, but thought better of mentioning it. 'We need a plan to put things right.' That should get a better reaction. 'And for that, we'll want Tony's input.'

Right on cue, he bundled through the doorway, complete with a pint of Hobsons Twisted Spire and his dog, Captain.

Bella made a fuss of the black labrador as John and Jeannie greeted Tony and he took his seat at the head of the table. It made him look like the king at a banquet, which was bound to please him.

'So,' he said, making himself comfortable, 'sad business, this.' He turned to John. 'Bella explained you and Clemmie were friends. Sorry for your loss.'

John swallowed and nodded.

'Like I said on the phone, it was an overdose of a common sleeping tablet that caused her death. Our boy Barry's taken on board your information on the tonic, Bella, and on Clemmie's efforts to contact Adam Davies. He likes your theory, that someone with a secret stopped her from talking, and they've already got a suspect.'

They all sat forward as he swigged his drink. 'Who?'

He pulled some crumpled paper from his back jeans pocket. Bella wished he'd keep confidential information secure. If he messed up, he'd probably lose his precious place on all those committees.

'Young lass called Daisy Birdwell. Works at the hospice.'

John put a hand over his face.

'What?' Bella asked, as Jeannie's eyes widened.

John sat back on the sofa, his shoulders sagging. 'Daisy is Poppy's sister.'

Poppy was a waitress at the Steps. Or what passed for one, anyway. She could just about be relied upon to transfer food from a to b, so long as there weren't too many distractions.

'It'll be devastating for her if her sister's guilty,' John said.

And ruinous for the rest of them, Bella imagined. Poppy would never concentrate with all that going on.

Jeannie shook her head violently. 'Why do they suspect the poor girl? I've met her and I don't believe she did it for a minute.'

Tony held up a hand. Jeannie tended to bring on gestures of helplessness, even in the toughest of people.

Bella leaped in on the back of what she'd said. 'She doesn't fit. When Clemmie mistook John for Adam Davies, she said she wanted to pass on something related to the Powells.'

Tony made a dampening motion with his hands. 'All right, all right. Give me a chance to explain. *Before* Daisy worked at the hospice, she did some cleaning at High Seat. And while she was with them, a couple of knick-knacks went missing. Nothing was ever proven, but the gossip went round, as gossip does.

'More recently, there's been a series of thefts at the hospice, and she came under suspicion. Now, it's come out that her dad takes the same brand of sleeping pills used to kill Clemmie Crowe. Most worrying of all, one of her friends at the hospice admits she knew Daisy had pinched some.'

'She stole his sleeping pills?' Jeannie looked horrified. 'But I suggested long walks and invited her to share her worries with me.'

Jeannie was touchingly unaware that her word wasn't law.

Bella leaned forward. 'Why was she worried?'

'Well, because of the accusations of theft, of course!' Jeannie said. 'She told me she couldn't sleep.'

Tony nodded. 'She claims she pinched the tablets for herself, and that she hasn't been able to rest since she was investigated. The evidence is all circumstantial, but Barry'll try to build a case.'

Jeannie was shaking her head. 'Ridiculous. You have other candidates, don't you, Bella?'

'Several.' Bella sipped her drink, John's partner Gareth's signature summer cup. 'And if Barry's homing in on Daisy, it makes sense for us to look elsewhere.' If she found something concrete, she might get him to shift focus. 'Top of my list is Rory Powell. Clemmie was a kind and reticent woman, yet she cut him out of her will, shortly before she died. It was a symbolic gesture – there was only two hundred and fifty pounds at stake – but he must have crossed a line. He and his dad got Clemmie to sign papers renouncing her rights to her rental cottage. It was grossly insensitive. Perhaps it was that which made her change her will, but I wouldn't be surprised if Rory's involved in something criminal too. From what I can see, he makes no effort to manage his money and expects other people to bail him out. Althea sees right through him, but his dad's another matter.' Bella relayed what she'd overheard at High Seat. 'It's infuriating that Bernard isn't firmer.'

Jeannie was frowning. 'I blame myself, really. I tried to offer him some coaching on how to take Rory in hand, but he wasn't receptive.'

No surprises there. Jeannie's advice could be rather heavy-handed at times.

'It still shocks me that Bernard gave him a house, when

Gregory lives at home,' Jeannie went on. 'Though I can imagine wanting Rory out from under my feet, of course. But it's very bad training. The worst of it is, Bernard doesn't appreciate how hard Gregory works. I heard him say the legal secretary job "isn't quite what he'd hoped for". Yet, does he complain about Rory's "work"?' She looked at them fiercely. 'He does not! Because Rory tells Bernard stories about smart-sounding "business ventures".' She tutted loudly. 'In reality they come to nothing, and I suspect him of gambling on the horses too. He's always sneaking over to the racecourse. He even had the nerve to offer my customers tips – in exchange for a percentage of their winnings if they got lucky. I ask you! He's a terrible influence.'

'I can't see him working hard enough to make money from anything legitimate,' Bella said. 'I'm planning to trace his contacts and see what I can find out. He mentioned someone called Foxy. But I wonder about Gregory too.' She glanced at John. 'You'd better explain what you saw when you nipped in to the solicitors.'

After John had summed up Gregory's shifty behaviour, Jeannie frowned. 'We mustn't get distracted. He was probably playing online games, or something like that.'

'And the notes he hid on his desk?'

Jeannie ruffled her metaphorical feathers. 'Confidential legal papers, no doubt.'

It was time for Bella to chip in. 'I'm afraid one of the hospice volunteers heard him having a suspicious conversation with Clemmie, too.'

'Not Gilbert Rowntree?' Jeannie's brows drew down. 'He's the most incorrigible gossip. I tried to point out the error of his ways, but he's irredeemable.'

'It was him. Gossip or not, the information's interesting. Gregory told Clemmie: "I didn't know you knew. You won't tell anyone, will you? Dad wouldn't understand if he found out."'

Jeannie waved a hand. 'That could be anything, from a secret passion for hopscotch to a love affair with an unsuitable woman. No, it's Rory we must focus on. He can't be allowed to ruin Leo's business.'

Tony met Bella's eye and winked.

John sat forward. 'If Poppy's sister's been falsely accused, Mum, we need to keep an open mind. Proving she's innocent has to be a priority. If we're blind to everyone but Rory, we might miss something important.'

Bella leaped in before Jeannie could rise again. 'Even if Rory isn't a killer, I'll bet he's guilty of *something*. We can look into that at the same time as everything else.'

Jeannie reached to grip Bella's arm as though it were a life raft. 'Yes, good. Thank you, Bella.'

'As well as Gregory, there's Paula to consider.' She explained about Gilbert seeing her accept a hundred pounds from Rufus Hartford. 'He's convinced she was trying to keep it secret. Do you know anything about him?'

Jeannie's brow drew down again. 'Yes. And he has a connection with the Powells.'

That was interesting.

'His family bought a lot of Powell land.' Jeannie shook her head. 'Selling must have been a sad blow to Bernard. He's such a proud man. I should try to get him involved in some community work. He needs to see the contribution he can make, even if he's no longer lord of the manor.'

Bella bet that would go down like a lead balloon.

'Althea's very different, of course,' Jeannie went on. 'She has a hint of the lady bountiful about her, but she's absolutely determined to do her best by the underdog.'

'She certainly doesn't want the rental properties sold off.'

Jeannie nodded. 'She visits her tenants, you know. Takes them apples and raspberries from the garden at High Seat, and gifts if they're unwell. She notices, and I take my hat off to her.'

Bella did too. She'd thought from the start that she genuinely cared.

'Any further ideas?' Tony asked.

'The dynamic between Paula and Rufus Hartford is interesting.' Bella thought it through. 'I could imagine Rory resenting Rufus's family for buying Powell land. He probably thinks it was his birthright. I doubt he'd like his girlfriend accepting cash from one of them.'

Tony nodded. 'Fair point. So, the upshot is, Paula and Gregory are both keeping secrets, and Rory is a nasty piece of work who Clemmie disinherited.'

'That's about it. I wonder if Barry's checked if any of them has access to the right brand of sleeping tablets. Whatever the truth, we need to get to the bottom of this. It's too cruel that Clemmie was killed while looking for justice, and we have to help Poppy's sister if she's innocent.' If she hadn't slept after the theft accusation, what would being a murder suspect do to her? 'We need to uncover the secrets we've identified, find out if Rory is hiding anything too, and work out who was stealing at the hospice. If it wasn't Daisy Birdwell, her motive for murder goes out of the window.'

Though if it was, it would be damning, even if she hadn't administered Clemmie's fatal dose. Bella sighed.

7

UNDERHAND DEALINGS

Bella was itching to get on with her research into Rory Powell's business dealings, Gregory's secret and Paula Richards' mysterious extra income. The sooner she had enough information to set Barry on them, the better. But she had to keep Vintage Winter afloat too. Stock was selling well, and she needed to source more. The following morning, the call for a lie-in was strong, but it was no good. There was an antiques and collectables fair at Long Marston Racecourse and she wouldn't miss it. She set herself six successive alarms to make sure she woke in time and hoped that Matt next door wouldn't be irritated by the noise. Ever since he'd mentioned her singing in the shower, she'd realised the soundproofing was unreliable.

The day promised to be hot, and Bella showered then donned a 1950s yellow-and-green floral dress with decorative Bakelite buttons. There wasn't time for more than a coffee for breakfast. Her plan was to attend the sale but be back in time to keep standard Sunday opening hours at Vintage Winter. It was John's day off, but he'd decided to come too. The news had put a spring in Bella's step – he'd be invaluable. Not just a second pair of hands, but of eyes too. He'd already learned just which items would interest her and their clientele.

'You're sure it's all right for us to sneak in early?' he said as she trundled her ex-London taxi, Thomasina, past dogwood hedgerows, oaks and fields to reach their destination.

'Everyone does it.' It wasn't the first time he'd asked. Bella had picked up spare tickets from a stallholder. Not officially allowed, but it would get them in at the same time as the dealers, before all the good stuff went. 'It's the only way I'll be back in time to open the shop.'

'And get a head start on the other buyers.'

'Only the ones who don't know the ropes.'

'What if we're found out?' John said.

'No one's going to notice.' The organisers had enough on their plates without worrying about Bella and John sneaking in.

'What does Robert say?'

'We've only been on one date; we're not joined at the hip.' She hadn't told him. She had a feeling he might be a stickler for the rules. 'Now we've got time to browse at our leisure while everyone gets set up.'

John sighed but gave in.

Within fifteen minutes she'd parked Thomasina and was looking around while the stallholders arranged their wares. It was a good time to assess everything – they were too distracted to shift into sales mode, so she could look in peace.

By nine o'clock, when the regular punters were starting to enter the fair, Bella had bought several items that delighted her. She considered her haul. The 1950s Royal Stuart Spencer Stevenson tea set and the hand-painted bowls from France were particularly good finds. The dealers she met were charming and it was nice to be distracted from poor Clemmie's death and the trouble that threatened the Steps. She was just wondering how John could cope in his suit – the sun was beating down – when a face in the crowd jolted her out of her bubble. 'What's *he* doing here? He's supposed to be skint.' She inclined her head very subtly towards Rory Powell, who stood amongst a gaggle of people beyond a stall selling reclaimed wicker baskets.

John raised an eyebrow as Bella walked towards the stall to get a better look.

She kept smiling as she approached the stallholder, despite the nasty taste Rory brought to her mouth. Forming a bond with a dealer was everything and she enjoyed the feeling of bonhomie. 'I love these.' She picked up a selection of the baskets. 'Is there any chance you'd let me have them at trade prices?'

The guy behind the table grinned. The sunshine seemed to have put everyone in a good mood. 'Reckon I can do that.'

The deal was done, money exchanged, and an agreement made to collect them when Bella was ready to leave. *Perfect.*

She handed the receipt to John who folded it very neatly then put it alongside several others in his bottle-green wallet.

'Rory's on the move,' he said quietly.

Bella had been monitoring him too. He was heading towards some trees. 'He looks shifty.'

John pushed his glasses up his nose. 'Who's the woman who's just joined him?'

'Paula Richards, Althea's niece.' After what Bella had witnessed, she wasn't surprised that Althea regretted their relationship. Presumably Paula had fallen for Rory's looks. He had a dash of wild allure, but you'd think she'd have seen past that. As if on cue, the pair started arguing – or that was what it looked like. 'Their romance makes me curious. You'd think Rory would go for someone with pots of cash. Paula's very pretty but I doubt she's well paid.' The most crucial jobs seldom were. 'I can only think he's with her to rile Althea. But why would Paula put up with him?'

Rory raised his hand, as though he didn't want Paula to follow him, and she put her hands on her hips. But a moment later, Rory's shoulders relaxed. He put an arm around her and herded her to a tent selling tea and cake. That would have been the limit for Bella. She couldn't bear to be herded.

She turned to John. 'I'm going to get closer. I'd like to know what Rory's game is.'

'Isn't that a bit risky? What if he killed Clemmie?'

'All the more reason to cling to his coat-tails. I won't let him see me. If you'd heard him in action, you'd want him to get his comeuppance too.'

John's brow was furrowed, but at last he sighed. 'All right. Shall I come too, or would you prefer me to scan the last few stalls?'

He was a gem. 'Scan the stalls. Thank you.'

Bella edged her way towards the tea and cake tent, keeping herself hidden in the crowds. The place was buzzing. She'd have to get close if she wanted to hear what Rory and Paula said.

In the end, she managed to sidle up to the red-and-white striped canvas and pause there. She could just see the pair of them through a gap between two tent panels.

'You can meet them next time,' Rory was saying. 'They're just a bit publicity shy.'

'I know.' Paula's expression was mutinous. 'You said.'

Rory was tucking a strand of Paula's hair behind her ear. Bella would have found that annoying too. From what she'd seen of Paula, she was surprised she'd tolerate it.

'I don't like being left out. I'm so bored, and you're having all the fun.' She sounded peevish, which was disappointing. Perhaps Bella had misread her. The thought was worrying. Divining people's personalities was supposed to be her specialist subject. It was central to dealing antiques.

Rory grinned and shrugged. 'It's not all glamour, you know.'

'It sounds exciting. Tell me, what are you taking them?'

'Something pretty. They like pretty things.'

'I do too.'

'Maybe I'll find you something nice as well.'

Only if he came into money, Bella reckoned, but perhaps he was about to. He was clearly here to sell something, and not as part of the main business of the fair.

'So it's a woman you're meeting, then?'

He sat up straight and his smile faded. 'It's not just women who like pretty trinkets.'

The deal sounded seriously dodgy. Why keep it secret from Paula, otherwise? He didn't even want her to know if he was selling to a man or a woman.

'Now, you stay right here,' Rory said, 'and I'll be back before you know it.' He strode off and his smile didn't falter, but he peered at Paula over his shoulder as he left. He really didn't want her following him. Bella could see the tension in Paula's body. She looked desperate to shoot out of her seat. In the end, she didn't, but her expression spoke volumes: the filthiest of looks, directed at Rory's retreating back. It was more than just momentary fury – there was disdain in her eyes. Bella felt a rush of realisation. Paula didn't truly like him at all.

She frowned. If she was right, Paula had to be playing him, but to what end? She might want to access his buyers, to do deals of her own. Or perhaps she wanted evidence Rory was a wrong 'un, for her own or her aunt's sake. Or to blackmail him, even.

Bella had the advantage over Paula. She wasn't being watched so she could move quickly – round the back of the tent in the direction Rory had taken. She was fast enough to track him through the trees and see him glance around again before doubling back smartly to the far side of the car park.

Bella darted a look at the tea tent and saw that Paula had moved too, now Rory wasn't watching. She was staring into the woods, at the space where Rory had recently stood, a look of frustration on her face. She hadn't seen where he'd gone. Once again, Bella wondered what was really driving her.

A moment later, Paula appeared to give up and wandered off. Bella kept half an eye on her, but most of her attention was focused on Rory, who was hiding in plain sight. There were hordes of legitimate fair attendees in the car park, wedging the goods they'd bought into car boots, vans and trucks. Bella adored the hubbub; it made her feel alive, and it worked in her favour too. She was able to slip between the vehicles and watch Rory close up. He was handing a small bubble-wrapped parcel, taken from his car boot, to a woman of around sixty in a well-tailored summer suit. Bella imagined she could pay handsomely for anything she wanted. She managed to get a surreptitious photo of the pair. Rory had his back to her camera but she could see his buyer clearly enough. The woman opened the bubble wrap, but not so Bella could see its contents, then handed Rory a large envelope, smiling. Payment, it had to be. Rory eased the envelope open and did some checking himself.

Bella glimpsed a bank note and then it was all stuffed away and he was on the move again, back towards the tea tent. She glanced around and saw Paula had returned to their table. She was all but certain she hadn't seen the transaction.

The dark-haired woman put her bubble-wrapped purchase into the boot of a Volvo, locked up and pottered into the crowds. Perhaps she'd arranged to do the deal here so it wouldn't look odd when she went home with a new acquisition.

Bella went closer to photograph the woman's numberplate and saw she had some kind of pass to use the car park. She must be part of the racing fraternity.

From a quiet spot within sight of the Volvo, she called John. 'I have a favour to ask, but I know what you're going to say...'

8

THE THRILL OF THE CHASE

Bella knew John was worried about not heading straight back to Hope Eaton. He always twitched if there was any danger of Vintage Winter opening late, and although he was all in favour of getting justice for Clemmie and saving the Steps, Bella suspected he wasn't sure about her methods. Meanwhile, she felt guilty because it was meant to be his day off. All the same, he agreed to do as she asked and round up their purchases. He'd revisit each stall and ferry goods to Thomasina while Bella kept watch next to the mystery woman's Volvo.

A short while later, he called her back to say he was ready to leave. '*And if we're not heading straight home, that needs to be sooner rather than later.*'

She imagined him looking anxiously at his neat gold-plated watch and biting his lip.

'If we get seriously delayed, I could always call Leo and ask if he can spare Poppy to open up for me. We're here trying to prove her sister's innocence, after all.'

'*Poppy?*' The word came as a yelp. '*Please tell me you're not serious.*'

It was true that she was neither the most reliable nor mature of workers, but in extremis, it would be better than nothing. Probably.

'The thing is—' She broke off mid-sentence. The mystery woman was approaching her Volvo. 'She's here. I'm coming to join you right now.'

By the time Bella was back in Thomasina's driving seat, the Volvo was leaving the car park. Bella drove off slowly, giving the mystery woman a head start – Thomasina was distinctly conspicuous in the Shropshire countryside.

'If I'm right, Rory sold her something dodgy and we need to get proof.'

John continued to look anxious. 'Couldn't you just tell Althea what you've seen and let her take it from here?'

Bella shook her head as she turned towards the village of Ditton Crossley. 'Rory's the sort to wriggle out of things. What's to stop him denying all knowledge? And it's his dad who needs convincing he's dishonest. He'll demand evidence. Imagine if it was Jeannie and one of you.' The landlady would no doubt fight to the death for any of her three sons.

She glanced at John for a second and he gave her a tired look.

'What I need is a photo of what Rory sold Ms Navy Volvo. He's got no money, so ten to one it's stolen. If I can prove it, the Powells will have to accept what he's up to. It could be why Clemmie died too.'

When she glanced at John again, he had a hand up to his forehead, as though he was developing a headache. 'How on earth do you propose to get a photo?'

'By relying on my knowledge of buyer behaviour. Whatever she bought, it's her new treasure. Rory called it "something pretty". If she runs true to form, she'll want to have a proper look as soon as she can. She'll probably head somewhere private – her own house perhaps – and if she's got the place to herself, I doubt she'll bother to go upstairs before she peels off the bubble wrap. She should be visible through a downstairs window. I just need to work out how to approach quietly. Once I'm in position, that's where you come in.' She glimpsed him close his eyes.

'I'm not sure I want to hear the next bit.'

Ms Navy Volvo was turning off the main road through the village, up a narrow lane with passing places. Bella slowed right down, then followed with caution. 'It's easy, I promise. I need you to be waiting just outside her house. If it all plays out as I think, I'll ping you a text the moment she's unwrapped her parcel.'

'And then?'

'The second you get my message, you march up the drive and knock on her door.'

'Do I have to?'

'It's to save the Steps and possibly get justice for Clemmie, remember. All you need to do is apologise for disturbing her, then say your car needs recharging, and can she direct you to the nearest charging point?' Thomasina was electric. 'Say your phone's out of battery, so you can't use that to check.'

'I'm bound to come across as shifty.'

'Honestly, John, you couldn't look more respectable if you tried.' She applauded the choice of the suit now, despite the summer heat. 'And I'll only need a few seconds to photograph whatever she bought. I'm betting she'll put it down when she goes to answer the door. If it's next to the bubble wrap, so much the better.' It would tell a story, along with the other pictures Bella had taken. 'I'll buy you lunch at the Blue Boar as a thank you.'

The mystery woman had driven up a driveway towards a substantial red-brick Georgian house with ivy growing up the wall. Bella pulled up in the entrance to a field and turned to John. 'Right, if you get in position, this shouldn't take long.'

He was glancing at his watch again, running a hand through his hair. 'What will you say if she spots you before I knock?'

'Don't worry – I'll think of something.' There was nothing like sudden pressure to get the creative juices flowing.

Her quarry was letting herself in through the front door as Bella reached the head of the drive. She listened hard, but no one called out a greeting and the house's windows were shut, despite the warm day. Two good signs that she was alone.

Bella surveyed the boundaries of the property. Hedges that could be squeezed through, which was good, and they backed onto fields. She dashed around the side of the house, glad that she'd worn her fifties-style flat sandals with the multiple cross straps. With any luck the mystery woman wouldn't have got further than nipping to the loo by the time Bella approached one of the windows.

She pushed through the hedge, feeling slightly worried for her Bakelite buttons, then approached a window carefully from one side. Sitting room. Empty. But through the open door, she could see another room opposite. A kitchen. That was where Bella would head, if she'd just come back from a fair. She'd want coffee.

She dashed round to the other side of the house, just in time to see the woman peeling open the bubble wrap.

When Bella saw what she had, she went hot and cold all over.

It was the three-panelled, gilded-bronze photo frame she'd valued the day before, at High Seat House. *But how had he picked that out to sell, just after she'd—*

And then suddenly it came to her. When she'd dashed for cover in the glorified alcove, she hadn't taken the book she'd been using to record her valuations. He must have been the person who'd entered the room while she was hiding. He'd used her information to steal from his father and line his pockets. This was terrible. Her carelessness had cost the Powells a possession. She'd been caught up in the thrill of hiding and acted too quickly.

But perhaps he'd stolen before too. It could explain the trinkets that had gone missing when Poppy's sister had worked at High Seat. The louse might have guessed she'd get the blame.

Silently, she cursed herself, then set to work on fixing Rory, the smarmy, selfish beast. She messaged John and within seconds saw the mystery woman pause, photo frame in hand, and glance towards the front of the house.

Go on, go on! It was essential to salvage something from this dreadful situation.

At last, the mystery woman put the frame down and turned towards the kitchen door. Bella got one shot of the frame and the woman's retreating back, and a second zoomed in on the stolen piece. She checked that the picture was clear, but her surge of triumph was tarnished by the way Rory had used her so easily. She was determined to make him pay.

By the time she'd worked her way round to Thomasina, John was in the passenger seat again.

Bella joined him and prepared to set off. 'What did she say, out of interest?'

John looked mystified. 'What?'

'About the nearest charging point? We might need it one day.'

He looked pained. 'I was too tense to take in the answer.'

'Never mind.' She showed him her photograph. 'We've caught Rory red-handed, but I've got a confession to make. I told him what to steal.' It was best to get it off her chest.

Bella made it back to Hope Eaton in time to open Vintage Winter. Just. She was still squirming at being responsible for picking out a suitable antique for Rory to sell. She'd have to explain to Althea. John had taken the news calmly, though.

'I don't think you can be held responsible for Rory Powell being a thief. My mother would say it's down to his upbringing.'

'She would, but all the same...'

Bella dropped John off at home and made him promise to have lunch with Gareth on her as a thank you. It was hard work getting him to accept and the treat would probably have to wait. Gareth was busy cooking that day, as head chef at the Blue Boar.

At Vintage Winter, one customer after another wanted to gossip about the murder at the hospice. Not everyone knew Clemmie, but they all talked as though they had – repeating what they'd heard from people with more details. Some of them were treating it like a TV drama, which Bella found hard to take; she was glad John wasn't there to hear it, but she bet he'd be getting it elsewhere. Poor Clemmie. The customers seemed to forget they were talking about a real person. Daisy Birdwell's name came up repeatedly. She hadn't been arrested yet, but the likes of Gilbert Rowntree had probably noticed her questioning by the police. Bella imagined her fear and upset; she was young to be dealing with something so horrific.

Bella was bursting with the need to do something, and between customers, she made plans. But beyond her investigations, she needed to talk to Althea about what she'd discovered. It would probably be best to let her break the news to her husband. She knew how carefully Bernard guarded his reputation. Humiliating him would be cruel, and counterproductive too. But he wouldn't go to the police; he'd never want his son in court. It left her in a quandary. If she went to Barry herself, he'd at least know that Rory was keeping a damaging secret, and that he was a potential suspect for the previous thefts at High Seat. But if he investigated to verify her story, the family would know Bella was his source. She had a feeling it wasn't only Bernard who'd cut her out as a result, but Althea too. Althea couldn't stand Rory, but she wouldn't want Bernard hurt, Bella was sure. And if Bella was banished from High Seat, she'd be powerless.

Whatever she decided, she hoped her discovery would at

least force Bernard to acknowledge Rory's wrongdoing. It ought to lessen his influence and give Althea ammunition to fight her corner over the rental properties. Perhaps Leo would breathe more easily over the fate of the Steps. The question was, had Clemmie got wind of Rory's thieving and decided to alert the police? Perhaps the woman he'd sold to that day was a repeat client. It would explain him sneaking off to the racecourse regularly, as spotted by Jeannie. If so, Clemmie could have cottoned on. Althea said she'd stayed at High Seat before she went to the hospice. And perhaps she'd wanted to tell sooner, but felt conflicted, worried that Bernard would blame her, and by association, Althea.

Paula was also a past High Seat resident, of course, and had probably been in and out of the house frequently over the years, given her relationship to Althea. She could have spotted Rory's antics too. What was her agenda?

Whatever the truth, Bella needed to try harder with Rory. Find something that would stick with the police. Because that could be the key to Clemmie's murder. Bella was determined to see him get his just deserts.

9

____

A SLIPPERY FISH

Bella was full of excitement at the thought of the tasks ahead, but she took a deep breath. One step at a time. She'd tell Althea what she'd found out about Rory, but before she went in, all guns blazing, she wanted the complete picture. Coming up with specific details would be more persuasive. It was time to call Tony again. Thank goodness he was nosy, enthusiastic and a gleeful rule-breaker. She needed someone to identify the Volvo woman, using her licence plate. Bernard Powell should know this wasn't just a family matter. Thanks to his son, she'd bought stolen goods and she looked well-to-do, perhaps with a reputation to maintain. Bella suspected she was complicit. Why sneak off to the car park at an antiques fair otherwise? But she wouldn't labour that point.

She called Tony and explained what she'd found out.

He whistled. *'Nice work. Proves your dad and I were right – you would have made a good cop. Not sure what your dad would've thought of you bowling in like that though. Sounds more your mum's style. Or mine!'*

The 'good cop' compliment made Bella glow, but the latest comparison with her mum set her teeth on edge. She and

Amanda were like chalk and cheese. They'd lived chaotically after her parents divorced, moving from Shrewsbury to a tumbledown house in London, full of her mum Amanda's random bohemian friends. Later on, they'd also shared with the three younger half-siblings Amanda had produced, via two unsuitable partners who'd come and gone. It had been Bella who'd kept order and made her younger sisters behave. Or tried to, anyway. Only one of them had ever been arrested. Not a bad average.

She took a deep breath and asked if he thought she should tell Barry Dixon what she'd discovered, pointing out the pros and cons.

He made a ruminating noise. '*I'd wait,*' he said at last. '*At the moment, you're an unofficial spy, able to see and hear things he'll never get access to. Why not preserve that for now, rather than upset old man Powell by reporting his favourite son? It's not as though he'd cooperate if the police pursued it. You can bet the case would be dropped before it came to trial.*'

'But what about Daisy Birdwell? Speaking up might help her.'

He puffed out some air. '*She could still have stolen from the Powells, despite your discovery. Someone's been nicking stuff from the hospice, after all. You need evidence that will stick, so keep your powder dry, that's my advice. You can always change tack if you don't find anything useful at the big house.*'

'Okay.' She felt shifty, and impatient too, but he was probably right. 'Anything new your end?'

He grunted. '*I asked Barry who else might have got hold of the sleeping tablets that killed Clemmie Crowe. Turns out Bernard Powell took that brand at one point. He had the old packet lying around, so anyone with access to High Seat could have pinched some. He can't remember how many were left. Or that's his story.*'

Interesting. 'And what about getting the address from the licence plate? Can you do it?'

He let out a throaty chuckle. '*Don't you worry about that. Sit tight and I'll be in touch.*'

She was labelling some new stock when Tony texted.

Vehicle at the racecourse belongs to Jonathan Teller, the Old Vicarage, Long Marston. You didn't hear it from me!

Jonathan Teller? It hadn't been him she'd seen, clearly. Perhaps the mystery woman was his wife.

She put his name into Google. Handsome, forty-ish maybe, probably around twenty years younger than the woman she'd seen. He was a racehorse trainer, so that explained the parking permit, but who was the woman?

Bella switched from general search results to images, and scanned them in turn, until she found one of Jonathan at a posh drinks do, with the woman she'd seen next to him.

The caption identified her as his mother, Margot Teller. Perhaps she'd borrowed his car so she could park at the racecourse without attracting attention. Bella googled her next. It turned out she was a bigwig in her own right, the mayoress of Long Marston, with a controlling stake in her son's stables, and an interiors shop in the town. That ought to make Bernard sit up and take notice – if she made a fuss, the whole of the Kite Valley would know about it. She sent Althea a text, saying how shocked and sorry she was that Clemmie's death hadn't been natural and expressing her renewed sympathy, then asking if she could visit the following day. She'd rather do it in person. Althea messaged back to say she could see Bella at eleven the following morning.

That evening, she went to dinner with Robert and told him about the evidence she'd gathered. Now she'd come to terms with tipping Rory off about the frame, she was on a bit of a high. She was building a case against him.

Robert sat back in his chair, his eyes wide, and she realised details of her hobby might be a bit more than he could cope with on a second date.

'I can't work out if I'm impressed or horrified,' he said at last.

'Impressed is the way to go.' She suspected he'd been about to come down on the other side.

He sipped his wine. 'I'll try. Seriously though, Bella, wouldn't you like to take up crosswords or something? I know you're worried about your friend's café, and you knew the lady who died, but it's not your battle.'

If someone had died at the hands of another, it was every-one's battle, surely? And didn't he appreciate what she'd achieved? Privately, she felt quite proud, and hooked too – bursting to carry on. Besides, she'd known and liked Clemmie, and missed the chance to help her before she'd died. And then there were John's feelings, and the future of the Steps to consider... 'We're all affected, Robert. Especially the Jenkses. You'd understand if you met them.' Or at least, she hoped he would. 'John, Leo and Matt are like brothers to me.' Actually, that was stretching a point. 'Sisterly' was far from the right word to describe the way she felt towards Matt, however unsuitable he was. He'd be a lot less distracting if he didn't live next door. Bella was so glad she was going out with someone like Robert instead.

The timing of Bella's meeting with Althea was ideal. Vintage Winter was closed on Mondays, so there was no issue making the appointment. Bella would do a couple of jobs at the shop before heading to High Seat, though it would be hard to concentrate. She couldn't wait to see what would happen.

She left her flat in a black halter-neck top and cigarette

pants. The July weather had been reliably warm and dry for weeks now. As she crossed the shared entranceway, she bent to stroke Cuthbert, who was making a determined effort to enter her flat. Perhaps it wasn't just the serenity that he was after, given the new-found tranquillity at Matt's place. Things had been quiet on the girlfriend front for two whole months now. She'd been wondering if he was sickening for something, though he'd looked as devil-may-care as usual. The thought of him sent a familiar spark firing inside her, but he wasn't her type. Robert Mead was.

Bella set off along the river, then cut up Boatman's Walk and St Giles's Steps to reach Vintage Winter. There were several of these sets of steps that led between Low and High Town in Hope Eaton. Along their route, snug cottages, tiny but hugely attractive, clung to the hillside. She knew that one of them, partway up St Giles's Steps, belonged to Rory, which was deeply annoying. He'd probably mortgaged it to the hilt after his dad had handed it over. Bella thought how undeserving he was and wondered about the background. Jeannie's words about his brother, Gregory, flitted through her mind. He must feel it, still living at home when Rory seemed to have got something for nothing. It wasn't as though Gregory would make up for it by inheriting High Seat instead. Althea had said it would go to him and Rory jointly.

As Bella passed Rory's cottage, she came face to face with Paula in her hospice uniform. Perhaps she'd stayed the night. The thought made Bella wonder, after the look of loathing she'd shot Rory at the racecourse. Was she genuinely keen on him after all?

It was time to find out, and to stir the pot more generally. If Clemmie had had something on Rory, Paula might know about it. She was probably at least aware of how things had stood between them. It still seemed odd that Rory had visited Clemmie, the day she died. And Bella was desperate to unearth Paula's secrets too. Why had Rufus Hartford given her money?

Bella reintroduced herself, then waded straight in. 'I've been meaning to say, but I hope you're okay. It must be hard, keeping going at the hospice after Clemmie's death. You knew her well, I suppose?'

Paula nodded. 'She and I were actually living at High Seat at the same time – I was a guest there briefly before I moved into one of Bernard's rental places. The place needed some repairs and they overran. I saw a lot of her over the years too, because she was Althea's closest friend.' She looked down. 'My mum died when I was still a young adult, so Althea was in loco parentis – not legally, but emotionally, you know?'

Poor woman. 'It must have been hard.' Bella's mind ran on. So, Paula had known Clemmie for years, and they'd overlapped at High Seat briefly too. If Clemmie knew Paula was doing something criminal, she'd probably have found it hard to report her. Bella could imagine her hesitating to act until the very end. 'I'm so sorry about Clemmie too,' she said aloud. 'The news about her death is shocking.' She watched Paula closely. Her eyes were damp.

'I still can't believe it.' Paula shook her head. 'The gossip is rife, of course. Everyone seems to have heard that Daisy Birdwell's under suspicion. People were asking me about it all day yesterday, but I don't know anything. It hurts, though. I liked Clemmie, and nursing her made us even closer.'

She certainly sounded cut-up. It was time to change tack, and focus on Paula's supposed love interest.

'It must be nice to have Rory supporting you at a time like this.' Bella nodded at the pretty cottage Paula had just left.

'Yes.' Her face became expressionless. Bella's younger sisters had often attempted the mask approach too. Paula was definitely holding back.

'Though not everyone's great at dealing with emotion.' His lack of sympathy might have upset her.

But she didn't comment.

'His cottage is so lovely.'

Bella had just been trying to keep the conversation going, but there was a flash in Paula's eye now. Her words had triggered something.

'Isn't it just?' she said at last. 'He's sitting pretty.' Bella couldn't miss the bitterness in her tone, though she covered it in an instant. 'Sitting pretty on the hillside, I mean. It's a beautiful view.'

But it was too late to hide her feelings. She was conscious of his good fortune, and she resented it. She really didn't like him, Bella was sure. So what was she up to? Looking for evidence to bring him down? Or perhaps she really did want his contacts, to make some money herself. Either way, she was going to some lengths to keep in with him. Staying under his roof would make Bella's skin crawl.

But she needed to focus and ploughed on. 'It's funny to think of Clemmie and Rory being related. He sounded a bit scratchy when he mentioned her at High Seat, though Clemmie said he'd been in to see her, so it was probably nothing.' Bella met Paula's eye and waited.

Paula gave a wry look. 'Truth to tell, I don't think he went because he wanted to see her. His dad's PA, Hester Harper, was visiting a relative that day with her little girl, and I saw him shout to her and follow her in. He must have wanted a word.'

Bernard had a PA? What in the name of Sweet Agnes was he thinking of? That couldn't come cheap.

'One of the staff assumed he was there for Clemmie,' Paula went on. 'I watched them usher him in.'

Half of Bella's mind was still on the PA. Surely Bernard didn't need a member of staff to help administer the rental properties? But she could see him keeping her on as a status symbol, or because he couldn't face the truth. She mentally shook her head. The take-home message was much more important. If Rory had dashed in to speak to her, it meant he'd been there by chance. He wouldn't have been armed with doctored tonic. Then again, if he was guilty, he'd have needed a reason to explain his presence, given he and Clemmie weren't close. Perhaps he knew Hester Harper's habits and had deliberately bumped into her. It would be a good way to make himself look innocent.

'Sorry,' Paula said, 'but I'd better get on, or I'll be late for my shift.' She turned rather awkwardly, thanks to the bulky bag she was carrying, and headed down to the river as Bella headed up, towards Vintage Winter. Passing the Steps, Bella thought of Leo and Carys. She'd left it to John to tell them about their discoveries the day before and Leo had sent her a wildly enthusiastic text just after midnight. It had given him a glimmer of hope at least.

When she entered the shop, ready to do some labelling and admin before heading up to High Seat, she reached for the coffee caddy and found it was empty. Of course, she'd finished the last lot the day before. What's more, she'd pinched the spare packet John had bought because she'd run out at home. It was time to get supplies.

She exited the shop, locked up, and dashed towards the high street via Old Percy's Lane. She was just in time to see someone ahead of her, turning right towards Uppergate, heading out of town.

Paula.

Still dressed for work at the hospice, but not heading in the hospice's direction. She'd certainly given the impression she was working that morning, but now here she was in High Town. She must have doubled back after she'd left Bella on the steps. Perhaps the hospice had sent her on an errand, but why was she still carrying the same bulky bag?

In that split second, Bella decided to follow her. She kept close to the town's half-timbered buildings and mingled with the morning shoppers. By the time Paula had cut through the high street, Bella was certain she wasn't fetching anything for the hospice. She walked purposefully, with the air of someone who still had a way to go.

Bella kept her distance as Paula ploughed on westwards. She was at the entrance to Dead Man's Walk now and there were no shops in that direction. Pottering off in her uniform for a stroll didn't make sense. This had to be something secret; Bella wondered what was in the bag she was carrying. At the end of Dead Man's Walk, she turned away from the stile that led to Gallows Hill, but a moment later, she glanced up, stopped abruptly and changed tack. She was going to use it after all.

Bella was just wondering how she could follow without being seen when Althea called to her from outside the chemist's on Market Street and the chance was lost.

Bella stood there, greeting Althea, petting Eustace, and resisting the urge to turn round and stare at Paula. She'd hate Althea to guess she'd been following her.

'I came out to buy coffee and decided to walk a little further as the weather's so nice. And then I'd have been on my way to see you.'

Althea nodded. 'Normally I love these balmy summer days, but they keep making me cry at the moment.'

It must have been bad enough when she'd been going through a standard bereavement. So much worse, now she knew someone had deliberately harmed her friend.

'I keep thinking of when Clemmie and I were young,' Althea went on. 'We'd walk off into the countryside. It was such an escape – especially for her.' She took a deep breath. 'I know our appointment was for later, but we can talk now, if you like? What about a coffee at the Steps? They're dog-friendly, aren't they?'

'Yes.' It might be all right, if they got a corner table and Bella discouraged Leo from listening in. She didn't want Althea to think they'd plotted the whole thing together to discredit Rory. Bella needed her research to come across as calmly factual, however she felt inside.

As they made their way to St Giles's Close, Bella reminded Althea of her offer to help with the Lammas Day feast. She needed to maintain friendly relations with the Powells, despite the bad news she had about Rory. Althea looked delighted and mentioned a load of white tablecloths that needed ironing.

Worse than she'd thought, but Bella pasted on a smile. 'Leave them to me.'

Once they reached the Steps, Leo peered at them curiously, and bobbed about in the background after they'd given Poppy their order. Bella gave him a back-off look, then turned to Althea once he'd retreated.

'I'm sorry, it's rather delicate.'

Althea waved a hand. 'I don't do delicate; I'm sure you've worked that out by now. I appreciate you warning me, but let's assume I won't be offended.'

Bella liked her style. 'Thank you. In that case, here goes.' She told her everything, from the mistake she'd made, leaving her notebook out when she'd gone to hide at High Seat, to following the woman who turned out to be Margot Teller and photographing the gilded-bronze photo frame which had come from the house. She only paused when Poppy arrived to deliver their order, at which point she leaned back. Poppy was a spiller; you had to leave a buffer zone. As she put their order down, Bella noticed her red eyes. It was probably down to the pressure Daisy and the whole family were under. They needed a resolution.

As Bella told her tale, angry red marks tinged Althea's cheeks. By the end, she was gripping her coffee cup so hard Bella was worried Leo would have a breakage on his hands.

Bella was full of adrenaline too. All the indignation came back, coupled with a surge of determination to use her skills to make things right. 'I'm so sorry. He took the most valuable item I'd found so far.'

'You don't have to apologise. I'm sorry they came back when I'd told you they wouldn't. I put you in a horrible position.'

Bella rejoiced that she was taking it like that. 'Obviously, it's none of my business, but would you like me to email you the photos and information?'

Althea nodded grimly. 'This will not stand. I'll let you know how I get on.'

Before Bella left the Steps, Leo pulled her to one side to ask how her talk with Althea had gone. He looked excited when she told him she was resolved to take a stand.

'If you've saved the Steps, it's free sausage sandwiches for you for life.'

'Just think of my waistline. How's Poppy bearing up?'

Leo sighed. 'The hospice has suspended Daisy while the police investigate the murder. The neighbours are twitching their curtains and my customers have been gossiping about it. They're almost as tactless as my mother and not as well-meaning.'

Bella put a hand on his arm. 'I'm sorry. We'll keep at it. Give it everything. We just need to make Barry Dixon realise there are other more promising suspects.'

He nodded dolefully.

The urgency to provide Barry with some leads that would stick felt overwhelming. Bella consoled herself with the progress on Rory. He deserved his comeuppance so richly. She spent the next hour imagining the conversation Althea and Bernard might be having, and even allowed herself to visualise snippets of her own discussions with Leo afterwards. It would be so lovely to feel Rory had had his day and was now persona non grata. Bella was sure Althea would have the upper hand, once Bernard saw Rory for what he was.

When her mobile rang and Althea's name flashed on the screen, she was quick to answer.

'*I should have known how this would go.*' Althea sounded deeply weary. '*Bernard would have me believe he gave Rory the photo frame to sell because he's "a bit short" just now. All lies, I'm afraid; I can always tell. But I can't prove it. I hoped your discovery would give me leverage, but I'm back to square one.*'

10

IDENTIFYING FOXY

Bella broke the news to John and Leo over lunch at the Steps. 'I'm so sorry. It's utterly infuriating. What's more, it makes Rory seem less likely as Clemmie's killer. Even if she saw him thieving at High Seat while she was staying there, he'd have no reason to worry if he realised his dad would protect him.' She was very glad she'd followed Tony's advice and not given Barry Dixon her evidence. Bernard would only have told him Rory was innocent. She'd have blotted her copybook with the Powells for nothing.

Leo's head was in his hands. It was vanishingly rare to see him deflated, which made it more disturbing.

Bella needed to give him hope. 'Althea's on our side, remember. Bernard won't sell any of the properties if she's got any say in it. We just need to do more to trip Rory up. I must look into his business dealings and find out who "Foxy" is.' The person he'd mentioned in the conversation with his dad. 'I can't see Rory being involved in anything honest. On the upside, I'm allowed into High Seat officially now. When Bernard told Althea that Rory had sold the frame with his permission, she rounded on him and said she'd thought he wasn't prepared to let anything go. So of course, Bernard had to backtrack. At which point, Althea pushed home her advantage and he's agreed to let me value everything.' One up to Althea. Bella was going to fetch the Lammas Day feast tablecloths to iron next time she went too. *Joy.* 'Rory's constantly on the scrounge, so he's sure to visit High Seat while I'm there. I'll watch him like a hawk.'

Over the next couple of days, Bella zoned in on Rory, Gregory and Paula. Being able to pop in and out of High Seat without hiding her presence was invaluable. She gritted her teeth and set her alarm early each day so she could be there by eight. It worked best to squeeze the visits in before Vintage Winter opened, and it meant she arrived before Gregory left for work too. If she wanted to know more about him, they needed to overlap. To the same end, she popped over at lunchtimes and after Vintage Winter closed too. It meant she'd finally clapped eyes on Bernard's PA, a tall, chestnut-haired woman in her mid-thirties.

It was just as well that the Powells' possessions were so plentiful. It would be ages before Bella ran out of things to value.

During one of her journeys to and fro, she'd spotted a young woman who looked so much like Poppy that it had to be her sister, Daisy. She looked so slight and vulnerable, scuttling along the high street, keeping close to the buildings, head down, but it didn't stop her being noticed. Bella saw Adele Lewis, the grocer, point at her and whisper behind her hand. Poor Daisy. Barry hadn't found enough evidence to arrest her, but she was suffering, just the same. It increased Bella's sense of urgency, if that were possible.

Between work and her visits to High Seat, she sat in her study at home – the room her father had used before her, all those years ago. Perched on her vintage captain's chair, she felt in control. She imagined her dad looking over her shoulder, urging her on as she searched for Rory's supposed 'business contact', Foxy. General googling produced little, which was a blow. Foxy sounded like the nickname of a close friend, but there was no one named Fox amongst his Facebook friends.

She sat there thinking. Nicknames were most common at school. LinkedIn might tell her where Rory had been educated, if he had a profile. It turned out he did. His photo looked glossy, but his experience sounded invented. It was full of words like 'facilitator' and 'consultant' but without the detail to back it up.

Still, it gave her his school: Acton Palgrave – a private establishment, the other end of the county. It must have been before the family's money ran out. After that, she searched for 'Acton Palgrave' and 'Rory Powell' to see what came up. Nothing except the LinkedIn page.

Where else might Foxy appear? Rory could have mentioned him to Bernard because he was known to be successful. If so, perhaps he could afford to be generous to his old school.

Bella clicked on Acton Palgrave's benefactors' tab, then searched by year, according to when the donors had attended the place.

No Foxes for the year Rory had graduated. But as Bella scanned the screen, she felt a spark of excitement. *Evan Todd*.

Beatrix Potter's Mr Todd was a fox. She remembered reading that blessed book to her younger sisters, over and over again. Her mother had found it in a second-hand sale. When Bella looked it up, she found 'tod' meant 'fox' in Middle English, and was still used in Scottish English.

It didn't follow that it was him, but he had to be worth investigating. After that, she was away. Thanks to the internet, she found Evan owned a successful wine-making business and a bar and restaurant in Herefordshire. Not too far away.

At Vintage Winter, she sank into a Regency mahogany elbow chair, wishing she could buy it for herself, and reported back to John. 'I'm going to go and see him. I think arriving unannounced would be best.'

He winced. 'What on earth will you say?'

'Don't worry. I've got a cover story. I'll tell him I have a friend who's fallen madly in love with Rory but, with her best interests at heart, I'm worried he's unsuitable. I'll hint at dodgy dealings, promise to keep anything he tells me quiet, and play on his sympathies. If I get a sniff of anything serious, I'll push further or dig elsewhere.'

'He'll probably lie if they're good friends.'

'No doubt, but I'm good at spotting tells.' She could do this; she knew she could. 'In any case, I'm not sure I buy them being close. Evan Todd's got a great reputation, judging by his reviews, and he's clearly hardworking and successful. I can't imagine them being soulmates.'

'And what will you do if he's not Rory's Foxy at all?'

That was easy, though it would be disappointing. 'I'll simply apologise and leave. What's the worst that could happen?'

John opened his mouth, so she carried on talking. 'You can stop worrying for the moment, anyway. He's gone to a wine festival in Bath, according to a press release on his website, so I'll have to wait until he's back.' It was a long shot, of course. But nothing ventured, nothing gained, and investigating would be simple. If Evan Todd was Rory's 'Foxy', he might know if he was a criminal. If he had any proof, she could use it to exert some pressure; perhaps Rory would say something he shouldn't.

11

HAM ACTING AND SECRET NOTES

On Thursday before work, Bella finally returned the duly ironed and now-hated Lammas Day tablecloths to High Seat, and the next major development occurred. Despite visiting early each day, she'd barely seen Gregory. He tended to leave for work with his head down, marching straight from his rooms to the front door.

Bella wasn't going to let him slip through her fingers again; this time, she latched on to him as he left.

She fell into step with him. 'I've finished for now. I need to get back to Vintage Winter to open up. You're heading to Butler & Co? Tom's a cousin of my colleague, John.'

Gregory shifted away from her, as though he wished she wasn't there. *Nice try.* She shifted too, closing the gap.

At last, he nodded. 'I've been there five years now.' Then suddenly he turned to her, his words coming out in a rush. 'There's no point you doing your valuations, you know. Not unless you find something that's worth a fortune. Dad's up to his ears in debt. He just can't—' He stopped abruptly. 'It doesn't matter. Selling High Seat's the only answer. The rent I pay takes up almost all my earnings. I'm sure he'd charge me more if he could. I can't get out from under.'

It seemed desperately unfair, and Gregory clearly thought so too. His fists were clenched, face reddening. She was sure he'd boil over if she gave him an extra nudge, so she went for it. 'How come you're expected to pay, when Rory gets a free house to live in? I'd be livid if it were me.' Even as it was, she was filled with indignation.

For a moment, he paused, and everything seemed to hang in the balance, but then it all came out on a tide of fury. 'It wasn't free to start with! Rory was paying rent, but then he "fell on hard times".' Gregory made angry air quotes with his fingers. 'He told Dad he couldn't afford it any more.' He shook his head. 'Althea said he should move back to High Seat and pay the same as me.

'She's got a strong sense of fair play, but she saw through Rory years back, and she doesn't hide it.' His anger was making Bella's job easy. If she kept quiet, she knew he'd carry on, and sure enough, he did.

'Rory told Dad he couldn't move back because Althea hated him, and he'd feel it every day.' Bella's adrenaline ratcheted up further. Rory was so manipulative... 'In the end, Dad gave in and let him stay on at the cottage, rent-free. There was an even bigger row when Althea learned Rory had talked Dad into signing it over to him, so he could "feel secure".' His hand shook. 'Dad said he'd have done the same for me, if I'd been struggling. But in his eyes, I'm not.' He paused, and when he spoke again, his tone had turned bitter. 'I toe the line and there are no rewards for that. Despite Althea's principles, she let it go in the end. She won't do anything that would hurt Dad. She finds his weakness over Rory agonising, but she's still fond of him. They're the archetypal old married couple, and nothing will change.

'So, I can't look to Althea to break the deadlock. The most

she manages is to maintain the status quo. If you make them just enough to struggle on, I'll never be free. What with Rory ranting on about getting shot of the rentals, and Althea protecting Dad's feelings, selling High Seat is out of reach.'

He stopped, and Bella let him catch his breath again as she began processing the windfall of information. 'It must be hard. But if I find something truly valuable, it *could* make a difference.'

He grunted. 'If Dad had anything like that it would have gone long ago.'

'I found a nice photo frame...'

Gregory's fist clenched. 'I overheard Althea and Dad arguing about it. And that flaming brother of mine... But even if Rory hadn't walked off with it, it wouldn't have solved our problems. Nothing will, while *he's* around. I need something big to shift the dial.' He sounded worryingly desperate.

'All this on top of Clemmie's death. I'm sorry. The news about what happened must be hugely upsetting. And I'm sure you must miss her too; she was a good listener, wasn't she? Did you ever share your worries with her?' What Gilbert had overheard weighed heavy in her mind.

'Clemmie?' He was instantly tense, shoulders up. 'No. What? Why would I? What have you heard?'

'Nothing. It doesn't matter.' Not the most reassuring response he could have given.

Bella crossed the high street to open the shop, but after closing time, she headed straight back to High Seat. As well as Gregory, she'd been monitoring Rory when he visited and spying on Bernard Powell's PA Hester Harper, too. Had Rory really rushed into the hospice the day Clemmie died to talk to Hester, or was that just a ruse to explain his presence? And what on earth was Bernard doing, employing Hester, when the family was desperately short of money? Bella had discovered on the grapevine that she was a single mum and that her parents lived in a Powell property. She was glad she was in work, but it must infuriate Gregory. It would certainly push Bella's buttons.

She was approaching High Seat when she heard voices coming from the room she'd identified as Hester's office. The open windows of summer were a definite benefit when it came to eavesdropping. Bella recognised Rory's angry, entitled tones. She peered around the side of the building and glimpsed him inside, looming over Hester. She was enviably attractive, with her flowing hair and high cheekbones.

'Good lord, you haven't changed!' Rory spat out the words. 'Just the same petty, pathetic, unfeeling—'

'You can talk! You faithless rat! You don't care about anyone but yourself. I'm so glad I saw through you when I did! I don't want you anywhere near me!'

Just beyond them, Bella caught movement. Someone else was listening in. She stared at the sliver of the figure, mostly hidden behind a viburnum bush. A tuft of grey hair and the toe of a polished shoe.

Bernard.

She was proved correct a moment later when Althea called his name and tuft and toe disappeared.

Rory and Hester carried on for another few seconds, then Hester put her hands on her hips. 'It's all right. He's gone.'

'Thank God for that. My throat was getting sore. Think he bought it?'

Hester turned towards him, her rich, reddish hair glinting in the sun. 'I think so.'

What in the name of Sweet Agnes were they up to?

That night, Bella and John arranged to meet Tony in the snug at the Blue Boar. Jeannie was just as quick off the blocks to join them as last time. Impressive, really. She sat down without being invited.

Bella filled them in on what she'd discovered that day. 'So, Gregory's desperate. And when I mentioned him confiding in Clemmie, he panicked and asked me if someone had said something. He's definitely keeping a secret, and Clemmie had uncovered it; I just need to work out what it is. As for Rory, on top of selling stolen goods, he and Bernard's secretary are pretending they're at daggers drawn for Bernard's benefit. I need to know why.'

'Initial thoughts?' Tony asked.

'Perhaps they're having an affair. If Bernard had begun to suspect, it could make sense to put him off the scent. Rory's meant to be dating Althea's niece, after all. I already had a hunch that was driven by his hatred for Althea. He loves taunting her. Althea thinks he wants to drive her away from High Seat.'

'Ridiculous,' said Jeannie. 'That will never work.'

Bella was inclined to agree. 'Of course, Hester herself is a puzzle. I can't imagine why Bernard has a PA. You'd think he'd let her go if things are as bad as Gregory and Althea say. Then again, he's still a member of the golf club, too. He seems fond of his status symbols. What news from the police, Tony? Have they asked the family why Clemmie might have wanted to talk to Adam Davies?'

Tony raised an eyebrow. 'They all claim to be mystified.'

Bella bet someone knew something. 'Please tell me Barry's at least considering the Powells as suspects, alongside poor Daisy.'

'He hasn't discounted them.' Tony sipped his pint. 'But it's only really Rory who's on his radar, and Hester Harper supports his claim that he entered the hospice to speak to her. It looks like chance that he got swept into Clemmie's room by one of the staff, and if that's the case, he wouldn't have been armed with sleeping pills.'

Jeannie was on her feet in an instant. 'Poppycock! I'm sure the man can lie like the devil himself.'

Bella agreed. Hester might believe what she was saying, or she and Rory could be in it together, given their joint shenanigans earlier.

But on the other hand, it might be someone else entirely. She didn't voice the thought to Jeannie, though. If she got any more impassioned, their drinks and crisps would be in serious danger. Bella needed to find evidence and thrust it under Barry Dixon's nose. It was the only way.

It was fully dark and late by the time she left the Blue Boar. The jolly sounds of the clientele faded, along with the glow from the strings of lights across the inn's cobbled courtyard. She was about to cross the high street towards St Giles's Close, the Steps and home, when she caught sight of a dark shape. A man, she thought, moving stealthily towards Lookout Walk. Instantly, she was on high alert. The gait and the hunched shoulders were distinctive. She was almost certain it was Gregory.

The way he moved told her he didn't want to be seen. Thoughts of her cosy flat faded. She needed to know what he was hiding. She followed, glad of her neat black dress, swing coat and dark hair. She ought to blend into the shadows.

On Lookout Walk, Low Town spread out below her, its twinkling lights arrayed around the inky darkness of the River Kite. Behind her, the ruins of the castle loomed, jagged and leaning. Bella could hear footfalls on the Cliff Steps. Following Gregory down the lonely route didn't feel like the best of plans, but she didn't have an option if she wanted to see where he went. She tiptoed after him, treading carefully in her slingbacks, to avoid any unfortunate clacking. Every so often she paused and strained to hear how far he'd got. If she moved too fast, he might turn and see her.

The steps felt longer than usual and the hewn sides of the cliff higher. She breathed a sigh of relief once she reached the bottom.

She could see Gregory better now. He was skulking along, close to the ivy-clad bank to the side of Maid's Lane, but despite his efforts, the glow of a street lamp revealed his dark curly hair. Every so often he looked round, forcing her to hang back. She carried on following stealthily until she saw him enter the Hanged Man. It was the exact opposite of the Blue Boar – dingy and intimidating. Bella had come across small-time crooks who used it. She wouldn't have said it was Gregory's natural territory at all. Nor was it Bella's, but if she didn't get in there, she'd never find out what he was up to.

She glanced through the window, to size up the situation before committing herself. The moment she entered she'd draw attention for not sporting jeans or leathers.

She saw Gregory pause in the entrance lobby before removing an envelope from the dark jacket he wore. A moment later, he'd entered the gents'.

Not good news. She'd stick out a hundred times worse if she went in there. She imagined what must be going on inside. Him handing the envelope to a contact perhaps, away from prying eyes.

Thoughts of the other customers set Bella's mind working. She knew a couple of Hanged Man regulars. There was no accounting for taste, but it could be useful. She pushed the pub's door open and dashed inside, scanning the room.

Her neighbour, John and Leo's youngest brother Matt, was by her side before she'd managed to weave round the nearest table to join him.

He raised an eyebrow. 'Not your regular haunt. I don't like to assume, but were you looking for me?'

She ignored the heat that fired up inside her at the sight of him and explained what was going on. A moment later, Matt entered the men's loos. Bella went outside again. Propping up the bar alone would trigger whispers. She hid round the side of the pub, where she could see if Gregory left.

Sure enough, he was out of there again in under a minute, collar turned up, glancing this way and that. He looked relieved, his shoulders more relaxed.

Matt came to find her half a minute later. 'There was no one else in the gents'. Your man jumped like a scalded cat when I appeared, but he wasn't holding anything. As soon as he left, I scouted round and found the envelope, tucked behind the cistern in the cubicle.'

He handed it to her. 'I thought of leaving it in place, to see who came for it, but I reckoned you'd want a look first.' He shook his head. 'Why don't you open it while I see who goes into the gents'?'

Bella held the envelope up to the street light. If only she could see what was inside without breaking the seal. But it was no good. The paper was too thick. At last, she eased it open as best she could, but it tore. Bella cursed under her breath. Whoever came for it would know someone had snooped.

But there was nothing at all inside.

12

———

PROGRESS ON PAULA

Bella left Matt at the pub. He'd put the envelope back for her and promised to see who else went into the gents'.

When she got back to her flat in Southwell Hall, she heard Cuthbert yowling on the wrong side of her door. Honestly, you'd think he'd learn not to trespass if he didn't want to get stuck.

She opened up, ready for the tabby cat to whisk into the entryway, but instead he slunk around her legs, looking up at her adoringly, then went back into her flat.

She sat down on the softly cushioned bench in her inner hall, and reflected on what had happened. She was glad now that she'd taken Tony's advice and not yet passed on Gilbert Rowntree's gossip to Barry Dixon. Gregory mightn't have dared make that evening's clandestine trip if the police had come sniffing around. But what she'd discovered didn't help. There was no way Barry would haul him in for an interview because he'd left an empty envelope in the Hanged Man. She'd need to find something concrete if she wanted to interest the police. She felt keener than ever.

It was an hour later when Matt texted.

I'm back. Still up?

She went to open her door and Cuthbert wandered out. He trousered Matt, who was already in the shared entryway, then slunk back into her flat again.

Matt raised an eyebrow. 'I'm starting to feel insulted.'

Bella just smiled. 'What happened at the pub?'

'Several regulars went to the gents' but the envelope was still there when I left.'

'And there was nothing in it anyway.' Bella was mystified. 'I can't get my head around it. Unless it's a message, and an empty envelope means something. In which case there'd be no need for anyone to take it away. They'd just see it and understand. If so, they'll realise someone got there first, thanks to me breaking the seal.'

Matt shrugged. 'I might have opened it myself, if I'd found it. Anyone could have got curious.'

'You're right. I doubt the intended recipient will get the wind up. It's frustrating, though. What in the name of Sweet Agnes is Gregory Powell up to?'

'Good question. And there was I, thinking *I* was the mystery man around here.'

Bella rolled her eyes. 'It's certainly a mystery why you hang out at the Hanged Man, when your parents own the best inn in town.'

'I think you'll find you've just answered your own question.'

It was true that Jeannie would try to steer Matt if he spent an evening under her nose, but Bella could see why she wanted to. On the one hand, he had hidden depths. He produced some of the most beautifully carved furniture she'd ever seen. But he seemed happily rootless, took any random work that came along, and until recently had collected girlfriends like she collected antiques and vintage.

She was secretly glad he didn't frequent the Blue Boar; it

would ruin her composure there. He made her uneasy – that was all. Not like Robert, who was pleasantly soothing.

'No need to ask why you're interested in Gregory, of course,' Matt said. 'I'm sorry about what happened to Clemmie Crowe. What have you found out about the Powells?'

Bella gave him the highlights as she picked up Cuthbert, who was purring extravagantly. The weight of him always surprised her. A moment later she handed him to Matt without any feline protest. She finished her summing up. 'I was thinking about Paula as well as the others. Do you know her?'

'Hardly at all.'

One of the few women in Hope Eaton he hadn't been out with, perhaps. 'I need to find out what her dealings are with a man called Rufus Hartford, and why she was sneaking onto Gallows Hill after claiming she was on her way to work.' She'd been carrying that big bag too. Perhaps she'd been off to a clandestine meeting to deliver something. Rufus could have been paying her for illicit goods.

Bella visualised her now, heading up Dead Man's Walk to the hill. 'When I saw Paula on Monday, she started off ignoring the stile to Gallows Hill. Then suddenly she looked up, stopped, and changed direction. Was the stile out of action recently?' Matt walked a lot; he probably knew. He frequently told her she should get out more.

He raised an eyebrow. 'Yes, for part of last week. You had to take the gate at the corner of the field. She probably hadn't realised it had reopened.'

'Interesting. If Paula knew the stile had been broken, she must make the journey regularly.' And that presented an opportunity.

She said goodnight to Matt and turned towards her flat, her mind on next steps. Moments later, she'd flumped down on her velvet sofa amongst tabby-cat hairs. *Honestly...* As she picked them off, Bella resolved to see if Paula repeated her journey.

The question was, whether to lurk near to her house or Rory's. She hummed and hawed, but plumped for Rory's in the end. Whatever Paula really felt about him, she'd been there the previous morning. If she drew a blank, she could always try Paula's place next. One way or another, she hoped she'd find something to take to Barry Dixon.

The following morning, Bella set her alarm unpleasantly early, rather than risk missing anything.

She made an energetic march up St Giles's Steps the moment she'd finished her coffee. The gateway to another cottage, nestled in a red-brick wall, mellow with age, provided some cover from which to watch, just down the hill from Rory's place. If Paula was there, she'd hopefully head straight up the steps this time, if she thought no one was watching.

At last, Rory's cream-painted front door opened, and Bella saw she was in luck. Paula emerged in her hospice uniform, but once again, she carried the bulky bag. Bella felt a surge of excitement. She'd discover her game this time.

As expected, Paula set off uphill. Bella gave her a head start, then dashed to the top of the steps to check where she went. She was just in time to see her stride across St Giles's Close, and tailed her to the high street. After that, her direction was just as it had been before: along Market Street, then straight onto Dead Man's Walk. Bella watched Paula climb over the stile, then cross the common land on Gallows Hill. Eventually, she passed a field boundary and disappeared beyond some trees.

Bella rushed to catch up, now she'd got some cover, but when she got beyond the thicket, there was no sign of Paula – just a lone bay horse in a field. Bella was standing there silently cursing when she spotted movement near a barn and a figure appeared, dressed in leggings, T-shirt and riding hat.

What?

Bella almost laughed. Paula *had* been bound for a meeting, but not with a person, with a horse. A moment later she was standing next to the bay, surveying it carefully – checking the animal was fit and well, perhaps. And then she was saddling up, with what looked like an expert's ease. Within minutes she'd put a foot in a stirrup, swung her leg over the horse's back and was away. The bulky bag she was carrying must have held her riding clothes, but why come all the way in her hospice uniform? Even if she were going to work afterwards, it would be quicker to come dressed to ride. Why change twice?

She looked utterly fearless, flying across the field, and a moment later, she'd jumped a hedge and was tearing across another pasture. Bella had no desire to get on horseback herself – it sounded even worse than cycling – but there was something about Paula's body language that spoke of pure joy and freedom. Bella remembered thinking how healthy and tanned she'd looked alongside poor Clemmie. Perhaps this was a daily habit.

But why the secrecy?

Bella pondered the question as she watched her ride. Perhaps it was Rory she was fooling. If Paula owned the horse, he might decide she was richer than he'd thought and pester her for money. If that's what Paula feared, it seemed certain there was more to their relationship than met the eye. Why put up with him otherwise?

But if so, Bella still wasn't sure of her motivation. Paula could be the hospice thief, looking for buyers who didn't mind stolen goods. It would explain her interest in Rory's clients, and it might mean she'd killed Clemmie if Clemmie had found her out. Or she might be trying to prove Rory was a criminal. Dating him for either purpose would be quite drastic, but it would allow her to get close.

Bella had sensed Paula was secretly furious with him, and that might hold the key to the mystery. Taking a step back, it was easy to see why she might be. If Rory really was having an affair with Hester, she could have found out. And even if she hadn't, she probably knew he was pushing to sell the Powell properties, hers included. Without it, she might lose her independence. Bella would feel more than indignant in her shoes. Why should Rory get his own way over everything, and threaten everyone's stability? It would be a good fit with the disgusted look Bella had seen her shoot him at the racecourse, and Paula's bitter tone when she'd agreed he was 'sitting pretty'. Him being so secure when her future was under threat would rub salt in the wound. Though if Paula was wealthy enough to own a horse, she might be self-sufficient.

But as Bella turned to leave the field, her thoughts moved on. What were the chances that Paula owned a horse, on her salary? Slim to zero, Bella reckoned. But if she was exercising someone else's, she'd probably get paid for it. She took a deep breath. *Of course.* They were close to High Seat, and the Powells had sold off land to the Hartfords. She bet it was Rufus Hartford's horse, hence the cash he'd handed over.

Satisfaction rushed over her. It fitted with what Gilbert Rowntree had said about Paula turning away swiftly when Rory appeared, just as Rufus was paying her. He'd hate her accepting money from Rufus, and all the more so if he realised she was happily riding his horse on former Powell land. If Paula wanted to keep in with Rory, whatever her motivation, she'd want to avoid upsetting him.

She'd need to check her facts, but she bet that was it. It looked like Paula was a grafter, filling her days with hard work to earn her crust fair and square – the very opposite of Rory. If she was nursing a simmering anger towards him, it made total sense. Bella was starting to think she really was out to bring him down. *Good.*

. . .

After she left the fields, Bella returned to High Seat to do some more valuations, but she was worried Gregory was right. She hadn't found any stand-out pieces that would 'shift the dial', as he'd put it. For a moment, she got excited by a silver-plated mantel clock, thinking it was an Edgar Brandt. That sort of art deco piece, created by a leading French metalwork designer, would do wonderfully at auction. But the moment she looked more closely, hope drained away. It lacked his stamp, and although it was well-executed, it fell short of the exquisite detailing for which he was known.

She fantasised about leaving her notebook out for Rory to find, with a falsely high valuation for the clock. She'd love him to make off with it, only to get into hot water later when his client found he'd sold them a pup. The idea was almost enough to make up for the disappointment of it not being a Brandt. But the gambit would never work. Rory no doubt knew Bella was onto him after last time. He'd smell a rat if she was careless with her notes again.

She gave in to a moment of despondency but then pulled herself together. All was not lost. There were plenty more pieces to assess, and a single one might tip the balance, if it was truly special. In any case, she couldn't leave until she'd got to the bottom of the family's secrets. Tony was right: she had an advantage over Barry Dixon, being able to wander in and out.

She was about to leave for Vintage Winter when she heard a rumpus from the room next door. Bernard's study.

'What the devil?' He sounded shocked, angry and perplexed.

Bella went onto the landing and found Althea there too, with Eustace standing loyally at her heels. A second later, Bernard emerged from his room. He'd left the door open, and his eyes were wide. 'Someone's been messing with my papers.'

Althea frowned and put a hand on his arm.

As Bella drew nearer, she saw how chaotic the room looked.

But instead of investigating further, Bernard marched down the landing in a great hurry, and into another room where he slammed the door. Perhaps he didn't want Bella to see him looking upset. A moment later, she heard him shout, 'Damn!'

Bella wondered if Althea had noticed the smell of Rory's cologne, emanating from Bernard's study. He had to be a prime suspect for rifling through his dad's paperwork, but unless Bernard grew a backbone, nothing would be done.

13

A REMARKABLE REVELATION

That evening, it was finally time for the Lammas Feast, and Bella had resolved to ask Althea if she knew why Clemmie had wanted to talk to the police. She and the rest of the Powells had claimed they'd got no idea, but Bella would be surprised if Althea didn't have some inkling if she thought hard enough about it; she and Clemmie were each other's oldest friends, after all.

Bella was looking forward to the feast for its own sake, too. When she'd attended with her dad, back in the day, he'd told her it had been happening since Saxon times. The word 'Lammas' came from the Anglo-Saxon *hlafmaesse*, meaning loaf mass. It fell on 1 August each year and traditionally celebrated the first bread made from that year's harvest. Bella remembered a field full of celebrating Hope Eatoners, drinking beer and whisky, filling long tables and spilling onto picnic rugs, lounging in the summer evening's warmth. People made corn dollies and displayed traditional farm equipment and there was music and dancing. Most of the townsfolk dressed up. Bella didn't need to be asked twice. She'd bought a crimson medieval-style dress, but sadly Robert Mead wouldn't get to appreciate it. She'd invited him, but he had an early meeting with a buyer the following morning in Shrewsbury. She didn't really blame him. It wasn't as though they were a pair of teenagers. Carys had regarded her sceptically though, head on one side, when she'd explained why he wouldn't be coming. Bella could tell she thought it a feeble excuse.

Matt would be there, of course. Girlfriendless, as far as she knew. For a second, she wondered what he'd be wearing, but it was irrelevant. However he dressed, he'd still be a womanising chancer with no regular income. He was a world away from someone like Robert. She turned her attention to her own preparations instead. She'd already joined with other volunteers to ferry food, folding tables and the pristine tablecloths to the field. Now it was all about the party.

In her flat, Bella pinned her dark hair into an appropriate style and donned some suitably extravagant jewellery. Soon after, she was walking up St Giles's Steps in her flowing dress, appreciating the gentle evening warmth. She resisted the urge to look over her shoulder to see if Matt was on his way too.

Althea had invited her and the other helpers to High Seat for pre-event drinks, so she left the town for the countryside and passed High Seat's one neighbour – another Powell tenant, occupying a farm cottage. She was let into the house by Gregory, who was dressed in a khaki tunic and britches. The empty envelope he'd left in the Hanged Man filled her head. What on earth did it mean? She could only think it was a signal to someone, but who? Rory appeared at that moment, glanced at his brother's costume and laughed. He hadn't dressed up and was sporting a cream jacket, chinos and a striped shirt. Gregory flushed.

Althea was resplendent in a long purple dress, handing out drinks. The moment Bella mentioned she had something private to discuss, though, Althea ushered her up to her dressing room. 'There's something up there I need to show you anyway.

It's been on my conscience ever since you started your valuations.'

Her words made Bella ascend the stairs at speed, skirts swishing. Had Althea been holding something back that she was personally fond of? It could make all the difference.

Althea lowered her voice and turned to Bella. 'You go first. What was it you wanted to discuss?' She motioned Bella to a seat with upholstering that was going at the seams.

Bella got ready to press Althea on what the police had already asked her. It was essential to feign ignorance, or she might guess someone on the force had been talking.

'It was just that I bumped into a man called Adam Davies at the celebration of Clemmie's life. He's a trainee detective and Clemmie had asked to see him, only he didn't reach her before she died. It struck me as odd. Clemmie always seemed so diffident, yet she called him in. I wondered if she'd had worries that might relate to her death. Then again, I guess she'd have confided in you, if she had. Did you get any hint that something was wrong?'

Althea sank down slowly, frowning. 'The police asked too, for obvious reasons...' She clasped her hands together tightly, and Bella saw the emotion in her eyes. 'I can't think of anything, unless it was something I dismissed as a random worry. She was concerned about a lot of things near the end.' She looked up at Bella. 'It does seem odd, though. If she left something unresolved, I'd like to sort it out for her.'

Bella nodded, thinking of Clemmie, thin as a reed in her hospice bed, her brain fizzing with anxious final thoughts. She really wanted to sort out whatever it was, too.

Althea bit her lip. 'I'll keep thinking.' She blew her nose and took a deep breath. 'But now, I must tell you my guilty secret. There's one treasure which might be special that belongs to me.' Althea indicated a necklace which sat on a low stool.

Bella gasped. She couldn't help herself.

'It's very pretty, isn't it?' Althea said. 'I've been lying awake worrying about it ever since you suggested valuing our things.'

'It's divine.' It was an antique French cluster necklace with what Bella guessed were Burmese rubies. The pigeon-blood red was certainly vivid enough and they had that exceptional clarity you'd expect, too. They were encircled with bright white diamonds. Bella went hot and cold thinking how much the piece might be worth.

'I know what you're thinking,' Althea said. 'It would seem proper to donate anything I've got to the family cause, and bail Bernard out. He's so unhappy, and although he infuriates me sometimes, I love him very much.'

'I agree it would be an option, but you certainly shouldn't have to.' Bernard had got himself into this mess. He was paying a PA, a golf club and an errant son as well.

'Bernard knows I have them, of course,' Althea said, 'but he doesn't really "see" jewellery, if you know what I mean, and I rarely wear them in case they get lost. All the more reason to sell them, you might say.'

Bella was still trying to get her breath back. 'It should be your choice.' However much they were worth, why should she give them up to plug the gaps Rory had left?

'I don't suppose they're all that valuable,' Althea went on. 'And the proceeds would only get swallowed up – paying off Rory's overdraft probably.' She threw her head back and gave a humourless laugh. 'And as I said, they're my only significant possession. Everything else belongs to Bernard and will go to the boys. I want to keep the necklace to pass on to Paula. You understand?'

Bella nodded. She'd do the same in Althea's shoes. 'But I think it might be worth more than you realise. You've not got it insured?'

Althea looked surprised. 'You think I should do something about it separately?'

'Definitely.' *Sweet Agnes...* 'Did you inherit them?'

Althea nodded. 'From my mother. I'm afraid the story's a bit scandalous. She was given them by an Italian racing-car driver during an illicit affair. Luckily, her husband was like mine – not interested in trinkets – so she got to wear them occasionally, though I imagine she was cautious about it.' She held the necklace up to her throat for a moment and sighed, looking almost tearful. A moment later, she'd put it back on the stool again. 'I'd half wondered whether to wear them tonight, but it wouldn't be appropriate. I'd look as though I was showing off. All the same, I can't donate the necklace to Bernard's Rory fund. Paula must have it.'

She raised an eyebrow and Bella nodded. 'I totally see that – not that it's any of my business.'

Althea smiled suddenly. 'I do feel less guilty now I've confessed, though. Come on. Let's go.'

'You might want to lock the necklace up first.' It was all Bella could do not to physically stop Althea from leaving. 'In a safe, perhaps. I can have a proper look for you later. Confirm the value.'

'Thank you, but I'm afraid we don't have a safe. And I mustn't be late. I tell you what, I'll secure the deadlock as well as the Yale. We never normally do, but now you've mentioned it...' She shot Bella a sidelong glance. 'Rory only has the Yale key, in case you're wondering.'

'Could you hide it somewhere, as well?'

Althea looked amused by Bella's anxiety, not caught up in it. 'If you like. Why not?' She tucked the necklace under an old-fashioned dressing table so it rested on the floor, hidden behind its valance.

Job done, she snapped her fingers to get Eustace's attention then strode out of the door, the miniature schnauzer hard on her heels. 'I'm leaving him with our neighbour, Sue.' Bella pictured the cottage, just the other side of the viburnum hedge. 'I often do when we go out. It's so lonely up here and she's got a bad leg. She'd never be able to run if she had an intruder.'

Bella couldn't imagine the miniature schnauzer being much help, but maybe he was fiercer than he looked.

With Eustace happily installed at the neighbour's, they headed to the nearby field for the feast.

'I only hope Sue remembers to let him out,' Althea muttered. 'There'll be a mess if she doesn't, but I did remind her.'

They all left High Seat together, but Rory was looking back over his shoulder, as though he'd rather stay at home. Bella hoped he hadn't heard Althea talk about her rubies – they wouldn't be safe for long if he had.

14

———

THE LAMMAS DAY FEAST

Althea was instantly on Rory's case when they reached the field for the feast. For a moment, Bella was distracted by their exchange as Althea insisted Rory help with the hog roast.

'About time he earned his keep,' Gregory said, under his breath.

Then Bella took in the whole scene, the beauty of the rolling hills, lanterns in the trees round the field's edge, crowds of people laughing, chatting, dancing and singing.

Leo and Carys rushed up to her, Leo looking totally over the top in what he proudly informed Bella was a 'mystic prince' costume, Carys like a beauty from Arthurian legend with her long jet-black hair and ankle-length sapphire dress. She was the most glamorous primary school teacher Bella had met.

'Matt's here,' Carys said.

'Yes, thank you. I can see that.' Bella had already clocked him. She was trying to ignore the thought that some people carried off quirky costumes better than others. He was wearing a rough collarless stone-coloured shirt with a lace-up section near the neck and narrow-legged dark trousers. She watched as he chatted to a friend, his eyes sparkling. But he reminded her so much of her mother's disastrous boyfriends. He was unpredictable and the member of a band at that – just like her mother's post-divorce boyfriend number three, the father of her two youngest half-siblings.

John joined them and raised an eyebrow. 'How did it go with Althea?'

'My questions about Clemmie wanting to see Adam Davies didn't trigger any fresh thoughts, sadly. She showed me a very interesting piece, though.' Bella lowered her voice to a whisper and filled John in on the rubies. 'But it won't help the family fortunes and put the rental properties out of danger.' She gave Leo and Carys an apologetic look. 'She doesn't want to sell, and I can't say I blame her.'

'Sienna Hearst is still spreading rumours about buying Leo's premises,' Carys said bitterly. 'I'd been keeping it from Lucy but one of her schoolfriends had heard. It's so unsettling. I could cheerfully throttle Sienna.'

Bella felt for their teenage daughter. It was a lot of worry on young shoulders.

'Come on,' Leo said, taking Bella's hand in one of his and Carys's in the other. 'Let's forget about her and enjoy the evening.'

They went to a rug where people were making corn dollies. Most of them looked as though they could do it with their eyes shut, but Bella didn't manage to finish hers before someone offered to help. She managed to smile sweetly and vowed to do better by next year. The dollies would be distributed amongst the local farms and kept safe over winter, to be buried for good fortune in the spring when the crops were sown. So many of these ancient traditions had survived in Hope Eaton. Bella found it strangely comforting: a point of unchanging reference in an uncertain world. Today, it brought people together who might otherwise have no connection.

When they'd finished, she, John, Leo and Carys went to

find Gareth, Jeannie, and Jeannie's husband Peter. For once, they were all off-duty. It felt as though the entire town had decamped to this precious field on this warm summer evening, the sun lowering in the sky. People were drinking whisky and beer, because today was all about the grain, not the grape. Matt was at the top of the field, performing with a different group of musicians than usual. Bella hadn't realised he could play the violin as well as the guitar.

'Impressive, huh?' Carys said. 'A man of many talents.'

Bella decided it was best to ignore her. Thankfully there were other distractions. The hour had come for 'chasing the sheep', a spectacle she remembered from her childhood. A boy of around fifteen stood poised, a sheepskin draped over his hessian shirt, then hared off at the sound of a bell, chased by a gaggle of laughing youths. There was a lot of whooping involved. The sheepskin-draped lad managed a full ten minutes before he was caught, though he lost the sheepskin sooner. Bella had a feeling it might be the same one they'd used years back. It looked disturbingly grubby.

Her dad had explained the origins of the bizarre tradition. In medieval times, Lammas marked the end of haymaking, as well as the first harvest. To celebrate, a sheep would be loosed in the meadow by the landowner, to be kept by whoever caught it.

When their modern-day 'sheep' had got up from where he'd been lying on the grass, laughing, and the crowd's cheers had died down, Bella turned to John.

'Let's go and get some food.' She picked up her long skirts and made for one of the many tables covered in the white cloths, loaded with freshly baked breads and local cheeses. She spotted Bernard next to Hester Harper, which brought her sharply back to the problems they had. She wondered how much he paid her. It was infuriatingly impractical.

He looked a lot happier than she'd seen him lately, and his eyes were slightly unfocused. He'd probably been enjoying the libations quite freely. Then, as she watched, he slipped Hester a twenty-pound note.

'Buy yourself something pretty,' she heard him say as she squeezed through the crowds. His cheeks were rosy and he looked more than a little emotional.

Hell. So that was how the land lay. She should have realised it was a possibility, but Bernard had to be seventy if he was a day. At least twice as old as Hester. It had put her off the scent but now she kicked herself. He was hardly the first man to pursue a younger woman. Althea and Bernard might talk late into the night, but they'd been together a long time.

Carys had seen too. She raised her eyebrows. 'Poor Althea, but if Bernard's having an affair, then poor us too. If she walks out, there'll be no one left to fight our corner.'

She was right. Bella lowered her voice. 'And it's all more complicated than it seems.' She filled Carys in on Hester and Rory's fake row. 'Perhaps Hester's seeing Rory too, and Bernard got suspicious, so they set up that display to allay his fears. It makes me suspect Hester's carrying on with Bernard with an ulterior motive. Influence and income, perhaps. He probably stopped being able to afford her long ago, but he won't want to sack her if they're sleeping together, and perhaps she's encouraging him to be lenient with Rory.' It made Bella's blood boil. And poor Althea! She'd put up with a lot from Bernard, and this was how he'd repaid her loyalty.

Bella was still brooding as she, John, Gareth and most of the Jenkses settled on a rug. She tried to focus on the dancing rather than the worries that were plaguing her. Over by the roast, she saw Althea saying something to Rory. He pulled a face the moment her back was turned, the weasel... After that, he sidled away and helped himself to a plateful of bread and meat, looking watchful.

When Bella went to fetch more food, she overheard Althea talking to some of the Powell tenants.

'And how's Becky's collarbone? Fully healed now? So easily done when you come off a horse. If she's lost her nerve, I'm sure my niece would help. She loves horses – used to work as a jockey, in fact. And what about Frank? I hope that business with the neighbours has calmed down. If not, I can come and talk…'

Bella drifted away again. So Paula had been a jockey. That explained her confidence on horseback. She wondered why she'd given it up. It couldn't be an injury if she could still ride like that. She made a mental note to look into it.

After that, she sat back down next to John and thought about Althea. She clearly knew each of the tenants and their families inside out and it wasn't just for show. She was ready to wade in and help and Bella was sure she was genuinely interested. She wondered how many landladies were so invested. But of course, Althea wasn't the landlady. Her only power over the tenants' future came via her influence over Bernard, and that suddenly seemed fragile.

She was so deep in thought that a figure in front of her, disturbing the warm hazy air, made her jump.

It was Matt. 'Come on, you lot. You all look far too serious for Lammas Day. There's dancing to be done.'

Carys gave a half smile and gathered her skirts, getting to her feet. 'He's right. Let's eat, drink and be merry.' She grabbed Leo's hand and pulled him up too.

Jeannie and Gareth were on their feet as well, and Bella followed them, as did John, though Bella could tell he'd far rather be back on the blanket.

'I'm sure you can manage some light swaying,' she said to him. He looked especially horrified when people started to hold hands and whirl round in circles. She'd have to give him lots of strong coffee and let him sit in a quiet corner at work tomorrow to get over it.

Althea and Bernard were in the centre of things, their

dancing a good deal more courtly than the rest. Perhaps Bella was wrong to think Bernard might leave Althea for Hester. He was holding his wife's hand tenderly and gazing into her eyes. Bella spotted Gregory and Rory watching them. Neither looked pleased at the display of affection. If it weren't for Althea's protectiveness, Gregory might get his way and sell High Seat. And without her fierce principles, Rory would doubtless persuade Bernard to sell the rental properties. If her influence ended, it would be a race to see who'd convince Bernard first. Rory would win, Bella was sure.

Suddenly, Bella was pulled off into another group. It took half a second to realise it was Matt who'd taken her hand. He was grinning and his grip was warm, his hand rough. The result of the casual farm work he took on, perhaps, or the hours he spent after dark, working on his beautiful wooden carvings.

'Isn't your new boyfriend coming?'

'Prior engagement.'

'Wrong sense of priorities.' Matt's smile broadened as the group swung round. 'Does he like dancing?'

'I haven't asked him.' Bella couldn't imagine Robert joining in for a moment, but she wasn't going to tell Matt that.

Their group carried on into the small hours. Bella knew she would pay for it tomorrow. John had been trying to sneak off for ages and had finally managed it when Gareth decided his cheffing would suffer if he didn't get some sleep. He was ever a perfectionist. The pair of them disappeared with Jeannie and Peter. Carys and Leo's daughter Lucy had already left too – she was off to a friend's house for a sleepover.

Leo was well away though, and showed no signs of giving in, and as it was Saturday tomorrow and the summer holidays to boot, Carys was right there with him.

Matt was still there too. And Althea and Bernard.

'They always stay until the end,' Carys said. 'There's a committee that organises the festivities each year, but I'm sure they still feel like the hosts. I think it's a matter of pride for Bernard.'

Bella imagined she was right.

At last, Althea turned to the stragglers. 'Come to High Seat for a nightcap. And then perhaps we should all go to bed.'

Althea led the way towards High Seat, dark against the midnight-blue sky, dotted with stars. The beauty of it made Bella's eyes prick.

They'd just made it to the entrance hall when Bella saw Althea's smile morph into a frown. She was looking through the door to one of the sitting rooms.

Bella caught her up and saw one of the windows was open a crack.

A moment later, Althea was dashing upstairs, Bella at her heels. Bella watched her pull up the dressing-table valance to reveal the spot where she'd hidden the ruby necklace.

It was gone.

15

THE GUILTY PARTY

Bella had the most terrible sinking feeling inside. Guilt and regret. She should never have let Althea leave the house after abandoning the necklace, even if she had hidden it.

She was in a daze as Gregory offered them the nightcaps that Althea had mentioned. Rory didn't help, not that that was a surprise. In the end, most people opted for hot chocolate rather than more alcohol. Bella offered to muck in and her reward was to witness an urgently whispered conversation between Althea and Bernard.

'... my ruby necklace!' Althea was leaning forward.

'What's that? What necklace? I don't remember it.'

Althea raised her eyes to heaven and darted upstairs again. As Bella ferried a couple of hot drinks from the kitchen to the reception hall, Althea reappeared with a photograph. 'This one!' She sounded exasperated. 'I wore it for our silver wedding anniversary. Oh, never mind. The point is I left it in my dressing room and now there's a window open in the yellow sitting room and it's gone!' She grabbed Bella's arm, almost making her spill her load. 'You saw me leave it there, didn't you, Bella?'

Bella nodded.

'So someone's taken it. It would be easy. Everyone knew we were out.'

It was true: Althea and Bernard had been the centre of attention throughout the feast. No one would worry that they might slip back to High Seat. But who knew that Althea owned such a valuable thing? Bella could only think it was one of the household or Althea's niece, Paula. She'd said she hardly ever wore the necklace.

Everyone had gone quiet. Even if they hadn't caught the conversation, they knew something was up. Bella handed out the hot chocolates, then, in the hush, she heard a hesitant tapping at the door.

Gregory opened up to reveal the neighbour, Sue, and Eustace, the miniature schnauzer. Sue couldn't normally be up at this hour. She was wearing a padded floral dressing gown and some sturdy wine-coloured slippers.

'I wanted to check everything was all right,' she said. 'I was on my way to the bathroom when I noticed the warning light flashing on my security camera. It's the alert, you know, to tell me it's picked something up. It sends the footage to my phone, only I don't know how to look at it. It's never happened before.' She held out an ageing smartphone awkwardly, as if it were a grenade.

Althea's eyes met Bernard's. 'Let's have a look.'

Bella glanced at the assembled group. Rory was edging away. She'd never seen him look so tense.

Gregory seemed to spot it. 'Yes, let's have a look. Come on, Rory, you can help Sue find the right app.'

'I'm sure you can manage that. I'm going to get myself another drink.'

But Bernard stepped in. 'Not now, old man. If there's an intruder, he might still be lurking about. We need to stick together.'

Gregory fiddled with Sue's phone for a few moments, then played back the footage, holding the device at arm's length as they all crowded round.

It showed Rory creeping through the garden at High Seat. He stepped through a flowerbed, round some topiary, and approached the open window that Althea had spotted.

'What's all this, my boy?' Bernard's voice was higher than usual, his eyes scared. Then he turned to the rest of them. 'I'm sorry, there must be some mistake, but you'll appreciate we need to sort it out.'

The spell broke. Everyone was agreeing, moving back, and preparing to leave. They shuffled around, picking up their belongings, then exited the house, leaving undrunk mugs of chocolate on side tables. It was deeply frustrating to have to leave with the rest, but Bella had no choice. After that, she had to endure the awkward walk back to Southwell Hall with Matt. At least Leo and Carys were with them for part of the way.

Leo was goggling. 'What's he supposed to have done? I didn't hear.'

'Broken into High Seat and stolen the necklace I told you about.' Bella closed her eyes for a moment, then filled Matt in on the background. 'At first glance, I'd say it was worth around half a million pounds.'

Everyone was stunned into silence.

It was Matt who spoke first. 'That's quite some prize. You don't seem very surprised about him taking it.'

'It's not his first offence and he's the sort who never has enough money. It doesn't mean he's Clemmie's killer, though. Even if she realised he'd stolen from his dad, I'd guess she knew Bernard would always protect him. But this time it's different. Althea's not the pushover Bernard is. Even if we can't get Rory for murder, him being prosecuted for stealing the necklace ought to lessen his influence and protect the Steps.'

For just a second, she imagined Althea leaving the necklace

out to tempt him. She could prove he was guilty, get the rubies back and put paid to his shenanigans once and for all. But if that had been the plan, she'd surely have done it years ago, before he'd drained Bernard quite so dry.

Carys grinned. 'I'm looking forward to seeing Sienna's face.'

Bella couldn't suppress a flicker of hope too, but she wouldn't celebrate until she saw Rory sentenced and the rubies back in Althea's hands. Rory was good at wriggling out of things.

Bella woke later that morning to find a text from Althea, asking her to drop in as soon as she liked to continue her valuations. She said she'd fill Bella in about the theft too. *Tantalising.* Bella would have been sorely tempted to go to High Seat immediately if it weren't for opening the shop, with John likely in a reduced state. She dashed straight to Vintage Winter as planned, more awake than she might have been thanks to adrenaline and coffee. John arrived marginally after her, which was unheard of. He was still pristine in his grey suit, but he had post-Lammas feast eyes.

She put more coffee on and filled him in on what had happened in the small hours. 'I wonder if Althea's secretly pleased. When it was Bernard who Rory stole from, he wouldn't do anything. Now at last she's got the upper hand. And hopefully she's already retrieved the necklace from Rory's clutches.'

John blinked. 'True. It's certainly good news from our point of view.'

'I just wish it took us closer to finding out who killed Clemmie.'

He nodded and breathed in the coffee as though it was oxygen. *Very relatable.*

'I'll be all right here.' He took another deep inhale, then a sip, though it must still be scalding. 'You should get up there and find out what's going on.'

Bella hesitated.

'I can manage, and the adrenaline's coming off you in waves. It's not very soothing after a late night.'

She laughed. 'Put like that, I shall leave you to it without guilt.'

It was Bernard's PA Hester Harper who answered Bella's knock at High Seat. Bella instantly thought of her fake row with Rory and the money Bernard had slipped her to 'buy something pretty'. *Deeply unimpressive.*

'Welcome to the happy home,' Hester said, tucking a strand of chestnut hair behind her ear. She closed the door after Bella before disappearing.

Shouting emanated from a downstairs room. It was Althea and Gregory, by the sound of it.

'I can't believe you won't report him! The police would search his house. Find the necklace!'

Bella's excitement came crashing down. She'd thought Althea would leap at this opportunity. What on earth had gone wrong? If Rory wasn't prosecuted, the threat hanging over Leo and all the Powell tenants wasn't over, and Bella had seen for herself how much Althea minded about them.

'For pity's sake!' Gregory went on. 'You don't even know how much the necklace is worth. You and Dad are both useless! And why let Rory off the hook? You know as well as I do that he's played Dad for decades. And then finally, *finally* he's due his comeuppance and he gets off scot-free.'

'Not scot-free, Gregory.'

'As good as. And he can still sell the necklace and wallow in the cash.'

Bella couldn't make sense of any of this.

'For all of five minutes until he's spent it again. Money's worth more to some people than others.'

Gregory let out a groan and bounded from the room. He cursed as he saw Bella, then stormed upstairs.

Charming.

Althea appeared, looking exhausted. 'Come into my study,' she said. 'Let's talk. You know the background – I'd like to explain.'

Bella followed her and found Eustace lying flat under her desk, as though he'd had quite enough of humans for one day. 'You haven't got the necklace back?'

Althea shook her head. 'Give Bernard his due, he made Rory turn out his pockets and all the rest of it, but he didn't have it on him. He must have taken it home, hidden it or had a contact he knew would take it off his hands at the feast.' She sighed. 'I was a fool not to listen when you said I shouldn't leave without locking it up.'

'I should have been more forceful. A lot more. Althea, I can't be sure without having examined it closely, but I think the necklace could have been worth as much as half a million pounds.'

Althea's mouth fell open and she dropped into a chair. 'I always thought it was nice, but I never dreamed it could be that much. Are you sure?'

'Not absolutely, without assessing it properly. You had a photo of you wearing it, didn't you? I could take a closer look.'

Althea rummaged in a drawer and pulled out the one she'd shown Bernard the evening before. She was standing in front of a fireplace, eyes gleaming, looking a million dollars in a tailored black coat with a velvet collar. It had been taken at Christmastime. Bella could see baubles and tinsel in a beautiful green bowl on the table next to her. There was a miniature Christmas tree on the mantelpiece and tall, church-style candles in the grate. That bit of the photo was reasonably well in focus, but

Althea herself was a little blurry, as were the jewels. Bella would have to rely on memory.

She told Althea why she'd thought the necklace was special. If Bella was right, the proceeds from selling it would buy a house. It didn't bear thinking about.

'Poor Paula.' Althea was shaking her head. 'They should have been hers, but I never told her. She won't know what she's missed out on.'

'You might get the necklace back if you went to the police.' Bella would have been straight onto them if it had been her. Rory richly deserved to feel the consequences of his actions.

Althea's look was sober. 'Possibly, but I doubt it. I'm certain Rory has been up to this sort of thing for years, and he hasn't been caught yet. He's cleverer than you might think. He denies everything of course, but he couldn't explain why he was caught on camera climbing through a side window when we asked him last night. By this morning, he was claiming he'd been bored with the festivities and after some peace and quiet. He says he found I'd turned the deadlock but someone had left a window open, so he got in that way instead.'

She nodded at Bella's reaction. 'He's a past master at coming up with plausible stories. I suspect he listened to our conversation, including me saying I'd double lock the house. He'd have known he'd need another way in. I believe he left the window open.

'I'm furious about it. The police were my first thought when I realised what had happened, and if I thought I could prove he was guilty, I'd still be tempted. But it would be my word against his unless the police find the necklace. I can't do it to Bernard – it's too much risk with too little hope of reward. And if I did succeed, just think of it, Bella – a public split in the family, Rory on trial for stealing from his stepmum. I'd have to watch Bernard disintegrate. His self-esteem is so low these days and what he has left rests on being the owner of High Seat and his pride in his younger son. It's Gregory's achievements he should celebrate, but sadly that's not the case. Rory talks big and Bernard believes things will come right for him. I couldn't shatter Bernard's illusions like that. Besides, it might turn him against me. Even if I could bear the upset, I'd lose all my influence. No. No police.'

She sighed, leaned forward and lowered her voice still further. 'Though entirely between ourselves, I'm using what little savings I have to hire a private detective. I'll ask them to stick to Rory like glue. Unless he's already offloaded the rubies, he'll have to surface with them sooner or later. I just hope it's before my money runs out. I'm determined to have them back for Paula. Meanwhile, holding back gives me some soft power. In return for not reporting it, I've insisted Bernard cuts Rory out of his will and removes all say he has in the property business. I've also said he must be kept at a distance and I'm making Rory break up with Paula.' She folded her arms. 'I know it's heavy-handed, but he's an awful man and now he's stolen her inheritance. I can't keep waiting for her to see through him. At least he's unlikely to persuade Bernard to sell the rental properties now. The idea of Paula being nudged into moving in with Rory was appalling. She needs a bolthole. She could stay here, of course – she did when she first came to Hope Eaton – but she needs some independence at her age.'

It took Bella a full minute to assimilate what she'd said and accept that Althea's word was final. It seemed she really did still love Bernard. If she knew he was sleeping with his PA, her feelings might change, but perhaps she'd still want to maintain her influence for the sake of the Powell tenants. And Bernard was going along with her stipulations. That suggested he wasn't ready to end his marriage yet. He'd been looking lovingly at her the previous night as they'd danced. Perhaps he was excited and flattered by Hester's attentions but wanted the best of both worlds. The old story.

'Keep in mind that I've negotiated Rory's excommunication without dragging the family name through the mud,' Althea went on. 'That means a lot to Bernard.' Her eyes were on Bella's. 'It's horrifying to know I've probably paid half a million pounds for the privilege, but I still feel relieved.'

Her thinking was flawed, in Bella's opinion. How long before Rory wormed his way into his dad's good books again?

'I won't let him come weaselling back,' Althea said, as though she'd read Bella's mind. 'As I said before, over my dead body.'

16

THE WORST NEWS

Bella dashed across town to Vintage Winter after she'd finished at High Seat. She'd spent most of the day at the Powells' place, continuing the valuations after calling John to make sure he was coping. She'd be back just in time to help shut up the shop. She had much more energy than she'd thought after dancing half the night. It was probably pent-up tension. She was still reeling from Althea's decision. She sympathised with Gregory: how dare Rory, and how could Althea bear to let him get away with it? She knew it was concern for Bernard which had swayed her, but surely it was time he faced facts? He didn't deserve Althea's loyalty when he was carrying on with Hester Harper, either.

Her mind returned to poor Clemmie. Her murder and this theft were both significant crimes; it would be a huge coincidence if they weren't related. Yet Bella still doubted Rory would have killed Clemmie if she'd noticed him stealing from High Seat. He knew he'd got his dad where he wanted him.

Before getting to Vintage Winter, Bella went to the top of St Giles's Steps and looked down towards Rory's cottage. She wondered if Althea's private detective was already watching. Either way, Bella should be. She found it hard to believe Rory had got rid of the ruby necklace already. Surely he'd be too canny to hand over something so valuable at the feast unless his buyer had the money to pay him, and how could they? If the theft was last minute, Rory had had no time to strike a deal. But by the same token he'd probably hidden it, and hidden it well. He couldn't bank on Althea not calling the police.

Bella walked a little way down the steps until she was level with his cottage. He was definitely at home. The window was open, and raised voices were travelling through it. Paula was clearly visiting, despite the order to end their relationship.

Bella needed to get nearer to hear what was being said, but judging by the heated tone, neither of them would notice. She opened the low wooden gate and let herself into the garden to get up close to the house. The smell of honeysuckle filled the air.

'What the blazes have you done with it?' That was Paula. 'Have you sold it already? You're despicable. I thought you cared about me. It should have been mine! Althea would have left it to me.'

So much for Paula not knowing what she was missing.

Rory had the gall to laugh. 'You're just as greedy as I am! I suppose that's better than putting on fake waterworks and pretending the thing had sentimental value. I'll bet you don't even remember it, do you? Althea said she hardly wore it.'

'That's not the point!' Paula sounded incandescent. 'Unlike you, I work like crazy and I've got next to nothing to show for it. It's not fair.'

'It's not fair!' The mimicry wound Bella up, despite not being on the receiving end. 'Read my lips: I. Didn't. Steal. It.'

'So why were you climbing through the window then?'

'I was fed up with Dad and your darling aunt ordering me about at the feast. I walked back to High Seat for a break, found I couldn't get in, then realised someone had left a window open. Simple as that.' The same story he'd told Althea – but only after several hours to think about it. 'I told Dad,' Rory went on, 'but he went all mealy-mouthed over it. I'd hoped better of you.'

'If you didn't take the necklace, then where is it?'

Bella imagined him shrugging. 'Who knows? Perhaps Althea set me up.'

'She never left the field.'

Paula was right; she hadn't. And it was as Bella had thought earlier, if Althea was minded to trap Rory, she'd have done it long ago. She was more than sharp enough to come up with the plan.

'Okay, so she didn't then, but I promise you, I'm innocent. Look at me! Look into my eyes. You know what I get up to sometimes, but I'd never take something that should have been yours.'

This from the man who had something going with Hester Harper behind Paula's back. Bella imagined he'd sell his own grandmother and smile as he did it. There was a long pause. Paula's quiet reply sounded like, 'Okay'. There followed a hiatus when what they were doing was left to Bella's imagination. Unpleasantly vivid images came to mind.

Paula had to be acting if Bella's previous conclusions about their relationship were correct. It would make her either very calculating, or very angry and out for revenge, and Bella was betting on the latter. Bella no longer bought her as a thief, out to make money. She needed to double check, but it seemed Paula was working two jobs, not the sort to take shortcuts. But that work ethic would make someone like Rory all the more infuriating. She could imagine her becoming obsessed with bringing him down. He hadn't given two hoots about her welfare when he tried to get Bernard to sell her house. And now he appeared to have stolen her inheritance too.

'You and I are going to have to lie low for now,' Rory said at last. 'Dad'll soften up before long; he always does. Then we can see each other again.'

'I wouldn't bank on Althea changing her mind.'

'Oh, I'm not,' Rory said. 'But we're evenly matched when it comes to bending Dad's ear.' When he spoke again, his voice was like ice. 'I'm going to find a way to pay her back. She looked so damned happy when she made her demands. Taking the place of my mum, then forcing Dad to cut me out of his will...'

'I think we should carry on seeing each other on the quiet.' Paula was clearly focused on her goals, not Rory's hurt feelings. 'I had fun at the racecourse. I want to come with you again. Get involved. Will you sell that client more stuff?'

Rory laughed. 'Don't you think you're being a touch hypo-critical, after objecting to the idea of me stealing the rubies?' After a momentary pause, he rushed on, 'All right, all right – I see that's different. You're a woman after my own heart. As for that client, yes, I'm planning to swing by their place. They're a valuable customer, but no can do on the joint venture, I'm afraid. I'll never get Dad back on side if he sees me breaking the rules. You can come once we're official again. Maybe I really will show you the ropes.'

Paula let out a groan, which held a lot of anger. 'I'm bored with waiting. Althea ruins everything for me. I push doors open and she shuts each one in my face. She won't even force the issue of the necklace when I'm the one who'll suffer. I've heard whispers that it was special.'

Rory grunted. 'Special? Never mind that. I've heard it was worth a small fortune.'

He'd probably been listening in as Althea and Bella talked, just as Althea thought.

As for Paula – Bella had guessed she'd be angry. Althea might be acting with the best of intentions, but she was breaking up Paula's relationship. A relationship Bella now guessed Paula had entered with a clear-sighted aim: most probably to ruin Rory, which was what Althea wanted too. Paula might feel Althea was treating her like a child. And that her desire to protect Bernard's feelings had trumped her fondness for Paula too, leading her to let the necklace go without a fuss. If only Paula knew that Althea had hired a private detective to try to get the rubies back, but Bella could see why she hadn't told her. She thought Rory had got Paula onside; if he convinced her he was innocent, Paula might tell him Althea had hired a spy.

Bella had been so intent on her thoughts that the sound of the cottage's front door opening took her by surprise. She crept further into the garden so she was hidden behind a pergola festooned with climbing roses.

She could hear enough to gather that Rory and Paula were allowing themselves a revolting goodbye kiss on the doorstep. Paula appeared moments later and let herself out of the gate, then stood there for a moment, staring back at the house, frowning. Maybe she hoped Rory would risk carrying on the relationship, which would mean she could surreptitiously search the house at some point. But at an upper-floor window, Bella glimpsed movement. She was pretty sure Rory was looking down at Paula. He'd know she was suspicious. If he did have the necklace, he'd never be so careless as to let her see it.

Paula retreated down St Giles's Steps, her fists clenched, mouth working as though she couldn't contain her feelings.

A minute later, Bella had returned to St Giles's Close and was just about to rescue John when she caught sight of a familiar figure on the other side of the church. Bernard Powell. He looked anxious, checking repeatedly over his shoulder.

On impulse, Bella walked quietly after him and as she got nearer, she spotted a bouquet of flowers sticking out of the plastic bag he was carrying. Three guesses who they were for. A moment later, he knocked at one of the tiniest, snuggest cottages on Old Percy's Lane. Hester Harper opened the door. She beamed and ushered him in.

. . .

The following day at Vintage Winter, Bella was eagerly awaiting John's arrival. It was his day off but he'd promised to pop in to pool ideas. She'd been desperate to unpick everything the day before, but there'd been no time. They'd barely overlapped during the day, then he'd dashed off to meet Gareth and she'd had to have dinner with Robert. It had gone okay. As far as she could remember. She'd been so preoccupied, it had been hard to focus.

Bella dashed to the door the moment John appeared. 'Come on in!' They had customers but she'd already established that none of them needed help. It was best to leave them be; pushing never worked. 'You're here for the lowdown?' She'd texted him the basics, but none of the detail.

John blinked quickly behind his glasses. 'I'm afraid not. You haven't heard the news?'

Bella felt a sinking feeling in her stomach as possibilities flitted through her head. 'No. What is it?'

'It's Althea. I'm so sorry. She went to an event down the valley last night. She must have been shattered after all the hoo-hah the night before, on top of the Lammas Day feast...'

'What happened?' She felt cold to her very core.

'It looks as though she fell asleep at the wheel. Her car came off the Brynway and crashed into the valley. They only found her this morning.'

17

SIENNA THE SERPENT

John refused to leave Bella until he'd made her coffee and let the news of Althea's death sink in.

'You should go and be with Gareth. Hasn't he got the day off?'

John nodded. 'It doesn't matter. He understands, and you know what he's like. I left him practising a new soufflé recipe and thumping around the kitchen because it wasn't quite right.'

He gave the ghost of a smile, but she could see how upset he was.

'This is too much of a coincidence after Clemmie, John.'

He frowned. 'I thought the same. Or that it might be to do with the ruby necklace.'

That had occurred to her too. It felt hugely unlikely that two monumental events in quick succession weren't related, let alone three. A connection between Althea's death and the theft of the necklace, she could see, and possibly between Clemmie and Althea's deaths too. But how would a link between all three work?

'Maybe Rory is guilty of something much more serious than theft, and he committed both murders. I heard him only yesterday saying he wanted to pay Althea back.' His tone came back to her, sending icy waves down her spine. 'If Althea suspected him of murder as well as theft, he'd have every reason to get rid of her.'

John gave a helpless shrug. 'I doubt convincing the police will be easy. No one's suggesting there was anyone else involved, and she must have been exhausted.'

'True, but it's far too convenient.'

'Leo said the same.'

Thoughts of John's brother made Bella look beyond her upset to the knock-on effects of Althea's death. No one to stick up for the Steps and the Powells' other renters. No one to care about Becky with the broken collarbone and Frank with the troublesome neighbour. No one to make sure Bernard wrote Rory out of his will. Gregory would be at his wits' end and Rory had motives coming out of his ears.

'I'm going to call Tony. I want to get his thoughts. I'll try to get him to come to the Blue Boar tonight. Will you join us?'

John nodded. 'I'll be there.'

Tony agreed to the meet-up too. He promised he'd find out all he could and be there by eight.

For a moment, Bella wondered if she should invite Robert. If she got him involved with her sideline, he might understand her motivations better. But they'd only seen each other the night before, and although John got on with everyone, she wasn't sure Robert would gel with Tony.

Instead, she messaged Barry Dixon to suggest someone could have forced Althea off the road and to tell him about the aggro with Rory and his threats to pay her back.

There was no reply. He'd be running around of course, but this was important. She hoped he'd at least take the message seriously. She needed the lowdown from Tony badly, but it was hours before they were due to meet.

In the meantime, Vintage Winter was busy. The customers

who came in asked questions and bought, but at least half of them wanted to talk about Althea's crash, so Bella was focused on it all day. She'd liked her so much. Visions of her bright, intelligent eyes kept rearing up in her mind. Her laughter and her pep. She'd been more alive than most people Bella knew; it was almost impossible to think of her gone, just like Clemmie. In quiet moments, she thought of her fear too. What must she have felt as the car careered off the road? Bella knew that stretch. There were barriers by the very steepest drop but they stopped when there was still a mighty fall, replaced by occasional bollards – not enough to offer proper protection. She imagined the car rolling, and Althea knowing there was nothing she could do. She kept thinking of Eustace too, and how lost he'd be without his mistress. Partway through the afternoon she had to dive into Vintage Winter's office to have a good cry.

Later on, Sienna Hearst came in. Of all the people Bella didn't want to see... She fantasised about taking a leaf out of Jeannie's book and barring her, but it would only allow her to take the role of martyr.

'Tragic news about Althea Powell, isn't it?' Sienna was smiling as Bella imagined deflating the tyres of her 4x4. 'Now she's no longer around, I imagine the family will go ahead and sell the Steps.'

Bella took a deep breath. The woman really was mind-bogglingly horrible. 'I doubt it. Gregory doesn't approve.'

Sienna pursed her lips. 'But he's such an ineffectual man, isn't he? Takes after his father. Whereas Rory knows what he wants. Just like me. It was Althea who held the balance of power. Now she's dead, I'm sure it's just a matter of time.'

She gave Bella a little wave and walked out of the door.

The worst of it was, there was no doubt that she was right.

Bella decided to have supper at the Blue Boar before Tony's update and complained to Jeannie about Sienna, which made her feel marginally better.

'We must stop her,' Jeannie said. 'I won't have these malign influences in my town. I ask you, what would people do without the Steps?'

18

A VISIT FROM THE GODFATHER

Just before eight, Bella approached the Blue Room to find Tony had slipped in unnoticed and beaten her to it.

He was in the process of winkling out a couple of stray drinkers, so they could have some privacy. Jeannie wouldn't approve, but Bella couldn't help admiring his technique. He seemed to have trained Captain to sniff people to order, to a disconcerting degree. That, combined with his offer to show the incumbents the tattoo on his knee, did the trick. Tony smiled and gave a retreating couple a friendly wave as they picked up their drinks and scuttled off.

Bella went to sit next to him. 'You are awful. Do you really have a tattoo on your knee?'

'No, but no one's ever called my bluff.' He gave her a half hug and looked unrepentant as Captain pottered over so she could fuss him.

Within minutes, John arrived too, and since Jeannie knew Tony was expected Bella had a feeling she'd be joining them before long.

Sure enough, she sailed through the door the moment John

was seated. 'I must be a part of this,' she said, sinking into a sofa. 'I can't have my town thrown into fear and chaos.'

As usual, Tony had taken the throne-like chair at the head of the table. He sighed. 'And so say all of us. Sad business this. I've looked at the reports and the word on the street's correct. No sign anyone else was involved. No skid marks on the road except hers, and no hope of telling if her car made contact with another vehicle before she came off the road. The damage from the fall will have disguised any dents made beforehand.'

Bella had her favourite notebook out, with its blue marbled cover and edges, her mind on the skid marks. 'So if she did fall asleep at the wheel, she must have woken and braked before she left the road.'

Tony nodded.

'And if someone actually drove into her, we'll have to rely on finding the damage on their car to prove it, maybe with traces of Althea's car's paint to help join the dots.'

'Yup,' Tony replied.

'Or maybe it wasn't another car. Someone could have put an obstacle in the road.'

Tony grunted. 'If so, they cleared it away smartish. The team have a witness they reckon drove down the Brynway fifty minutes after she did, and there was no sign of any blockage then. They didn't notice the accident either. Althea Powell was way below them, of course. They just carried on their merry way until they saw the appeal for information today.

'Upshot is, if you think something's off, you'll have a job convincing our boy Barry. Might have been a straightforward accident, to be fair. It wasn't a reliable way to kill her. She could have regained control and stayed on the road or crashed to the bottom without fatal injuries. And nodding off at the wheel fits. Her family say she was up all night, the night before.'

Bella's frustration built. It was so plausible. Very handy for anyone who might have run her off the road. 'I can think of multiple reasons why Althea's closest connections might want her dead. And I can't help feeling it relates to Clemmie too. The timing's too much of a coincidence.' She stroked Captain's head. 'How do the police know when she crashed, if the witness didn't see the accident?'

Tony sat back in his chair. 'There's no modern tech in the car to help, but a rough estimate based on journey times fits with the doc's estimated time of death. She'd been to a private view at a gallery near Church Stretton – left earlier than planned, before the artist's speech, which makes sense if she was knackered. She set off at nine fifteen, which would put her on the Brynway by nine thirty.'

'What did Bernard do when she didn't arrive home?'

He grunted. 'Nothing. Says he went to bed early after the previous night's high jinks and fell sound asleep. They've got adjoining bedrooms – not a shared one – and he'd no idea she was missing until breakfast time. Or so he says.' He checked his notes. 'Same applies to the son who lives at the house.'

'So Bernard and Gregory can't alibi each other,' Bella said. Not that a father–son alibi would be worth that much.

Tony shook his head.

John blinked. 'Did the police check where Rory was?'

'They did, as a matter of fact. Good dotting of the 'i's there, given there was no sign of foul play. They'd got wind of bad blood between Althea and Rory from Gregory, who told them all about the necklace.'

That was good news. Perhaps her text combined with Gregory's evidence might sway Barry's thinking.

Tony held his notes at arm's length and Bella wished he'd get round to updating his reading glasses. 'Rory was home alone, Paula having been warned off by Althea. And Paula was back at her place, also unaccompanied. She's down on Kite Close in Low Town.'

It was all very unsatisfactory. Bella's thoughts turned to

Gregory and how furious he'd been when Althea failed to report the stolen necklace. She wasn't surprised he'd dropped Rory in it. 'So they'll investigate the theft of the rubies now?'

Jeannie sat up straight and looked full of righteous indignation. 'I should jolly well hope so!'

Tony sighed and sipped his Hobsons Twisted Spire. 'Afraid not. Bernard's saying it was all a misunderstanding.'

'But the necklace should have gone to Paula.' Bella remembered her fierce row about it with Rory. She suspected she didn't truly believe he was innocent.

'Just the same, unless Althea has specifically left her the necklace in her will, she won't find it easy if Bernard won't even admit the thing's missing,' Tony said.

It was so frustrating, but Bella had been a witness. She made a note to impress upon Barry that it had not in fact been 'a misunderstanding'. Perhaps that would help if Paula wanted to pursue it. Bella wondered how she felt now.

'So let's take this from the top,' Tony said. 'What do we have?'

John gave Bella a sidelong glance. 'We should start with Clemmie.'

'Yes.' Bella still felt her murder and Althea's death had to be connected. 'Our theory that Clemmie had damning information about someone and was killed because of it still holds.'

Tony nodded.

'We're looking for someone with access to Clemmie, and to the brand of sleeping tablets used to kill her. If she was going to report someone, Rory seems most likely, simply because we know he's a criminal, and she'd cut him out of her will. He'd clearly done something she couldn't stick. But for him to kill, it would have to be something so serious that his father couldn't protect him.

'And he's not the only one with secrets. I'm fairly certain Paula took money from Rufus Hartford for innocent reasons now, but I need to check, and I'd like some proof to back up my theories about her. I suspect her relationship with Rory's a sham, and that she's angry with him, probably because he's been pushing to sell her house from under her. And he's so vain he hasn't realised she's playing him. My guess is she wants to bring him down in revenge, but I need to be sure.

'Meanwhile, Gregory left that weird empty envelope in the gents' at the Hanged Man. It's hard to think of an above-board reason for that.'

'Or any reason,' John said.

'You have a point. Beyond that, Gilbert overheard him panicking about a secret that Clemmie had picked up on.

'Then there's Hester Harper, who appears to be carrying on with both Bernard and Rory, and Bernard, who might have been caught out in an affair. Hester and Rory are pulling the wool over Bernard's eyes, pretending to be at daggers drawn.'

'So Rory knows Hester and Bernard are together but he doesn't mind?' Jeannie's eyelashes fluttered with indignation.

'That's what it looks like.'

'Outrageous!'

'Perhaps Rory could have killed Clemmie to stop her talking about *that*.' Bella followed the thought through. 'If Bernard's sleeping with Hester, I guess he'd be deeply humiliated if he discovered she was double-crossing him. And humiliation is the one thing he can't stand, according to Althea.' Pain shot through her as she thought of the dead woman. 'It wouldn't just be that Hester was two-timing him, but that Rory was in on it. They'd have been laughing at Bernard behind his back. If Clemmie knew and told him, he might finally have turned against Rory for real and I'm sure Rory would do anything to prevent that. Plus, the killing must have seemed low risk. The stumbling block is that there's nothing criminal about Hester cheating on Bernard, so although Rory might kill to keep it secret, it wouldn't explain Clemmie involving the police. But perhaps there's more to it than meets the eye.'

'Hester and Rory must be getting something out of it,' Tony said, 'unless it's just for kicks.'

'Exactly.' Bella continued to mull over the facts. 'Bernard slipped Hester twenty pounds at the Lammas Feast, but I can't believe she's sleeping with him just so she and Rory can share the odd tips he gives her.'

'Any thoughts when you put it together with Althea's death?' Tony peered at her keenly. 'Assuming it was murder?' He liked to put Bella through her paces, having decided she'd missed her vocation in CID.

'It could be a much more elaborate scheme. Perhaps their plan is for Hester to marry Bernard, so she gets the sort of control that Althea had. She could guard Rory's interests, and push for the sale of the cottages as he wants. She'd have to move into High Seat, but I'm sure she could keep Bernard at bay and spend most of her time sneaking off to be with Rory.'

'Grotesque!' Jeannie looked as though she could barely stomach her drink, which was relatable.

'But why kill Althea? You don't think Bernard would just have divorced her?' Tony slurped his beer.

Bella thought of the fond look in Bernard's eye as he'd danced with poor Althea at the feast. 'I think it's unlikely. I believe he was still very fond of her, and he minds about his reputation. He wouldn't have liked the idea of a messy breakup, followed by marriage to a much younger woman. I guess people will still talk if they marry, but the situation will be much more seemly.'

'Really!' Jeannie ruffled her feathers. 'This is most unsuitable, and any sort of connection with Rory is to be abhorred too. I must see if I can steer Hester towards someone more appropriate next time she comes in. I'll make a list. Perhaps that will encourage her to mend her ways.'

She wouldn't know what had hit her... 'Of course, Hester and Rory might have plotted all this together, and it could have been Rory who drove Althea off the road. He was already furious with her, and threatening revenge. And as well as emotional satisfaction, and potentially clearing the way for Hester, killing her would have been a great practical benefit to him personally too.

'You can bet Althea would have ensured Bernard kept his promise to cut Rory out of his will. And she could have told the truth about the necklace any time she liked. There were witnesses at the after-feast drinks at High Seat who would have backed her story. And she'd either hired or was planning to hire a private investigator to try to get the necklace back. It's possible she'd have been able to prove it was theft in the end. Now she's gone, Rory can start his campaign to rejoin the family fold. And if he knew about the investigator, he's neutralised that threat too.' Her thoughts ran on to practicalities. 'Rory could have guessed Althea's route, waited until he saw her car approaching then driven at her. She was tired – there's no denying that. I could see her making the fatal swerve on autopilot, without his car touching hers. There are no cameras around there, I suppose?' It was so lonely.

Tony shook his grizzled head.

Bella was scribbling notes as thoughts flew through her mind. 'As for Paula, it seems as though her secret income has an innocent explanation, and the way she's playing Rory hardly suggests they'd be in cahoots over murder. That makes her look less likely for Clemmie, and for Althea, if Althea was killed because she'd guessed who had committed the first murder.' And Paula had dealt with Clemmie very tenderly on their last visit, too. 'But I need that proof that I mentioned. And she was angry with Althea about the necklace, and ruining her plans by making her break up with Rory. We can't discount her.'

Tony grunted. 'Fair enough. What about the others?'

'Bernard could have done it. Even if he was still fond of Althea, he might have wanted to marry Hester, and I'll bet he wants to bring Rory back into the fold. On top of all that, he hates confrontation. If he was going to kill, I could imagine him opting for this method. He could almost kid himself it was an accident.'

Jeannie looked scandalised, but Bella couldn't write the idea off. She leaned forward. 'As well as hating conflict, it's as I said before. Bernard would loathe people gossiping about him. And if he divorced Althea, her decision to keep quiet about Rory's criminality might change.'

'He knew where Althea was going,' Tony put in, 'and he could probably guess which route she'd take too.'

Bella nodded. 'He could have waited in the road, without acknowledging to himself what he was planning. Then right at the last minute he could have driven at her, to solve all his problems at once.'

Tony cocked his head. 'Not impossible, if you reckon it would be in character, but if it was premeditated then whoever did it took a risk. Althea could have survived. And the killer's car might have been hit. Hard to explain the damage away.'

Annoyingly, that was true. 'Emotions were running high. Maybe anger or fear and desperation won through and they weren't thinking logically.'

'You said Gregory could have killed Clemmie over something he was hiding too.' Tony stroked Captain's head.

Bella nodded. 'And he's another one who was furious with Althea, just like Rory and Paula. He'd had it up to here with everyone letting Rory off, and he blew a gasket when he realised Althea wasn't going to report him.' Bella could see why. 'I'm not sure he'd kill over it – there was still a chance he could change her mind, after all. And to an extent they were allies. She acknowledged how poisonous Rory was and like Gregory, she didn't want the rental properties sold. But they clashed over letting High Seat go. She thought it would be too painful for Bernard.'

'But you'd cross him off the list, if it weren't for this other secret he's keeping?' Tony asked.

Bella nodded. 'I think so. But as it stands, he might have had a motive for killing Clemmie, and Althea could have found him out. We know Clemmie was on to something, and that he begged her not to tell.'

'So any of them could have done it?' John slumped back on the sofa.

'What do you think, Bella?' Tony was eyeing her like his favourite pupil again. It was very irritating.

'It's true. Though I'd guess Hester's least likely to have slipped Clemmie dodgy tonic; she wasn't at the hospice to visit her and nipping into her room would probably have caused talk. But we can't discount her. She was there that day.

'I'd say she's less likely to have acted personally in Althea's case, too. She's got a young daughter. She'd have to have left her home alone last night, unless she got a babysitter, which would seem risky.'

'So what's the plan?' Tony leaned forward.

Bella rallied her thoughts. 'We need to gather evidence and get Barry Dixon to accept that Althea's so-called accident was murder. I believe the deaths are connected and the ruby necklace feels significant too. Though maybe it just fed into Althea's murder – by making Rory, Gregory or even Paula furious with her, for example.

'It's delicate when the family's grieving, but I must get back inside High Seat. Althea had talked Bernard into letting me value the contents, but I'm sure it's only a matter of time before Rory persuades him to sell the rental properties instead. My guess is that Bernard will make him wait a week or so, for appearances' sake, then give in.'

It was bad news for Leo and Carys. Bella couldn't let them lose the Steps.

'Inside High Seat, I'll look for evidence that one of the household's guilty – any damage to Bernard's car, for instance. I'll try to get a look at the others' vehicles too.' Even if the killer had been lucky, and their vehicle and Althea's hadn't collided, they might have acquired some scrapes if they'd hit the hillside opposite the drop as they struggled to regain control.

'For Rory, we know he's guilty of theft, even if he's not a killer and there's no proof he took the rubies. I want to find someone who's willing to testify against him. If we can show the police he's a criminal, I hope we can save the Steps.' That was a must, as well as justice for Clemmie and Althea.

'While I'm at High Seat, I'll want to keep a very close eye on Gregory too. I hope I can find out what he's up to. And I'll dog Hester Harper's steps as well. I need to understand the end game of this plot of hers and Rory's. As for Paula, she's still on the list. I must check my guess about Rufus Hartford is correct, and keep watching her to verify my other theories.'

Thoughts of her dad filled her head. He'd taught her all he knew about policing. He might not have been CID, but he'd understood people and Bella reckoned she did too. That was everything.

'I've got one more bit of news for you.' Tony turned to Jeannie. 'You'll like this. There's been another theft at the hospice, and this time, Daisy Birdwell looks unlikely for it. She's still on suspension.'

Jeannie clapped her hands. 'I knew she was innocent. Didn't I say so?'

Tony nodded. 'And to you and me, it rules Daisy out, but our boy Barry reckons one of her friends could have staged it to make her look innocent.'

Jeannie thumped the table. 'What is the matter with the man?'

'He says he's "covering all angles". I shall be asking questions to make sure he really is. He's not a bad copper; he just needs a bit of guiding.'

Bella leaned forward. 'What was taken?'

'A powder compact – the sort that opens out, with a mirror. Antique, as a matter of fact, and worth a grand according to the lady who owns it.' He looked utterly incredulous.

Bella wondered. No one who knew Daisy had believed she was the thief. Was there any chance Bella was wrong about Paula, and it had been her instead?

19

ROWS AND RESEARCH

By the following day, Bella had spent a lot of time thinking over the news of the latest theft from the hospice. The more she thought about it, the less she believed Paula was guilty. It seemed she was prepared to work hard for her money, but even without that, it was difficult to believe. She was too sharp to do it when it would rule out the absent Daisy. In fact, unless someone was truly desperate for cash, Bella couldn't imagine anyone risking it.

The other oddity was the thief's choice of the compact. It wasn't the sort of object that screamed high value. But that thought led her nowhere. The only people she knew who would have guessed its worth were herself, John and Robert Mead. Unless Rory had developed an eye for a saleable antique... Even if Bernard and Althea had banned him from seeing Paula, he could still have sneaked into the hospice for an illicit meet-up.

Bella continued to mull on the puzzle at Vintage Winter. The shop was closed, but there was always lots to do. She spent all morning there, barring a quick march to High Seat to deliver a letter of condolence to Bernard. After that, she interspersed bouts of Powell-related research with labelling stock and rear-ranging the displays.

John and Gareth popped in – Gareth in edgy black from head to toe, John without his suit jacket, which Bella always found slightly startling.

'What news?' John sounded strained.

'I've written to Bernard to express my condolences and assure him I'm keen to carry on my work. I suggested it might stop the boys fighting over what to do next.' Boys… honestly, Gregory and Rory had to be in their late thirties, but it really didn't feel like it, and Bernard didn't treat them as adults either. 'I said I appreciated that emotions run high at times like this, and he can rely on me to be discreet.'

John looked uncomfortable.

'You do have some faith in me, I presume? I was tact itself, and we can't progress this if I'm on the outside. I'm hoping I'll hear back from him once he's got over the initial shock of Althea's death.' If he was that desperate for money, the poor man probably couldn't afford to hang around. For a moment, she imagined *him* sneaking in to steal from the hospice, but even if he was immoral enough, he'd never risk being caught, she was sure. The shame would be too unbearable. 'I feel for him, but Althea might have been a thorn in his side. He was going behind her back with both Rory and Hester Harper. Whether Clemmie found out or not, there's no excuse for it. And if she did find out, perhaps he killed her too.' It wouldn't explain Clemmie asking Adam Davies to visit, but it was as she'd thought before: there might be more to it than Bella knew. Poor, poor Clemmie. The memory of her, pale and fragile against her pillow, was vivid.

Bella was just as focused on the other suspects. She'd been in touch with Tony, to ask if he could get one of his former colleagues to find out what cars Rory and Hester drove. It would be easy to check Bernard's and Paula's for damage that might have been caused on Saturday night – their cars would be outside their houses – but the others must rely on on-street parking. It would be like looking for a needle in a haystack. It was just as well that Tony was happy to stretch the rules. She told John and Gareth he'd promised to help. 'At least they can't sack him when he's already retired.

'And I've been looking for evidence to back my theory that Rufus hired Paula to exercise his horse. The fields where she was riding are definitely owned by the Hartfords, according to an article I found about the sale. So far, so good.' She shook her head. 'I'll bet Bernard hated that publicity.'

At lunchtime, Bella nipped to the Steps, where Leo pressed her for news.

'It's early days. I need to get Bernard to invite me back to High Seat.'

She was partway through a sustaining Eaton sausage sand-wich, when Leo started waving his long arms and gesticulating out of the window.

She leaped up, bringing sandwich and plate with her, and saw that Paula was outside Rory's place again. She thrust her plate into Leo's hand. 'I'm going. I'll be back for that.' It was worth saying, just in case he finished it off in her absence.

She pelted down the sun-dappled steps, slowing her pace as she neared the rear of Rory's cottage in case they heard her, but once again, they sounded too involved to notice. Bella peered round the side of the building and saw Paula in the front garden, in floods of tears.

'I thought you'd be pleased!' Rory's tone was exasperated. 'You told me she'd ruined your career by reporting you to the stud manager.'

Wait, what was that all about?

'Now she's gone, and it's good riddance,' Rory went on. 'Dad'll come grovelling back before you can say knife and we can be together again. Isn't that what you wanted?'

'For Pete's sake, Rory – she was like a mum to me. She might have got my goat but that doesn't mean I'm pleased she's dead. She reported me to save my life.'

Paula was bent double now. She was genuinely devastated – no doubt about that.

'I'll miss her so much.'

'I've never known anyone so contrary and hypocritical. Well, forgive me for getting it wrong.' Rory didn't sound contrite. 'Personally, I'm not sorry she's dead at all. She was about to force Dad to cut me out of his will. And all because of that stupid ruby necklace, which I didn't even take.'

'Someone must have left that window open on purpose.'

'Well, it wasn't me!' He definitely sounded shifty now.

'Yet it was you who sneaked off to High Seat, climbed in through it and got caught on camera. What do you take me for? It's not like I don't know you're involved in underhand dealings. And you don't trust me. You wouldn't let me come with you to meet your contact at the racecourse.'

Rory paused a moment. Bella saw him take a step towards Paula. 'But I said you could join me on one of my adventures soon, and now we can relax.'

Paula didn't reply immediately. Bella was still convinced she didn't really like him. She must be deciding if she could bear to carry on faking it.

'You want to take me with you back to Long Marston?' she said, at last.

He had a hand on her arm now. 'Not there. I swung by their home yesterday, but something's spooked them. Still, it was good while it lasted – I made a lot. But I've got a fresh enquiry from someone in Upper Bewley. Sounds like an excellent opportunity. Go on! You'll enjoy it! It's what you've been after.'

He'd moved in close, and Bella was convinced they were going to kiss and make up. But then, suddenly, Paula pulled away.

'Actually, forget it! I only wanted to come along to prove you're a thief, but it doesn't matter any more. I'm finished with you.'

So that answered that one. She could understand Paula not feeling able to go through the motions any more. It must have been a hideous challenge, from the start. She'd probably wanted to protect Althea by proving Rory was a wrong 'un, but with her gone, that no longer mattered. Yet the threat he posed was greater than ever. Without Althea's influence, it was only a matter of time before he persuaded his dad to sell Paula's cottage, along with all the rest. Paula was crying harder now. Perhaps that thought had just run through her head.

'I can't believe your holier-than-thou attitude!' Rory screeched. 'If you hadn't been a drug-addled disaster zone, you'd still be a jockey.'

'But I've come good.' Paula's voice was low and dangerous. 'I've been clean for years and I work hard. That's a lot more than can be said for you.'

Bella crept back up the steps as quickly as she could before Paula could storm out and catch her. Back at the café, she checked for any reduction in the size of her remaining sausage sandwich, then filled Leo in on what she'd heard as she drained her cooling coffee.

'You think she's out of it, then?' Leo said, his wavy hair catching the sunlight slanting through the window.

'Probably, but it's not conclusive. If she'd run Althea off the road, I imagine she'd still be devastated at what she'd done – especially if it was impromptu. And even if she was trying to bring Rory down, she and Althea had issues. She didn't know Althea had hired a PI to try to get the rubies back, so she was angry and hurt that her inheritance seemingly meant so little to her aunt. And Rory said something about Althea losing Paula her job by reporting her to the stud manager when she was working as a jockey. It sounds as though Paula was doing drugs at the time. She said Althea reported her to save her life, but who knows how she really felt about it?'

It was definitely something to look into.

Back at Vintage Winter, she googled 'Paula Richards' and 'jockey' in quotes, and found a potted biography. She'd started off as a stable hand, then got an apprenticeship at a small yard. Eventually she'd been taken on at the Mansel Stud, down the other end of the Kite Valley. Bella found details of several wins, but then the successful races petered out. An old press release from the stud said she'd retired, and there was a quote from her saying the pressure had been too much, following the death of her mum. Poor Paula. Perhaps she'd taken drugs to numb her grief. She could imagine how terrified Althea must have been if she'd seen her go downhill. She could easily have got hurt or even killed while under the influence, and involved other riders and animals in the ensuing melee too. Bella could see why Althea had told the management, though it must have been a terrible decision to take. And life-changing for Paula. The stud must have hushed up the seamier details. They'd want to avoid reputational damage. But Bella bet word had got around; it would explain why Paula had never gone back to riding professionally.

She could certainly have resented Althea bitterly, whatever she claimed. But all this was years ago. Althea had interfered again, of course, by stopping her from seeing Rory, but Paula hadn't really been hooked on him, and she'd thrown in the towel of her own accord, even when they were free to carry on.

Having said all that, Paula still had one major reason to be livid with Althea: she didn't know she'd made secret plans to get her inheritance back. It was just possible that had sent her along the Brynway to have it out with Althea, only to meet her coming home.

But she had no obvious motive for Clemmie. If Paula had started doing drugs again, it could have ended her career at the hospice, but Bella had never seen her look anything less than sober and competent. And even if she had slipped up, Bella couldn't imagine the police being Clemmie's first port of call. She'd surely have gone to Althea about something like that, so they could take action privately.

Unless someone else had killed Clemmie, and her and Althea's murders were unconnected, Paula was starting to feel less likely as a suspect. But Bella knew she didn't have all the facts yet.

20

BERNARD'S SECRET TRIP

In the end, it was Gregory who invited Bella back to High Seat House.

Bella was drinking a reviving cup of proper coffee, the light streaming into her period flat's long living room, when his call came through.

'*Dad won't even consider selling this place, and now Althea's dead I know he'll revert to wanting to offload the rental properties instead, which is crazy.*' Bella could hear the pain in his voice. He didn't wield the same influence as his spendthrift brother, and certainly not as much as Althea had done. '*I know I said yours was a sticking-plaster solution, but it's all I've got. The only way I'll stop Dad doing what Rory wants is to find something valuable to sell instead.*' He sighed. '*To think that Althea had those rubies. Not that I can really blame her. If you get your hands on anything valuable in this place it's best to keep quiet about it.*'

Bella wondered again about his secret trip to the Hanged Man, and if he was hiding a legally dubious money-making scheme.

'*Anyway,*' Gregory went on, '*come along tomorrow, if you're free. Dad's agreed to it. He knows he's got to be practical.*'

Vintage Winter would be open again, but she told Gregory that she'd come early and maybe stay while John opened the shop. Just after she'd rung off, she drained her delicious coffee, then called her right-hand man to see what he thought.

'*I'll come with you to help before opening time.*'

He was such a gem. 'You're sure?'

'*I want to save the Steps and get justice for Clemmie and Althea as much as you do.*'

When Gregory let them in the following morning, they found Bernard in his drawing room. They expressed their condolences, but Bella wasn't sure he'd heard. He was making a clumsy effort to hide something on the coffee table in front of him, but he bungled it. Two plane tickets to France.

Bernard was blushing but he looked Bella in the eye, as though he could hypnotise her into forgetting what she'd seen. *Fat chance.* 'Thank you for coming. Althea thought it was right that you should do the valuations. We should honour her memory and stick to that.'

Bella dropped her gaze to the tickets, now half-hidden under Bernard's arm. It was rude, but she wanted him to feel forced to explain. She was sure Gregory had seen too. He looked thunderous.

As Bella continued to stare, Bernard's flush deepened. 'Friend of mine thought I might like a break. After the funeral, you understand. Althea hated France. Her father was killed in a car crash in Paris when she was six and she never went back. My friend very kindly bought the tickets. Ticket.'

He wasn't cut out for lying. Bella thought of her younger sisters and how they'd laugh at his pathetic efforts. Gregory was staring at the ceiling, a tic going in his cheek.

Upstairs, in the room where Bella had worked previously, she and John talked to Gregory about how to prioritise their search.

'It feels horrible to be so practical, but I assume Clemmie's half-sister Myra's estate came to your side of the family, as it didn't go to Clemmie. Is there any chance there might be anything of note amongst those things?'

Gregory gave a hollow laugh. 'I'm afraid not. My grandfather was a lot more organised than my dad. He had the whole lot auctioned off the moment he took possession. It paid to fix the roof here and for a couple more rentals. There were a few odds and bits left, though. They can't have been worth much or they'd have been sold, but you can have a look. I know there were some boxes in the attic with Myra's name on them.'

It was hardly worth it, but they might as well check. Some trinkets went in and out of fashion. It could make a difference. Gregory headed off to the third floor and Bella peered up to see him pulling down a ladder from an attic hatch.

He reappeared with two boxes, one balanced on top of the other. 'There are more up there too, but I'll have to leave for work soon.'

Bella shook her head. 'Don't worry. I can go and look myself if you don't mind.' Shame she'd worn her black Audrey-Hepburn dress. Every bit of dust would show.

Gregory nodded. 'Thanks.' As he left the room his mobile went. He glanced at the screen and something in his eye made Bella pause.

He picked up hurriedly, then shut himself in a room down the corridor, which increased her interest. She turned to John. 'Don't mind me.'

A moment later she had her ear to the door. John looked horrified, hopefully just at the thought of discovery and not her morals. Still, Bernard was downstairs and she was quite sure Gregory wouldn't emerge until he'd finished.

His words were muffled, but she caught snippets.

'... can't talk long... wouldn't be good if this got out.' Then something about having to review some details all over again. 'It's an appalling mess.' He sounded agitated, but it was his next words that really made Bella sit up. 'He said eighty K at first, but now he's after a hundred, which is really bad news. I'm not sure I can do it. Look, I've got to go. I'll call you soon.'

Thank goodness the Powells' landing carpet was there to deaden her footsteps. She moved quickly along the corridor and made it up the next flight of stairs before Gregory reappeared.

John risked his tidy suit by joining Bella in the attic, which had its advantages – nice and private.

He pushed his glasses up his nose. 'What did you hear?'

Bella filled him in. 'Glad I listened in now?'

He nodded slowly, his eyes wide.

'I think it's fair to assume he's got personal money worries as well as the family ones. It can happen to anyone of course, but his situation sounds precarious. He could be in hock to a loan shark, or maybe it's a case of blackmail. He said "they", so it sounds as though it's more than one person. I guess at least one of them might be male, given he left that envelope in the gents' loos. And that certainly suggests whoever he owes isn't above board. But the envelope didn't contain money.' What on earth did it mean? 'If he needs to raise that kind of cash, he might have wanted Althea's ruby necklace too, but it can't be him. If he'd managed it, he'd have no problem paying a hundred K and besides, it was Rory who was caught on camera. He doesn't fit for the hospice thief either. I could see Rory sneaking in – still in the role of a desperate lover, forced to see his girlfriend in secret – but any visit by Gregory would cause gossip, now poor Clemmie's dead.'

John grunted. 'It puts things in a new light, though. If he is being blackmailed, then what did he do to earn that? It could have been him Clemmie was planning to report to Adam Davies.'

He was right. Once again, Bella thought how anxious Clemmie must have felt when she finally decided to tell the police, and how cruelly someone had silenced her.

21

SLEUTHING IN GREGORY'S STUDY

Bella desperately needed to know what Gregory was up to. She'd start by letting herself into the room where he'd taken the call, once he was safely at work. He'd gone past several doors before shutting himself away, rather than diving into the nearest. Perhaps it was his study.

'Let's have a look at these other boxes of Myra's now we're up here.'

She pulled them open one by one, but the contents were as uninspiring as Gregory had suggested. A tea set that wouldn't fetch more than fifty pounds, old tablecloths, even towels with laundry labels still pinned to them. They clearly hadn't heard of charity shops or recycling... What was the point of keeping all this stuff?

'There are still the boxes that Gregory took downstairs.' John was folding the attic ones shut again.

But back in the room where Gregory had left them, they found they were full of letters, photos and paperwork.

John gave her a sympathetic look. 'At least there's plenty more to value in the house. We should get started.'

But Bella had just glimpsed Gregory through the window,

leaving for work. Now was her chance to get some of the more dangerous jobs out of the way while John was around to stand guard. She broke her plans to him gently. 'You carry on, and listen out for Bernard. I'm going to find the room where Gregory took his call.'

John went pale. 'Are you sure it's worth the risk to go poking around?'

'It'll be fine, honestly. Just leap out and distract Bernard if you hear him come upstairs.'

'What on earth will I say?'

Bella glanced around the room and picked up a pair of carved elephants from the mantelpiece. 'Ask if he knows anything about the history of these.'

John nodded, though he looked deeply uncertain. 'Okay. If you ever readvertise my role, you might need to write a more honest job description.'

'Sorry. Call it career development. Did I ever tell you you're one in a million?'

She did feel guilty for the anxiety she was causing him, but you couldn't make an omelette without breaking eggs.

On opening the relevant door, she found a study, with paperwork suggesting Gregory was the regular user. But when Bella searched, there was nothing suspicious – just records relating to his day job. There was a locked drawer though, and that was interesting in itself... Bella glanced at her watch. John was adept at lock picking. It wasn't uncommon for her to buy antique boxes without their keys. But there was no time to tackle it before he left to open Vintage Winter, and it wouldn't be fair anyway. The chances of discovery were too great.

She was about to leave the room when she noticed the pristine pad of paper on Gregory's desk wasn't quite as blank as she'd thought. She went closer and saw faint indentations on it. He'd written something on a sheet then ripped it out, she guessed. It was probably nothing, but she tore the sheet off anyway. She couldn't make out the marks, but she'd examine it properly later. Gregory would never notice, and he might be guilty of a double murder. That was reason enough to snoop.

When she rejoined John, she found he'd put several nice pieces aside, but as before, none of them was stand-out. Not even as valuable as the photo frame Rory had made off with. She took a deep breath to quell her frustration.

'Thanks, John.'

He nodded. 'I'll go and open up.'

'I'll join you by lunchtime.' Their afternoons were always busiest. She watched him leave, then got on with the job, wondering if she'd find anything useful from Gregory's pad of paper.

It was late morning when she heard voices on the ground floor. Paula, talking to Bernard. She was clearly upset and it sounded as though he was making a hash of dealing with her. Bella tried not to blame him. He must still be in shock despite the plane tickets.

Bella gathered her things and went downstairs. It was time for her to go, anyway. She wanted to check Bernard's car for damage on her way out, but only once she'd talked to Paula.

As it happened, Paula had just burst into tears as Bella reached the ground floor. Bernard was gaping at her like a goldfish, which wasn't at all helpful, and poor Eustace sat at Paula's feet, whining. Bella walked over, said how sorry she was about Althea and, after gauging Paula's state, pulled her into a hug.

Over her shoulder, she saw Bernard's look of relief. A moment later he pottered off, muttering something about tea. Probably not a bad idea, in fairness.

'I had to come,' Paula was saying, between sobs. 'Face up to her not being here any more. I haven't even got a photo of her — not a recent one.'

Bella remembered the one Althea had showed her, taken at Christmas. 'I think I can find you one. Why don't we wait for

Bernard to bring the tea, then I'll fetch it for you? And Paula, it feels like the wrong time to mention it, but if you ever want to pursue the theft of the ruby necklace with the police, I can testify that it disappeared, the night of the feast.' It felt important to say it, though she doubted Paula was taking it in.

Bernard reappeared at last. He hadn't managed to bring milk, but you couldn't expect miracles. Bella went to get it herself, then nipped upstairs to find the photo of Althea. She was wearing the necklace of course; perhaps it wasn't the most tactful picture to give Paula, but Bella doubted she'd mind in her current state. She took a quick photograph of it for reference before re-entering the room where Paula sat.

Paula clutched the photo tight, blinking through her tears, and Bella thought of how she'd felt when her dad died. The emptiness, and desperation to turn back the clock, however impossible that was.

She crouched down. 'I'll leave you in peace, but if there's anything I can do or if you want company, pop in to Vintage Winter. Or call me. Any time.' She gave her a card.

Bella's feelings on Paula hadn't changed – it wasn't impossible that she was guilty. But it seemed she'd never truly wanted to join in with Rory's criminal activities and it looked as though the money from Rufus had an innocent explanation too. She might just be suffering like the blazes.

Bella was in luck when it came to checking Bernard's car. The garage was on the opposite side of the house from where he was 'looking after' Paula. What with the cups of tea, they weren't likely to leave the room and spot her.

On top of that, the family weren't very security conscious, and the garage door was half raised. Bella only had to duck to get in. There was space for two cars and Bella felt the lack of Althea's keenly. She wondered where it was now – in some police facility still being investigated, or at a breaker's yard perhaps. She and Clemmie had been so close, and now they were both gone. She clenched her fists against her sorrow and got to work.

There was nothing to suggest Bernard's car had recently crashed into another vehicle at speed, but it was covered in small dints and scrapes. There was no way of knowing if any of them had been acquired on Saturday night. As she walked away, she was alarmed he was allowed on the road at all.

Since Paula was safely occupied, she checked her vehicle before returning to Vintage Winter too. It was on the ancient side, but unlike Bernard's it was free of obvious damage. Frustratingly, that didn't prove anything, any more than the dints on Bernard's did.

Back at the shop, Bella filled John in on the latest valuations and the state of the two cars, then took the paper she'd lifted from Gregory's study through to the cosy office between the front and back showrooms – her and John's inner sanctum.

She laid it on her beloved architect's drawing board and rubbed over it very gently in the softest pencil she had, angling it so she was using the side of the lead, not the point.

A moment later, letters came up.

Kevin, Black Swan, 9 p.m., Tuesday

And just underneath that,

Arabella N, Esmerelda's Terrace Bar, 7 p.m., Thursday

Unless the note was a week old, Gregory was meeting 'Kevin' tonight, and in the Black Swan too. A rough-and-ready pub down the valley, already known to Bella for its iffy clientele. She'd have to find out where Esmerelda's was as well. This felt like a proper lead.

22

SKULDUGGERY AND SATNAVS

John and Bella went to the Blue Boar for lunch and found Carys there, so they filled her in on the latest.

They sat in the sun in the inn's courtyard at one of the pretty cornflower-blue tables. Bella jiggled her chair on the ancient cobbles until it stopped wobbling, then tucked into her sumptuous flatbread with hummus, roasted vegetables, and Shropshire blue cheese.

Carys gave her a sidelong glance. 'So, what are you going to do about Gregory's appointment this evening?'

'Show up and see what he does.'

John twisted his napkin nervously. 'You shouldn't go on your own. And what if he sees you?'

Carys was grinning. 'I'll come. Unless you're inviting Robert.'

It was Bella's turn to feel uncomfortable. She'd thought of inviting him – she'd like to see him – but she knew he wouldn't approve of her sleuthing. 'I'm not sure he's free, so if you want in, then company gladly accepted.' Leo would be bound to turn up too. Their daughter Lucy was old enough to stay at home or hang out with a friend.

'But John's got a point,' Carys added. 'What if he sees you?'

'I've checked and there's live music at the pub tonight.' Not Matt's band, like the last time she'd been there, but she imagined the result would be similar. 'It ought to be crowded. We can blend in, then keep an eye on things.' She wondered if that was why Gregory and this Kevin person had chosen the venue. It would be easy to talk privately if you found a spot far away enough from the band, where everyone's focus would be.

Bella turned to John. 'Fancy coming along, assuming Gareth's working? If Gregory does see us, he'll assume we're there for the music.'

He looked uncertain; he'd probably been hoping for a quiet night in with a crossword, but at last he nodded. 'We need to know what's going on.'

'Of course we do.' Jeannie had appeared during their conversation as if by magic and dropped into a spare chair. 'Though I think your focus should be on Rory. If we're to save the Steps, then that's the way forward. You can bet your bottom dollar that he committed this latest theft at the hospice too.'

Everyone had heard about it, naturally. Ironically, Jeannie blaming Rory so firmly made Bella rethink his possible guilt. It didn't feel quite right. Like a bit of jigsaw that had been put in the wrong place. It would have involved him hunting through residents' rooms, unless Paula had tipped him off, and Bella was sure she wouldn't.

And Paula still didn't seem like a realistic suspect either. It was as Bella had thought before, she and the other members of staff would never risk it; it would take them from being in the clear, to in the frame, not just for theft, but potentially for murder. Unless a young colleague of Daisy Birdwell's really was responsible. Perhaps Barry Dixon was right after all, and the latest theft *was* to make Daisy look innocent.

Bella came back to the present, and saw John was glancing at Jeannie. 'Rory might not be guilty, Mum.'

'Of course he's guilty. You only have to look at him. The way he skulks.'

'Don't worry, Jeannie.' Bella put a hand on the landlady's arm. 'We're not neglecting him. In fact, I'm going to focus on him right now.' She'd just seen him through the inn's window, skulking, as Jeannie said. Who'd choose to drink indoors on a glorious day like this?

There was no time to explain, so she left John and Carys to finish their food and slipped into the Blue Boar's shaded interior, where soft lights were glowing cosily, brightening its dark corners.

Bother it. Rory had disappeared.

She walked through the rear bar, which dated all the way back to the 1400s, past the shining taps and beautifully polished glassware, then round towards the snug. The interior of the inn was sparsely populated but she could see two figures in the shadows, close to the sweeping oak stairs.

'What is it?' It was Bernard's PA, Hester Harper, her tone sharp and impatient.

'Like I told you, we need to talk.' Rory sounded calmer, but there was an edge to his voice too.

'I don't see why.'

He scoffed. 'I'll bet you don't. But seriously! You're getting an awful lot out of Dad, aren't you?'

'It's not as though I can stop him if he wants to give me presents.'

'And now Paris? Seriously? How d'you think he'd feel if he found out the truth?'

Hester laughed now, full of scorn. 'Only he won't, will he? Not unless you want him to see you for who you really are. There's nothing you can do about it, so stop making waves and be grateful for what you've got. It's way more than you deserve. Good grief, you're despicable. The very idea that there'd ever be anything between us!'

She turned on her heel and marched out of the inn, but Bella stood in the shadows until Rory moved back to the bar and the coast was clear.

A moment later, she'd returned to her seat outside, and was telling the others what she'd heard. It had Jeannie rubbing her hands.

Bella's mind was whirring. 'I think I was wrong. They sure as hell don't sound like lovers. Rory is getting jealous, but of what Hester's getting out of Bernard, not of having to share *her*.' What did it mean? 'I'm starting to wonder if the set-up's even more cynical than I'd thought. Maybe the arrangement's entirely practical. Hester's agreed to make up to Bernard to benefit the pair of them. But it makes no sense. If they're not lovers, then why does Hester need Rory? She could operate alone and keep everything Bernard gives her. And why have that fake argument in front of him? If they're not involved, it's unlikely Bernard would imagine that they were.'

They all stared into space but no one offered a solution. It was mind-boggling.

'I can't explain it,' Jeannie said at last, 'but I'm very disappointed in Bernard for cheating on poor Althea. I must keep an eye on what happens next. Perhaps I'll introduce him to some suitable companions of his own age. I'll invite him along to Poetry Pals night.'

Bella couldn't imagine him agreeing for a minute, though Jeannie could be quite forceful... 'Maybe Rory knows something damning about Hester and he's using that to extort money out of her, having discovered her affair with his dad. But it still doesn't explain the fake lover's tiff. And she clearly knows something damaging about him, too. She said he wasn't in a position to reveal her duplicity to Bernard without showing his true colours.'

'What about her as the killer?' John said, his voice low.

'I suppose she could have run Althea off the road if she

wanted to marry Bernard and didn't think he'd get a divorce. And it's possible Clemmie had found out about the affair, given both Hester and Bernard had been visiting the hospice. But I come back to the same objection as before: it's a damning secret, but it's not criminal, so why would Clemmie involve Adam Davies? And I still think Hester would have found it hardest to spike Clemmie's tonic, too.

'But if Clemmie wanted to report Rory – for theft, say, from someone who wouldn't protect him – then it's another matter. He and Hester would have different reasons to want Clemmie dead, him to escape jail and her to keep the affair quiet. They could have collaborated over the killing.' It was a horrific thought. If only Bella had persuaded Clemmie to share her worries, when they'd talked months ago in Vintage Winter. She'd had no inkling of how important it might be.

It was just as Bella and John left the pub that the text came through from Tony with Rory and Hester's makes of car and registration plates. Bella showed John.

'I'll have to look online to see where the residents' parking is for Rory.' It was anyone's guess when his house was on the hill and only accessible via St Giles's Steps.

A moment later, she found it on the local council site: Old Percy's Lane, the same road where Hester lived. Inconveniently distant from his point of view, but perfect from Bella's. She could examine both his and Hester's vehicles at once.

'I'll open the shop while you have a look,' John murmured as they crossed St Giles's Close.

'Thanks.'

As he headed towards the antiques centre, she skirted the beautiful old church, and neared the trees that sat between the close and the lane, leaves looking rich and green in the sun. She was just approaching the short run of worn steps that led to Old Percy's Lane when she saw Paula, already down there, walking next to the line of parked cars.

Bella paused and peered at her from behind a linden tree. She'd slowed next to a red BMW. Rory's car, according to Tony's invaluable information. How he'd managed to get it was anyone's guess.

Paula stood still for a moment and Bella wondered what she was up to. Then, after a surreptitious glance over her shoulder, she took a mobile from her pocket. A second later the door of the BMW was open, and Paula had slipped into the driver's seat.

What on earth was going on? Had she managed to pinch Rory's phone so she could unlock the car? She must have. But why?

As Bella watched, Paula fiddled with the satnav. Checking where he'd been on Saturday night? It was one up on the basic check that Bella had been planning. Paula might have decided she couldn't bear to continue her sham relationship with Rory, but it seemed her investigations were ongoing.

Catching Rory out should neutralise the threat he posed to her home, but if she thought he'd killed her aunt, it took her motivation to a whole new level. Sweet Agnes, she was playing a dangerous game, though.

Bella was all for catching Rory, but if he was a killer, Paula might be next. She couldn't just watch as she put herself at risk. And besides, if she had some firm hint that Althea's death wasn't accidental, Bella needed to hear it.

Paula jumped out of her skin when Bella tapped on the car window. She got out immediately.

'Sorry,' Bella said. 'I didn't mean to startle you.'

She looked terrified. 'This is actually Rory's car. I thought you were him.'

'Paula, if you suspect your aunt was killed as well as Clemmie, and you think Rory's to blame, it would be safest to tell the police. Did you find anything?' Bella nodded at the satnav.

Her shoulders sagged. 'No. If he was on the Brynway on

Saturday he's wiped the journey.' Bella sensed she was relieved to share the burden. 'But I can't go to the police. I've got nothing. Just fear and suspicion.' She was shaking.

'How did you get his phone?'

She climbed out and closed the car door. 'It was opportunistic. I saw him through the window at the Blue Boar just now, and he had it out on the table. He was yakking away to someone, so I went in and swiped it.'

Bella took a deep breath. 'Want me to hand it in to one of the bar staff? Hopefully he'll think he dropped it or it slipped onto the floor.' It would certainly be safest if he never found out it had been pinched.

Paula nodded at last. 'I'd be really grateful. I'm sorry. I never really liked Rory as much as I made out.'

Bella nodded. 'It's all right, I understand. Even I'd worked out he was dishonest. I can't prove it, but I know he stole a lovely photo frame that I'd valued at High Seat and sold it at Long Marston Racecourse.' The way he'd used Bella still rankled, and she wanted Paula to know that they were on the same side.

Her eyes opened wide. 'How do you know?'

'John and I were at the antiques fair.'

She let out a long breath. 'I was too. Did you see the buyer?' Bella could see the hope in her eyes.

Bella nodded. 'But I'm afraid it's no good. I told Althea about it, but when she faced Bernard with the news, he claimed he'd given Rory permission to sell the frame. There's no way the police will be interested.'

Her shoulders drooped again and she clenched her fist. 'Damn!'

Bella had rarely seen someone look so frustrated and pained, but it was no use crying over spilled milk. Time to check on something else. 'Paula, I was out for a walk the other day and I saw you riding. It was amazing.'

It took her a moment to reply. Bella sensed she'd been too disappointed to respond immediately. 'Thanks.'

'You ride Rufus Hartford's horse for him?'

She nodded. 'It's a crying shame. He works in some fancy office in Birmingham and hardly ever sees the poor animal. But he pays me to do something I love, so there's an upside.'

It was good to have it confirmed. Five minutes later, Bella handed Rory's mobile to Bill the barman. She told him someone had picked it up from under a table and she'd offered to hand it in. She didn't want Rory to think she'd been involved either.

After that, she went back to Old Percy's Lane, but neither Hester's ancient Ford nor Rory's flashy BMW had any marks on them. She returned to Vintage Winter, feeling frustrated.

Between customers, Bella filled John in.

'It makes me afraid for Paula. I think what she's doing is fuelled by her anger at Rory and her sense of injustice. And if she thinks he killed her aunt, I guess it's sent her into overdrive. It's dangerous because it's making her reckless. But at least Rory didn't catch her at it, and it was good to confirm my guess about her exercising Rufus Hartford's horse.'

'So she's out of it?'

'Never say never, but I can't see why she'd kill Clemmie, and she clearly suspects Rory. She can't have been putting it on for show — she had no idea I was there and she'd already pinched his phone.'

He let out a sigh. 'It feels like progress.'

He was right, but it was all too slow. Justice felt far away and the Steps still wasn't safe, any more than Paula's cottage was.

23

AN OLD LAG

The afternoon at Vintage Winter was busy, which was just as well, as Bella was impatient to follow Gregory that evening. Every customer-free moment dragged.

She snatched a snacky supper – glad that Gareth couldn't see her eating a fish finger sandwich. In her defence, she'd paired it with some remarkably delicious tartar sauce and had splashed out on artisan bread: squidgy with the perfect crust.

After that, she changed. Customer fashions at the Black Swan were similar to those at the Hanged Man. Anyone not in jeans would stand out. She really ought to get a pair as a disguise, only she hadn't imagined being a regular at either venue. As it was, she opted for 1950s cigarette pants in self-effacing black, a black halter neck, and black Mary-Jane shoes. Good enough.

She bumped into Matt as she was leaving. 'Going some-where nice with the boyfriend?'

'The Black Swan.' She decided not to elaborate.

He raised an eyebrow. 'Wouldn't have thought that would be his scene. I deduce you're off sleuthing instead, and probably not with him.'

Bella just smiled and went on her way.

Soon afterwards, she was driving John, Carys and Leo down the valley to reach the pub. She had the windows down, the sweet summer air blowing through the cab.

They'd arranged to reach the Black Swan well before Gregory's meeting with the mysterious Kevin. It would be a lot more subtle to hide themselves in the crowd and watch their quarry arrive than the other way round.

Leo was craning forward from one of the rear seats with enough nervous energy to trigger Bella's adrenaline too. 'What's the plan?'

'If I can manage it, I'd like to get a photo of the man he meets. It's possible Tony will know him if he's got a record. Hearing what they say might be too much to hope for – though perhaps one of us could slip past unobtrusively and catch the odd snippet.'

Leo was bouncing now. 'Me, for instance.'

'Mr Unobtrusive himself,' Carys muttered, to a disgruntled look from her husband.

Bella didn't like to rub salt in the wound, but she was right. 'Maybe you could do it, Carys. You don't move as though you're on springs.'

Carys nodded. 'Common sense prevails. I'll be ready.'

'Other than that,' Bella signalled to enter the pub car park, 'we should watch their body language. It sounds to me like Gregory's being blackmailed. "Kevin" could be the guy doing it.'

Inside, Bella ordered Hobsons Twisted Spires for the others and a Coke for herself, ignoring the way the barman looked at her clothes. Leo and Carys had found a corner spot with a good view across the interior. The place was filling up nicely. They shouldn't be spotted.

'Was Robert really not available this evening?' Carys eyed her.

Bella hesitated for a moment too long.

'You didn't ask him, did you?'

'He's a lovely man. Perfect for me. But he wouldn't have approved of an escapade like this.'

Carys gave her a look, but said nothing, and Bella felt irritated. Before she could analyse why, Gregory walked in.

'He's early.' John didn't need to lower his voice; the band had started and it was hard to hear him.

'It suggests he's nervous.' Bella watched as he approached the bar, glancing left and right.

A moment later he'd ordered a half of lager and sat on a bar stool, fiddling with a beer mat, his gaze roving over the clientele. Every half minute, he peered at his phone, then looked at the crowd again.

'Perhaps he hasn't met Kevin before. It looks as though he's trying to match a photo to someone here.'

It was another few minutes before a man of around seventy, heavily built, entered the pub. If Bella had been asked to sketch her idea of an old lag, he would be it. Rough around the edges was putting it kindly.

Gregory looked round immediately, checked his phone and started. This had to be Kevin, then, and Bella was sure it *was* a first meeting. Gregory motioned the man to the bar, but he shook his head, beckoning Gregory to him. Words were said, then Gregory returned to order a pint of something and carried it back to the sturdily built stranger. They sat at a table near the door, heads bent, ignoring the rest of the customers.

They'd barely exchanged a word before Gregory handed the man an envelope. Leo tapped Bella's shoulder and pointed, as though she might not have noticed.

Bella watched as Kevin slipped the envelope under the table, eased it open and peered at the contents. Presumably this one wasn't empty, as he nodded, then leaned forward. Kevin was talking rapidly now.

'On my way,' Carys said, in response to Bella's look. 'I'll

pretend I'm leaving, then see if I can hover behind them.' She picked up her bag.

Bella took surreptitious glances as Carys loitered just beyond the pair. Wisely, she didn't dally for too long. Bella had a nasty feeling Kevin was aware of her presence. He'd hunkered down, his head sunk between his shoulders like a vulture, and as Carys moved away, he'd flicked a look in her direction. It was as well that Gregory and Carys's paths rarely crossed. Bella doubted he'd recognise her.

Carys exited the pub, but moments later she reappeared through a door close to their table.

They looked at her as she sat down.

'I don't know what it was all about; I couldn't hear most of it, but the man called Kevin clenched his fist and thumped the table. The only words I caught were something about someone having it coming, and him crushing all the bones in someone's hand.'

'Sweet Agnes. I hope he didn't see you watching him.'

Carys smiled. 'Yes. Me too.'

Bella managed to get a photo of Kevin by pretending she was taking a group selfie. It wasn't great, she got him through the crowds in a low-lit room, but she couldn't exactly ask him to say 'cheese'. A moment later she was texting Tony.

'Anyone up for a trip to the godfather before we go home for the night?'

It was well past sunset when they left the Black Swan and dark by the time they reached Shrewsbury. Tony stood in the porch light of his snug Georgian cottage, looking too big for it, and rather like a long-suffering dad whose kids had come home later than promised.

'In you come, then.'

Captain was blocking the way, tail wagging, so Tony gave him an affectionate push-cum-pat and they trailed inside.

He offered them drinks, though the range was limited – water, whisky, tea or more Hobsons Twisted Spire. Bella doubted anyone could civilise him now.

'So then,' he said, as they sat down on the squashy sofas in his front room, a table lamp glowing. 'What've you got?'

Bella showed him the photo she'd managed to take, using her finger and thumb to enlarge it. It was badly pixelated but the sturdy man was quite distinctive. 'He's called Kevin. Met him on your travels?'

Tony whistled. 'I'll say. Kevin "Crusher" Baker. He's called Crusher because—'

'I think we already know.' His nauseating comment about bones and hands was still fresh in Bella's mind. 'He was saying something about it to Gregory Powell.'

Tony nodded. 'What can I tell you? He's probably spent more time in jail than he has in his own home. I thought he'd calmed down of late. Finally got sick of the late nights and the violence. But old habits die hard, naturally. Tell me what you saw.'

Bella and Carys filled him in.

Tony nodded. 'Interesting. So money changed hands right at the start, then Baker regaled Powell with tales from his CV. What does that tell you?'

Cue the performing-seal routine. 'I'd guess Gregory wants to hire him for a job. John and I heard him panicking to someone on the phone about a third party upping their demands from eighty to a hundred K and how Gregory couldn't manage it. Maybe he wants to get rid of a blackmailer and Kevin Baker's his solution.'

Tony nodded. 'A hit. It's possible, though that'd be pricy. Still, he'd be cheaper than some – a punter with more cash might opt for someone younger. Age discrimination, obviously, but it happens.'

Bella looked out of the window at the quiet, homely lane with its soft street lights to check they really were in a quaint Shropshire town and not on the set of a police drama. 'Not only that, but if they go ahead, what's to stop Baker blackmailing him too?'

But Tony shook his head. 'He wouldn't do that. He'd never get repeat business if he did.'

The question of payment ran through Bella's mind. Once again, she wondered if there was any way Gregory could have stolen the ruby necklace rather than Rory, but that wouldn't wash. It was as she'd thought before: he might still want to avoid paying a blackmailer, but he wouldn't be panicking over a hundred K if he had access to five hundred. Besides, it was indisputably Rory who'd climbed in through the window and who had form as a thief. 'I'll contact Barry about what I saw, anyway. Send him the photo.' She couldn't bear to leave it any longer and surely this had to count for something.

Tony sucked in a breath. 'No harm in having a go, but I can imagine what he'll say.'

Bella could too. She couldn't prove there'd been money in the envelope and it wasn't a crime to chat to a man in a pub, even Kevin 'Crusher' Baker.

She sent the photo anyway, then left a message on Barry's voicemail with an explanation, glad of the chance to put her case uninterrupted.

24

THE PRODIGAL SON

Bella and John were back at High Seat before opening time on Wednesday morning. Barry had sent her a message, thanking her for her information but making exactly the points she'd anticipated. He'd ended by saying he'd 'keep it all in mind', which sounded far too vague.

Then he'd asked if she had any idea how to get children to eat cabbage but Bella hadn't replied. Her childcare knowledge had been hard-earned and it didn't come for free. If he wouldn't promise firm action on Gregory and Kevin Baker, she was withdrawing her services.

Instead, she focused on next steps with John, talking in a low voice. 'I need to ask about Althea's will.' She held up a hand as John winced. 'Don't worry – it'll be a legitimate query. Althea said Paula would have got the rubies if they hadn't been stolen, and presumably that was the case for anything else she owned. If Althea listed her belongings in her bequests, that will help us identify what's off-limits. Checking is fair enough.'

John nodded. 'Okay.'

Bella prowled the wide landing and found Bernard in his study. When she asked about the will, he teared up, wiping furiously at his eyes with a hanky. Maybe her death was finally sinking in. Even if he'd been infatuated with Hester, it wasn't the same as having shared her life for decades. He motioned Bella out of the door and took her to Althea's room.

'She called this her dressing room, but it's where she kept her official bits and pieces too.' He opened the door of a Victorian mahogany cupboard – scuffed like everything else – to reveal a series of envelope files. He pulled out one labelled 'Will' and handed it to her.

'Here. We agreed everything she owned should go to Paula, a long while back, when...' he coloured... 'when we Powells had more money. Even now, we have more than Paula does.' He sounded relieved about that, and busied himself turning the pages. 'Here. No, there's nothing mentioned individually – it just refers to Althea's personal money and her effects. What you see in this room, together with the books in that case there, and the watch and jewellery on her dressing table.' He turned away – to try to hide his tears, Bella guessed. 'I'm her executor. I'll need to sort it all out for Paula. Excuse me.' He left the room.

The combination of his upset and his desperate attempts not to show it pulled at Bella's heartstrings. She found it hard to forgive him for planning a trip to France with Hester just after Althea's crash, though. Rory mentioning it to Hester put paid to his story of a friend standing him the fare.

But it was no good just feeling angry. She was in Althea's inner sanctum, with the chance to look through her papers as well as her possessions. Paula no longer seemed like a top suspect, but it would be worth gauging how much she'd had to gain from Althea's death.

Divining how much money she'd stood to inherit wouldn't be easy. Few people got paper bank statements these days. But on looking in the filing system, Bella found some annual interest summaries which gave her an idea. Althea hadn't been well off, if those were anything to go by. Next, she checked the jewellery box on the dressing table. There was a pretty Edwardian cocktail watch which ought to fetch four or five thousand. Yellow gold with platinum settings, decorated with diamonds. It was the most valuable thing there – definitely desirable but nothing compared with the ruby necklace. Bella shook her head. Althea might have imagined the watch was the more valuable of the two. In some ways, it was showier.

She couldn't see Paula killing for anything Althea had possessed when she died. It was a shame the will didn't mention the necklace specifically, but it made it clear that all Althea's possessions should go to her. That, coupled with the photo of Althea wearing it, and Bella's offer to testify that it had gone missing meant Paula could pursue its whereabouts more officially now, if she chose to.

In a corner of the room, Bella found a large Victorian camphorwood campaign trunk. That would be popular at auction – but not for large sums. She bent to open it, just in case Althea had kept anything valuable there.

But inside, she found treasure of a different sort. It was a box of nostalgic memorabilia, and it set Bella off. So many memories. Happy times and sad. Things that must have meant a lot to Althea, amassed over the years, the collection brought to an abrupt halt.

Saddest of all were several items relating to Clemmie. It was a reminder of her and Althea's closeness.

She found a thank-you note from Clemmie dated 30 December 1969, with a hand-drawn picture of a cat on the front. Clemmie had signed the drawing. Bella hadn't known she'd been good at art. Inside, she'd written:

> *What you've given me is far too much. I feel terrible accepting*
> *it but you're a true friend.*

People made the same protest all the time, of course, but the words seemed heartfelt. It made Bella think of Clemmie's low self-esteem, which brought a fresh wave of sadness.

Bella found other notes from Clemmie, too. She'd clearly been very unhappy living with her half-sister, Myra. There was a tear-stained letter, telling Althea that Myra had banned her from leaving the house for two weeks, except to go to school. She had to do all the chores at home too. She said she was tired and hadn't had time to do her homework.

Decades hence, Bella was full of frustration that no one had stepped in to make things better.

There were notes from after Clemmie went to live with her new guardian, too. She'd clearly got happier over time, but the first ones were still tear-stained, with ink that had run. She said how she wished Myra was still alive. *Poor kid.* She must have got used to the shabby treatment and hated the change. She remembered her childminder's children saying she wouldn't come out of her room for days after Myra's death.

Bella found umpteen photos of Paula in Althea's chest too. Several showed her on horseback, one dressed in full jockey regalia, her hands raised in triumph, her smile radiant.

A while after John had left to open Vintage Winter, Bella heard quiet voices from the ground floor and went to peer down from the galleried landing. Perhaps Hester was talking to Bernard; she might learn more about their relationship. But no, it sounded like two men. She'd already seen Gregory leave for work, so it couldn't be him. She tiptoed down the carpeted stairs, switching her phone to silent.

At last, around five steps up, she was close enough to identify them.

Bernard and Rory.

'I want to bring you back into the fold, dear boy! You know that. But I have to honour Althea's memory. Allow a decent amount of time, so people don't think...'

He let the sentence tail off.

'You mean it wouldn't be seemly!' Rory sounded livid.

'Several of our guests saw the recording of you climbing through the window the night Althea's necklace went missing.' *Was stolen.* He really wasn't one for facing facts. 'What will they say if I forgive you the moment Althea's gone?'

'Isn't it about time you got past what other people think?' Rory's voice was full of disdain, but then his tone changed. 'The plain truth is, I can't bear to be kept at arm's length when you're suffering. It isn't right for us to be apart at a time like this.'

Bella's teeth were gritted. It was infuriating to listen to his cynical change of tack to get Bernard back on side.

'Ah, my boy.'

Bella imagined them embracing and could barely contain herself.

'And we really do need to crack on with selling the rental properties too,' Rory went on. 'I've been talking to Sienna Hearst about the Steps. She's biting my hand off, Dad. Just think how it would help solve your problems. I know Gregory won't like it, but he's got his own agenda, and it's a selfish one.'

Seriously? The way he twisted things beggared belief. As for him and Sienna joining forces, it sent Bella's heart rate into overdrive.

After a moment, Bernard spoke again. 'I see your point, and of course I understand the urgency too. We must act soon, though how I'll break it to Gregory... But I'll set everything in motion shortly, and reinstate you in my will.'

'What?' Rory's one-word reply shot out like a bullet.

Bella guessed he hadn't realised Bernard had already changed it. She was surprised too. She was sure he'd never wanted to, and there'd been less than twenty-four hours between the discovery of the theft and Althea's death. Once she was gone, there was no way Bernard would have progressed things.

'It was Althea who pushed me on, dear boy. She wanted it

done immediately.' Bella could see the sense in that. 'She called Tom Butler out of hours and took me to his house to sort it out. You know they were friends and there was nothing I—'

'She hated me, and you let her do what she liked!'

'My dear chap, she was upset. Her precious necklace... In any case, I'm planning to talk to Tom—'

'Planning to?' Rory's true colours were coming out, loud and clear.

'I'll go this afternoon.' After the briefest pause Bernard added. 'In fact, I'll go now.' Bella was certain he was reacting to his son's anger – anxious to avoid a fight as ever. 'I'm sure he'll fit me in. A good man, is Tom. I'll just have to explain to Bella Winter that I'm going out.'

Time to beat a hasty retreat. She heard Rory complaining about her presence as she dashed back upstairs.

She'd just re-entered the room where she'd been working when Bernard appeared. She tried to breathe evenly and look busy.

'No problem,' she said, when he told her he needed to walk into town. 'I'll finish up for now.'

As she left High Seat ahead of Bernard, she noticed Rory hadn't gone yet. She found herself shredding a tissue in her pocket as she focused on him. *Appalling man.*

He was skirting the side of the house, glancing over his shoulder. *Shifty.* Perhaps he wanted to talk to Hester Harper again.

She followed him, taking care not to be seen, until she saw him slip inside the house through some French windows.

She crept closer, stepping around a beautifully scented rose-bush to position herself next to the open doors, then risked a careful glance inside.

It was as she'd thought. She could see Hester standing in the shadows.

'Right then,' Rory said. 'Cough up. He must have given you the latest lot and I want my half!'

Hester pulled a sour face but a moment later she handed over a wad of notes.

Bella hid behind the rosebush and watched Rory leave again.

He followed Bernard out of the grounds – to make sure he visited the solicitor, probably.

She followed the pair too, at a distance. What on earth was going on with Hester and Rory? She'd already figured they were in league and getting money out of Bernard. It sounded as though halving what Hester got was a long-standing arrangement. But Rory's reference to 'the latest lot' was unexpected. It was obviously something regular, yet not wages, Bella reckoned. The way Rory phrased it hadn't been right. He'd have said 'He must have paid you' or something like that.

If Bella was right, Bernard was giving Hester extra money regularly, as though she was an old-fashioned kept woman, as in the days of yore. Unless she was blackmailing him... But Bella didn't believe it. The look on his face when he'd presented himself at her door with flowers had been fond. Unpleasantly soupy, in fact.

There was more to this than met the eye.

25

A TERRIBLE EVENT

Bella followed Bernard past the half-timbered, lopsided buildings on Hope Eaton's high street, with their jettied upper floors, all the way to Butler & Co. She kept behind Rory, who was also in hot pursuit. He really was a toad. Neither she nor Rory could follow Bernard inside, of course. She waited close by, in a narrow side alley where the buildings almost touched, and watched him.

Bernard reappeared around three minutes after he'd entered the solicitor's and rushed over to Rory. Bella crept closer, to hear what was said.

'I'm sorry, dear boy! Poor old Tom's off with a stomach bug and the rest of the staff are booked solid picking up the slack.'

Rory was red in the face. 'I still can't believe you changed the will in the first place! You should have talked Althea round!'

Bernard shook his head sadly. 'Well, you know what she was like. And I couldn't blame her. You tell me you didn't steal the rubies,' he held up a hand hastily, 'and I believe you. Naturally I do. But try to see it from her point of view. She was convinced you were responsible, and it did look that way...'

Rory was pacing up and down the pavement. 'Well, when *can* the solicitors see you?'

Bernard put a hand on his son's arm. 'They've promised to call me to sort something out, but it will be done. And there's no immediate rush. If only Gregory had trained as a proper solicitor. He could have sorted all this out for us.'

He must be in the office, working. Bella wondered if he knew or guessed why his father was there. If so, he'd be livid. If ever someone deserved to remain disinherited it was Rory.

Bella went back to Vintage Winter in time to help with a gaggle of customers who were pleasingly absorbed by the pieces on display. As usual, she'd organised the front and back showrooms like a stage set, so her clients could imagine how it would feel to live in rooms filled with the wonderful antique and vintage goods she sold. She'd tucked smaller pieces away in a mahogany blanket box and an antique specimen cabinet. It meant customers could poke around and discover things for themselves. There was no greater pleasure, in Bella's view.

As soon as they closed for lunch, she updated John.

'It's so frustrating. Bernard didn't want to bring Rory back into the fold too quickly for appearances' sake, but Rory's pushing on an open door. I think Bernard will approve the sale of the Steps within days. I'm so sorry, John.'

He shook his head. 'I'm beginning to feel we'll never stop him.'

Bella made John coffee in lieu of putting an arm around his shoulder. 'Maybe Foxy – Evan Todd – will know something damning that we can use. There must be some reason he decided not to pursue the business venture Rory was talking about.'

'Assuming it wasn't fictitious.' John's look was bleak.

Bella wanted to give him hope, but in truth, she wouldn't be surprised if Rory had made it up. Or perhaps Evan Todd had pulled out because Rory was lazy and unreliable, without discovering anything worse. 'I could still see Rory having killed Althea, and Clemmie too, if he'd done something so unspeakable his father couldn't protect him.'

'Hmm.' John looked unconvinced as he took the coffee from her and opened a packed lunch of braised chicken with three different salads.

That evening, Bella and John went to the Blue Boar to talk things over and try to make sense of them. Jeannie appeared too, of course, the moment she realised something was going on.

Bella relayed the scene she'd witnessed between Rory and Bernard.

'He really is the most despicable man!' Jeannie took a large swig of her drink.

'It doesn't take us any further forward when it comes to working out who killed Clemmie, I'm afraid.' They went through the key players again, but without more information, Bella felt that nothing would click. 'Mind you, it's possible there are two different killers. Or as Tony would say, that Althea wasn't murdered at all.'

At that moment, Gareth dashed into the snug in his chef's whites. He looked as pale as his uniform and took a second to catch his breath. 'I'm sorry – this is going to be a shock. The crowd who've just come into the bar are saying Bernard Powell's been found dead.'

They rushed out into the main bar, where a cacophony of voices repeated the terrible news. People were saying he'd been found bludgeoned to death on Dead Man's Walk.

Jeannie had lost all her colour. 'I think it was most ill-advised to give the lane that name. It's tempting fate.'

It dated to when Gallows Hill had still been a place of execution, but Bella didn't bother to remind her of the fact.

'Poor, poor Bernard,' Jeannie went on. 'He was a bit of a snob of course, and sadly a very weak character.' She wasn't one to stop critiquing people just because they were dead. 'But he certainly didn't deserve this. We should have been able to prevent it. It was foolish of DS Dixon not to believe you about Althea being run off the road, Bella. He'd have been more focused on the Powell family and less on Poppy's sister.'

People were spilling out of the inn now. Jeannie had to go back to work, but John and Bella went with the flow. The police would keep them back, but Bella found it impossible to stay behind. The horror of it made her want to be with everyone else. And however terrible it was to approach the site where it had happened, something they saw might help them piece things together.

Bella felt as though she'd been punched in the stomach. Her thoughts were on Rory earlier in the day, hounding his dad about visiting the solicitors. She doubted Bernard had managed to change his will back before he was killed. That made Rory a lot less likely as the killer. But if Gregory knew what Bernard was planning, he'd have been furious and went right up the list. And he certainly could have known, or guessed. He worked at the solicitors, after all, and Bernard's move was entirely predictable.

Rory had spent years burning through his and Gregory's inheritance, yet Gregory was badly in need of money himself. If Kevin 'Crusher' Baker hadn't put paid to his blackmailer, perhaps Gregory had decided to take control of the Powell finances and sell High Seat to save himself.

Bella could see Barry Dixon and several other officers behind some police tape. A white tent stood just beyond. That must be where Bernard's body was.

And then, Bella saw Gregory arrive, his mouth hanging open, followed shortly by Rory, whose fists were bunched.

Rory rushed up to his brother and grabbed him by the collar. 'You did this! I know you did! You knew Dad was about to write me back into his will!'

It took two officers to drag him off.

26

____

NEWS FROM THE GODFATHER

Bella was on the phone to Tony the minute she was back at her flat. She filled him in.

'*Blimey O'Reilly. Right, I'll find out what I can. I'll be at the Steps tomorrow lunchtime.*'

He'd developed a soft spot for Leo's Eaton sausage sandwiches. He'd hate it if Sienna Hearst took over and dished up nouvelle cuisine. Quantity was very important to him.

After he'd rung off, she was out of jobs. No more normality to hang on to. She stood in her spacious bathroom, clinging to the basin, and felt overwhelmed. She hadn't warmed to Bernard – she rather agreed with Jeannie about his character – but the way he'd been dispatched so brutally was horrific. Robert phoned her mid-evening and she found herself not wanting to explain what had happened because he wouldn't understand or feel the brunt of it like she did. She ended up passing it off as something distant from her too, and they moved onto small talk about their shops. They arranged to meet again on Saturday evening and Bella set a phone reminder so she wouldn't forget.

. . .

The following morning, between customers, Bella and John speculated endlessly about Bernard's murder. Bella could hardly concentrate for wondering what Tony might tell them. It was a great relief each time someone came in and she could switch to saleswoman mode, banishing other thoughts.

They met Tony at the Steps at one. He already had his sausage sandwich in front of him, ketchup and English mustard at his elbow. Captain was looking on mournfully but padded over to Bella and John when they approached. Bella found it soothing to ruffle his fur.

Leo swooped in, leaving Poppy at the counter.

'Is she all right?' Bella said, looking over.

'Better than she was,' Leo replied in a low voice. 'I'd hoped the latest theft would take the pressure off her sister. If she's innocent, Clemmie can't have been about to report her. It seems so obvious. But people are coming up with crazy conspiracy theories – that she managed to sneak back in, or the compact was already missing when Daisy was suspended.' He rolled his eyes. 'It's like they've already jumped on that bandwagon, so they don't want to be wrong.'

'Poor kid.'

Leo nodded. 'It's horrendous. And the upshot is, Poppy's still more distracted than usual.'

'*More?*'

'She put brown sauce on a scone yesterday.'

'Ah.'

Leo shuddered. 'We need to get this sorted, for all our sakes. Mum knows you're meeting Tony here, by the way. I promised you'd send her updates.'

Bella ordered a sausage sandwich, so she didn't feel jealous of Tony, and John asked for a garden salad with coronation chicken. Bella still wasn't sure what a garden salad was.

She sat down next to Tony. 'What news?' He'd already

finished his sandwich and was embarking on his tea with enthusiastic gulps.

'Time of death was between seven forty-five and nine, when
he was discovered. Killed by a bash over the head using a rock,
which was discarded by the roadside – so it could have been
spur of the moment, just like Althea, if she was killed. No
prints, sadly. The surface was too rough.' He put his mug down.
'His wallet was taken, so it *might* be a standard mugging gone
wrong. Barry's not ruling anything out.'

'Has it changed his thinking on Althea's death?'

Tony shook his large head. ''Fraid not. He'll have it in the
back of his mind, of course, but there's no evidence the crash
was anything more than an accident.'

'I hope he's looking at whether it might relate to Clemmie's
murder at least.' Dixon needed to get his act together.

Tony nodded. 'I'll make sure of it. And I reckon it'll make
him rethink Daisy Birdwell too. He was still banging on about
someone stealing that compact to make her look innocent, last
time I heard. But even he'll have to admit her attacking Bernard
Powell looks like a stretch. She's a waif of a thing. Can't be more
than four foot ten. I don't see her going at him with a rock. And
in the unlikely event Daisy killed Clemmie Crowe, how would
Bernard have found out, well after the event? It's not as though
they move in the same circles.'

'It'll be a welcome breakthrough if Barry rules Daisy out.'
Bella glanced at Poppy. 'She must have been having a horrible
time. What about alibis?'

'None of the key players has one. Daisy says she'd gone for a
walk up the river. No witnesses, unfortunately. Gregory and
Paula had left work and they each claim they were at home, but
again, there's no one to vouch for them. Nor Rory neither.

'Gregory says he saw Bernard leave the house, dashing out
at a rate of knots, but there's no one to back him up because
Hester Harper had already left for the day. And Hester's alibi-

less too. Her daughter was on a play date. Not much help, I'm afraid. But it's Bernard's will that makes things really interesting.' He grinned for a moment.

Milking it for all it was worth...

She and John leaned forward and Leo, sensing something momentous, dashed over again.

'As you know, Bernard cut Rory out and he never got the chance to reinstate him, but Gregory doesn't get everything – he's left with the rental properties, plus all proceeds raised from High Seat's contents. There's a very small amount in Bernard's bank account too, but it's nothing much. High Seat itself is to be sold, the proceeds going to... Hester Harper.'

Bella gasped in spite of herself. She had wondered if Bernard might do *something* for her, but she'd decided he couldn't have. It sounded as though Althea had been breathing down his neck when he'd updated his will. He'd hardly have put in a bequest for his lover with her watching – or so she'd thought. So Tony's news was shocking. Bernard had finally agreed that his beloved High Seat should be sold, and not even so the money could go to Rory. 'I can't believe Hester gets it.' She was still goggling. What would Althea have said, and why on earth had she agreed? Bella must be missing something.

'Interestingly,' Tony peered at his notes, 'he's also left an antique clockwork toy to Hester Harper's daughter, Phoebe.'

To Phoebe? Goodness. Bella's thoughts reeled. Was it possible that Bernard was her dad? But then suddenly, the truth came clear. Facts rushed together at speed, like iron filings flying onto a magnet and memories filled her head. *If only you'd felt able to do what was right*, Bernard had said to Rory. And what were people usually referring to when they talked about 'doing the right thing'? 'I think Phoebe Harper must be Rory's love child, making Bernard her grandpa.'

Leo gasped.

Tony nodded slowly, drained his tea and sat back in his chair. 'That could fit.'

And Althea must have known all about it. Bella could see her fingerprints all over the arrangements. She'd be determined for Bernard to do the right thing by Phoebe and she'd have decided Gregory could be relied upon not to sell the rental properties. By choosing him she was trying to protect Paula, Leo and the other tenants, but was she right? It was true that Gregory had favoured selling High Seat instead, but thanks to the will, he no longer had that option. And if he was desperate for cash...

It had been right to protect Hester and Phoebe's interests, though.

'So where are we on motives?' Tony said.

Bella rallied her thoughts. 'Well, we now know Hester had a big, fat one. She might have killed Bernard to get her bequest, for her own or Phoebe's benefit, especially if she guessed Rory would be back in favour soon, and the will revised.'

'And what about Rory?' John's frown was deep. 'If he knew, he might think he could squeeze money out of Hester more easily than from his dad.'

But Tony shook his head. 'I hear he went ballistic when he heard Hester was a beneficiary. Our boy Barry's convinced he had no idea.'

'And it would have been best for him if Bernard had redrawn his will anyway. I think Rory is out of it, for Bernard.' That came as a blow. 'He had every reason to want him alive for now.'

Tony nodded his agreement. They all paused, thinking it over, and Bella took the chance to text Jeannie an update. Her eyes widened at the response.

Leo spotted the words on her screen and his eyebrows shot up. 'To think she once told *me* off for swearing!' He trotted back to the counter, where Poppy had dropped some beans on toast.

Bella sought some crumbs of comfort; Jeannie would need them. 'On the upside, Rory has got no say in what happens to the rental properties now – or anything else for that matter. He's a toad and I'd love to see him jailed for something, but at least his influence is gone.' She relayed the thought to Jeannie.

'But Gregory has a motive, just like Hester, and conceivable ones for Clemmie and Althea too, given his secrets. Whereas I can't see Hester's motives for the first two murders, now we suspect Bernard was visiting as a doting grandpa, not a lover.

'Of course, Gregory's motive's even stronger if he thought he'd get the entire estate. Did he seem surprised about Hester's inclusion in the will, Tony?'

Her godfather referred to his notes. 'One hundred per cent gobsmacked.'

Presumably Bernard would have warned him at some stage, if he'd lived. Then again, given his character, perhaps not.

John slumped in his chair. 'So if Gregory killed Bernard because he's still in financial trouble, he might have to sell the Steps and all the rental properties.'

It was just what Bella had been worrying over. They both looked at Leo, who had wiped up the spilled beans and was serving a local. His laughter rang out, and Bella's heart ached. The issue was secondary to the murders, obviously, but it was still a thoroughly miserable thought.

She refused to accept the idea until it was upon them. She needed to focus on preventative action instead. 'Back to suspects. We haven't talked about Paula yet. Let's tick her off, for completeness's sake.' Bella reviewed what they knew. 'I'd basically written her off already. The secret she was keeping had an innocent explanation, which left her no motive for Clemmie. And I caught her checking Rory's satnav to see if he'd been on the Brynway on Saturday night. I can't see her motive for Bernard either, unless he'd found proof she'd killed Althea. The evidence says she didn't, but even if she had, I don't see how Bernard would know, far less prove it. Despite her car being ancient, it's got no dints, and certainly no satnav to check.'

Tony laced his fingers. 'So what we're coming down to is that Gregory Powell is top of the list now, with Hester still in the running, and Rory and Paula out of it, as far as we can tell.'

'And the Steps in a mess,' John said.

She needed to give him hope. If only there was some way.... Then suddenly Bella saw it. 'I am an idiot!'

John started, and Poppy dropped a cup.

'Sorry. But I got it wrong about Hester Harper. It doesn't fit. Why would she and Rory have to fake a row if they weren't trying to convince Bernard they were no longer lovers?'

'Maybe Bernard would have stopped paying Hester an allowance if he'd thought they'd made it up,' John said. 'So they needed to convince him they hadn't.'

'I don't think so. Bernard would have known Rory could never have supported Phoebe, whether he wanted to or not. He didn't have any money. And besides, I remember now. Hester made it clear they'd never been lovers when I heard them argue in the Blue Boar.' Irritatingly, the memory had escaped her until that moment: '"Good grief, you're despicable," Hester said. "The very idea that there'd ever be anything between us!"' Bella sighed and shook her head. 'And here's another thing. Why was Hester secretly giving Rory half the regular allowance Bernard must have been giving her for Phoebe?'

Tony shrugged. 'Maybe Rory had some kind of hold over Hester.'

'He could have, but I had the impression she had one over him too, so you'd think they'd be quits. Hester talked about the danger of Bernard finding out just what sort of a man Rory really was.

'There's something extra that Bernard didn't know! The truth is more complicated than we realise, and I think I know the answer. If I'm right, the Steps might be safe.' Or safer than it would have been, anyway. 'I need to talk to Hester Harper.'

27

HESTER'S SECRET

Bella went straight to Hester's cottage at the cheaper end of Old Percy's Lane, where the dwellings were tiny. On hearing that her visit might help put the Steps on a firmer footing, Leo had practically pushed her across St Giles's Close, while John had gone to Vintage Winter to open back up.

Bella knocked on the door. No reply. But she could hear a commotion within. Crying. She knocked again. Hester needed to know Bella wasn't going anywhere. With any luck, she'd assume Bella was the police and it was no use hiding.

When at last Hester opened the door a chink, her eyes red, Bella had the urge to hug her. She looked so bereft. But if her guesses were right, she had a lot of explaining to do.

'I'm sorry, Hester, but can we talk? I didn't want to go to the police, but I know the truth about you, Rory, Bernard and Phoebe.'

Hester paled, but it did the trick. She stood back to let Bella in. It wasn't the sort of conversation to have on the doorstep.

Bella peered through to the sitting room. 'Where is Phoebe?' She didn't want to upset her.

'At a friend's place.' Hester blew her nose and led the way, motioning Bella to a small sofa.

She sat on an armchair herself, perched on the edge, hunched and deeply unhappy. Despite the background, Hester must have become fond of Bernard.

'When did you and Rory decide to pretend that Phoebe was Rory's child?'

Hester started to cry again. 'Around a year ago. I've regretted it so many times since. It was like signing a pact with the devil. Rory suggested it. He needed more money – as always – and I knew how bad things were financially for the Powells. I was terrified that Bernard would end my contract. How would I support Phoebe then? Rory said Bernard would never let me go if he thought Phoebe was his granddaughter, and that he'd talk him into giving me a monthly allowance too, in return for half the cash.'

The arrangement was just as Bella had thought.

'I hated helping him,' Hester went on. 'He was pushing and pushing to get the Powells' rental properties sold, my parents' place included, but he would have done that anyway, whether I agreed or not. As it was, Bernard moved heaven and earth to carry on paying my salary, and I was able to give my parents my share of the allowance to build up a nest egg. I was desperate to help them. They'd have had to find a deposit for a new place if Rory got them chucked out.'

Bella could see how she'd been tempted, but it was still a horrible deception. 'So when I saw you and Rory pretending to argue in front of Bernard, it was to perpetuate the idea of you being ex-lovers? You never were together?'

Hester shuddered. 'No, never.' Her voice went small. 'I didn't know you'd seen us.'

'Wasn't it hard to lie to Bernard for so long?' Something about his weakness made the trickery seem even more unfair.

Hester drew herself up. 'Of course it was! But I could see that Bernard would sell my parents' house from under them if it weren't for Althea, so I did my best to harden my heart. If I lost my job, Phoebe and I would have nothing. I agreed in a moment of desperation, and after that it was hard to stop.'

Bella could imagine it getting complicated too. 'Does Phoebe think Bernard was her grandpa?'

Hester looked down. 'I tried to make it seem as though it was an honorary title, a bit like a courtesy uncle, so I wasn't lying to her. But it got messy.'

'She must have got fond of him.'

Hester was sobbing now. 'She did. Very. He played with her and bought her toys.' Her voice lowered to a quavery whisper. 'And I enjoyed his visits too. Whatever his faults, he was a kind man.'

'And Rory got jealous because it wasn't just the allowance that Bernard gave you?' Bella remembered the flowers he'd brought to the house, and the extra twenty pounds he'd slipped Hester to 'buy something nice'. He'd formed a bond with her and Phoebe, and Rory had complained to Bernard about 'favouritism'. Bella had thought he'd been jealous of Gregory, but it had been Hester all along.

She nodded. 'Bernard was very short of money himself, but he was generous, so I started feeling worse and worse. Most recently, he bought tickets for me and Phoebe to go to France before she starts year two in September. He said it would be educational.'

The tickets Bella had seen on his desk. 'He must have wanted to tell everyone about Phoebe. It sounds as though he was very proud of her.'

Hester's hands twisted in her lap. 'He did. But Rory and I told him we wanted to keep it secret.' She hung her head. 'I said I was still married when Phoebe was conceived and that although my husband had run off and wasn't giving me anything – which is true – I didn't want his parents to turn against her.'

So many layers of lies. Bella could see how they'd built and how hard it would have been to escape. 'Do they help you out at all?'

Hester nodded. 'With babysitting. And Phoebe loves them – they are her real grandparents. But they can't help financially. They're just as hard up as my parents are. I don't know what I'm going to do!' Her head was in her hands. 'I had no idea Bernard would write me into his will. It was stupid of me, I suppose, but I was living in the moment and now everything's gone wrong. Bernard intended me to use the money for Phoebe, of course, and I'd love her to have it, but accepting it is impossible. I got the bequest under false pretences. I couldn't live with myself if I let it go through. And think of the hold Rory would have over me. He'd blackmail me for the proceeds from High Seat, probably. Whereas if I confess, I'll feel marginally less terrible about myself, and the house will go to Gregory, presumably, along with everything else. Rory would do anything to avoid that, but it's not his decision.'

The situation would leave Rory raging. As if on cue, there was a tremendous pounding at the door and his voice, yelling through the letter box.

'Hester, you can't get away with this! If you don't want me shouting your business in the street you'd better let me in.'

His aggression sent Bella's adrenaline going. What an utter louse. And he was automatically assuming Hester would take the money and run, judging her by his own standards, clearly. Bella was delighted he was in for a disappointment, and glad she was there too. Hester shouldn't face him alone.

'What can I do?' Hester looked panic-stricken.

'I'll stay with you, and we can make a plan.' Bella got busy googling as Rory's pounding continued. 'According to this website, beneficiaries are free to refuse a bequest without giving a reason. If they do, it goes back into the estate, like you thought.' She turned to Hester. 'What if I call Tom Butler on the high street?' He'd hopefully be back at work. 'We could book you an appointment so you can tell him your decision. What do you think?'

28

DRAWING CONCLUSIONS

Hester agreed to Bella's plan, but the phone call would have to wait; Rory was making so much noise, she'd never hear the receptionist at the solicitors.

Hester let Rory in, but Bella's presence took some of the wind out of his sails. He demanded to see Hester alone, but when Bella refused and told him she'd worked out the truth, he seemed lost for words. It was horrible to be in such close proximity to him. His volatility and selfish fury filled the small room as he marched up and down. A second later he threw out his hands and turned on Hester.

'You can't keep it!' he said. He pointed at a photo of Phoebe. 'She has no right to it!'

Poor Hester was crying again. 'I know. I know she doesn't, and it's all my fault.'

'Not just yours,' Bella put in. 'And that being the case, I doubt Rory will want to tell Tom Butler the full story, any more than you do.' Bella was hoping it could all be resolved quietly, for Phoebe's sake if nothing else.

Rory rounded on Bella, fists bunched, and she tensed. But

then he looked at Hester and stormed out of the door, slamming it behind him so hard a picture shuddered on the wall.

A moment later, Bella made her call. The solicitor could see Hester that afternoon at five.

Bella spent another ten minutes with Hester, making her a soothing cup of tea, then returned to Vintage Winter to help John.

He was serving a customer as she arrived, and Bella took a moment to adjust, after witnessing Hester's despair. She'd been horribly dishonest, but Bella had sensed her desperation. She couldn't imagine doing anything similar, but she'd never stood in Hester's shoes. Money had been scarce during Bella's childhood, but her mother had tended to fall on her feet. There'd always been a friend who could help tide her over, dossing down in their flat and contributing to the rent, or offering her weird ad hoc jobs for when she wasn't writing her books.

John's customer left, carrying a beautiful Art Deco ball lightshade that Bella had picked up at Long Marston. Despite everything, the sale gave her a buzz of excitement and satisfaction. There was nothing like it.

John turned to her and raised an eyebrow. 'What news? Anything that tells us who the killer is?'

'I'm afraid not, but it might help the Steps.' Bella filled him in. 'I hope Hester can avoid being prosecuted for what she did. It's only really Gregory or Rory who might report her. Rory won't, for obvious reasons, and although Gregory will be mystified when she refuses the bequest, I doubt he'll guess the truth, or pursue it, if he ends up getting everything. I know it was a horrible way to treat Bernard, but Hester was clearly terrified about the future. And if she went to prison, it would be terrible for Phoebe.'

John polished his glasses. 'I see all that. So Gregory should be able to sell High Seat and keep the rental properties?'

Bella nodded and he sighed.

'That's a reassuring thought. Though we shouldn't count our chickens before they're hatched.' He got up to make coffee. 'So does this rule Hester out for Bernard's murder?'

Bella had been considering that. 'I think so. She'd have to be a very fine actress to have performed the scene I just witnessed without meaning it, and she's dead set on refusing the money.'

John set Bella's coffee down on the refectory table in front of her. 'I wonder how much the entire estate amounts to.'

'Good question. It could make quite a difference if there's a financial element to the motive for killing Bernard. I wouldn't be surprised if he'd borrowed against some of the properties. I can't imagine he'd have managed to pay Hester and bail out Rory otherwise. I'll try to snoop at his papers when I'm back in High Seat.'

John winced. 'I suppose the police will check. Couldn't you leave it to them?'

'I could, but I shan't.' There was no harm in duplicating and the matter was too urgent. Three deaths already... 'If Bernard did borrow against the properties, I'll bet he did it secretly. Imagine Althea and Gregory's reactions if they'd found out. The police are sure to check his more obvious financial records first, and even that will take time. But Bernard was old school. There are probably papers somewhere in High Seat that will reveal the truth. I just need to work out where he'd have hidden them. If I find anything, I can give it to Barry Dixon myself.' That would be pleasing...

John sipped his coffee gingerly. '*Please* be careful.'

'You do have some faith in me, I suppose.'

His look in response was somewhat sceptical. 'What about Hester killing Clemmie, if she'd found out about her and Rory's scam?'

Bella tried to picture her lifting Clemmie up to put some doctored tonic to her lips. Clemmie could have mistaken her for a carer in her confused state, but even so, she couldn't see it. 'She's too moral to accept Bernard's bequest and she's scared for Phoebe and her parents. Would she risk doing something so terrible and getting life in prison? And what's the worst that would have happened if Clemmie *had* told the police? Bernard would never have testified; the police would have no case. It would have meant letting the world know he'd been duped by his PA, and – far worse – his favourite son. Hester would have lost her job, of course, but she'd been facing redundancy anyway. She'd be no worse off than she would have been before Rory suggested the scheme.'

'Hmm.' John frowned. 'Put like that, I believe you. And I suppose the same applies if Althea had found out. She was protective of Bernard. She'd never have wanted him humiliated if the truth came out.'

Bella reckoned the same, and that Hester would have guessed that. 'I don't think Hester had a viable motive for any of them, which puts her in the same boat as Rory and Paula. It takes us back to Gregory as prime suspect. He's supposed to have that other meeting tonight. The second one we saw on the indents on his notepad. "Arabella N, Esmerelda's Terrace Bar, seven p.m. Thursday".'

'You think he'll still go, after his dad's murder?'

'I can't be sure, but the meeting with Kevin "Crusher" Baker felt high stakes. If this one's just as important, then he might.'

The moment they broke up, she texted Barry Dixon to remind him about Gregory's dodgy meeting at the Black Swan. Surely alarm bells must be ringing now. This was all taking too long. It felt like ages since she and John had said goodbye to poor Clemmie for the final time, little knowing her fate was already sealed.

29

GREGORY'S CLANDESTINE MEETING

Bella had already googled Esmerelda's and found the top hits led to a rooftop watering hole in London, near the West End. She hoped that was the one that Gregory was making for. She was forced to leave Vintage Winter early to reach the capital, changing trains at Birmingham. It took a tediously long time, but it was better than ploughing through traffic, and she had company on the journey.

She'd debated who to take as a co-conspirator. She might need to send them to listen in to Gregory's conversation, since he'd obviously recognise her. That ruled out John, naturally, and possibly Carys too, after she'd eavesdropped last time. She'd also dismissed Leo, who'd be a hoot but didn't have the required subtlety. Robert might have managed it, but he'd never have agreed. She bet Matt would have been up for it, but spending all evening with him might give him the wrong idea. In the end, she'd asked Tony.

She'd abandoned the idea of telling Barry Dixon about Gregory's meeting after his discouraging response to her Kevin Baker text. There was no way he'd send someone to London on spec to follow this latest lead. And at least Tony had some sway with the police, if they discovered anything useful.

The moment she entered Esmerelda's Terrace Bar, she wondered if she'd made a mistake bringing him. As expected from her research, it was swanky in the extreme. She'd spent some time warming Tony up to the idea of wearing a suit, and at last he'd agreed, but she could tell it had been years since he'd last put it on. There was a moth hole in one sleeve, and he'd filled out a bit so the fit was... less than ideal. In under two minutes he was complaining about the showiness of the place. She couldn't wait to hear what he said when he saw how much the drinks cost. She'd pay, of course, but for Tony, it would be the principle of the thing.

It was reasonably busy, which drowned out some of Tony's exclamations, but nowhere near as rowdy as the Black Swan. She managed to smooth over her godfather's horror when a couple at the bar ordered a bottle of Dom Pérignon for two hundred pounds, and he seemed relieved that he was allowed to ask for beer. (Though it didn't match up to Hobsons Twisted Spire, apparently.)

Bella and Tony had decided to hover in the most crowded part of the bar while they waited to see if Gregory and the mysterious Arabella turned up. Tony agreed that it was more than possible the meeting related to the secret he was keeping and the money he owed. They mingled while Bella kept an eagle eye out for her quarry. Gregory arrived early, just as he had at the Black Swan, looking tense and haggard. The meeting must be hugely important for him to keep it, after his dad's death.

He spoke to someone, then sat at one of the many tables next to a huge glass window giving views of London's skyline. His exhausted eyes, however, were on the door.

Bella and Tony made for a table close by, where they'd be hidden by palm tree fronds. After ten minutes of Gregory looking anxiously at his watch, a woman with long, blonde hair, excellent deportment and exquisite tailoring walked into the room. All eyes turned, but she took no notice, as though she was used to it. Gregory rose, reddening a little, and raised his hand. A moment later, she'd joined him and a waiter materialised. It seemed to be Gregory who was suggesting what they should drink. The woman nodded, then he put in the order. The waiter gave a slight bow and backed away.

So this must be Arabella N. Her smile was gracious rather than familiar, and she'd needed Gregory to wave to identify him. As with Kevin 'Crusher' Baker, Bella was certain they hadn't met before.

A moment later, the waiter reappeared and showed Gregory a bottle for his approval.

'Blimey.' Tony was drinking it all in too. 'That's two hundred quid down the drain.' They'd gone for the Dom Pérignon. 'What the hell's he playing at?'

It was a good question, given his straitened circumstances and the possible blackmail. Bernard's death wouldn't change his fortunes until probate had gone through. 'I can only assume Arabella's worth more than two hundred quid to him.' But why would she be?

Gregory certainly appeared to be schmoozing her, in an embarrassingly awkward way: leaning forward, indicating something she was wearing, paying a clumsy compliment, Bella imagined. He seemed very uncomfortable. In the unlikely event he succeeded in charming her, she might splash out on him. But that couldn't be his goal, surely, when it was clear they hadn't met before? Bella doubted a woman as beautiful and seemingly rich as Arabella would agree to a blind date with anyone less than a minor royal.

She watched as Gregory's gaze remained fixed on Arabella. Although he asked the odd question, she was doing most of the talking. He seemed to hang on her words.

'Right,' Tony said, after taking another swig of his 'pint of substandard' as he called it, 'I'll mosey past and see what I can find out.'

If only he looked a little more in keeping with his surroundings. Bella fitted in just fine in her figure-hugging black dress with her hair up, but Tony was attracting almost as many glances as Arabella. On the upside, the gents' was beyond Gregory's table, so he had a believable destination.

He arrived back a few minutes later. 'Interesting.'

Bella waited. He was such a showman.

He smiled. 'I only managed to catch the odd bit. On the outward journey the Arabella woman was talking about a route through Milan. I heard her mention the word sniper.'

'Seriously?'

He nodded. 'Thought you'd be interested. But on the way back, the topic had changed. She was pointing out her security detail to Gregory.'

'Security detail?'

'Yeah. I was so busy watching her that I'd missed them. Must be getting rusty. See the guy in black with the earpiece by the lift? And that suited hulk on the other side?'

'Sweet Agnes. Yes. Was she warning Gregory to mind his behaviour?'

'I couldn't say, but he looked a bit startled.' He chuckled. 'He certainly hadn't spotted them till that point either.'

'Damn. I was hoping to get a surreptitious photo of her so we can work out who she is.'

'Wouldn't if I were you.'

In the end, Bella waited until Arabella, Gregory and the two musclebound security guys had left, then went to sweet-talk a barman.

'Wasn't that Arabella what's her name?'

The guy grinned. 'Neville. Arabella Neville, yeah, that's

her. She comes in most weeks. Shame her security guys never drink more than a Coke. Still, she tends to make up for it.'

Bella could believe it. She'd got her answer so quickly that she and Tony had to slow up as they left to avoid bumping into their quarry. They watched from the foyer as Gregory got into a taxi and Arabella was driven off in a Range Rover by one of her two guards. The other sat in the back.

Before Gregory's taxi left, Bella saw him tapping furiously into his phone. Bella nodded in his direction, so Tony looked as well. 'Taking down Arabella Neville's licence plate, do you think?'

'But what would he do with it? Unless he's got a tame friend in the police, and he's hoping to discover Ms Neville's home address.'

For a second, Bella thought of Adam Davies, but he looked more like a head boy than a bent cop.

On the train home, Bella and Tony googled Arabella Neville exhaustively. It turned out she was a successful art dealer, with an oil-baron father and an heiress, ex-model mother. Arabella had been kidnapped as a child by a gang associated with drug trafficking. Poor kid – how on earth did you recover from something like that? Her father had paid up, according to news reports, but ultimately her kidnappers had been caught.

Bella was grateful to be solvent, rather than rich. 'No wonder she takes her security seriously. But Gregory must know all this. She's not going to let her guard down. It feels strange that he'd try to get her car's licence plate, so maybe he was typing something else. Overall, I can't imagine what he's hoping to achieve.'

'What about all that talk of the route through Milan and the sniper?'

'They could be planning something criminal together, but

what possible help might Gregory be? She's clearly as rich as Croesus. She could afford any professional she wants.'

'It's rum.' Tony closed his eyes. 'Don't mind me. I'm just thinking.'

He was snoring by the time Bella's mobile rang, two minutes later, and started awake with an alarming snort.

The caller ID said 'Gregory Powell'. *For heavens' sake!* They'd checked as carefully as they could, but it was still possible they were all on the same train home. She picked up hastily, hoping he wouldn't hear her answer in real life, as well as down the line.

'Gregory. I'm so very sorry for what you're going through.'

He cleared his throat. *'Thank you. I'm getting in touch because I've had the details of Dad's will. There's a query – well, it'll soon be sorted out. But whatever happens I'll need the rest of the contents of High Seat valued. The police have finished with the place, so I wondered if you'd be able to return tomorrow and carry on? As your work at Vintage Winter allows, obviously.'*

'Of course.' This was perfect. She wanted to see if she could find out how heavily mortgaged High Seat and the other properties were, and whether they'd been worth killing for. But whatever the truth, Bernard's murder must surely relate to Clemmie's, so perhaps money wasn't the issue. Her pent-up frustration was getting the better of her. Clemmie had been such a vulnerable victim; the lack of progress simply wouldn't do. And how in the name of Sweet Agnes did the thefts at the hospice fit in? She didn't know what to prioritise, but at least the mission at High Seat was something she could tick off. 'I'll be there first thing.'

The last thing Bella felt like was getting up early on Friday morning, but as soon as she was properly awake she remembered her mission and forced herself out of bed.

An hour later, she was with John at High Seat. They'd at last moved from the large upstairs sitting room with its many trinkets to a second smaller room along the corridor, but Bella wasn't focused on the contents yet. Gregory was downstairs having breakfast and she wanted to look at Bernard's papers while the going was good.

John was acting as a rather unwilling lookout.

The problem was where to search. Bernard might have something telling in his study, but there was no immediate sign of it. He'd probably opt for a less predictable hiding place. She could only imagine Althea and Gregory's wrath if they found out he'd been borrowing without their knowledge...

Then out of nowhere, a memory came to her. Last week at High Seat, Bernard had flown into a rage about someone snooping in his study. She was sure it had been Rory – she'd smelled his cologne in there. But rather than rifle through the papers on his desk to see if anything was missing, Bernard had marched up the corridor, looking panicky. Might that imply there was nothing important in his study, but something momentous elsewhere? Moments later, from behind the closed door of another room, Bernard had shouted, 'Damn!' Perhaps his worse fears had been confirmed, and someone had breached his defences.

She slipped onto the landing and stood there, trying to remember where he'd gone. It had been the third room on the left, she was pretty sure. As John made agonised faces, Bella quietly turned the handle of the relevant door. It was a box room, full of suitcases and out-of-season clothes. The luggage looked most promising. Bella went to investigate.

Inside an inner compartment of a suitcase that must be at least seventy years old was a wad of papers. It was lucky that Bernard had been the sort to keep hard copies...

And there it all was. Bella skim-read page after page, then sat back on her heels, taking in the enormity of it. Bernard had let things get totally out of control, dealing with multiple companies to remortgage every single property, including High Seat itself. He must surely have lied on the application forms, and even falsified documents, perhaps. All of that to keep subbing Rory and provide for his mythical granddaughter. Bella felt ready to cry with frustration. He could have, should have, put his foot down, but he never had. And Rory and Hester had used him in a way that was hard to forgive. She took photos and forwarded them straight to Barry, pointing out how it might affect the motive for Bernard's murder.

The properties would be worth next to nothing to Gregory, especially when you considered the repair work that needed doing to High Seat before or after any sale. The debts would surely wipe out Bernard's estate. Gregory might not have known about the remortgaging, but she was sure Bernard knew Rory had found out. It would explain the cry of 'damn' from inside this very room. Bernard had told Rory he was having to borrow. That might have triggered Rory's search. It would explain the smell of his cologne in the study.

30

A MOMENTOUS DISCOVERY

John looked intensely relieved when Bella returned to the small sitting room. She told him what she'd found.

'I think Rory knew the properties were all but worthless to him.'

'But he was desperate for his dad to write him back into his will.'

Bella could still see it. 'I believe he'd have done that anyway. I think it's a visceral thing. He'd loathe Gregory getting preferential treatment and be furious at the snub. And as for Hester being named when he wasn't, he'd never take that lying down. He's proud and jealous as well as greedy. Look how angry he was when Clemmie disinherited him, with only two hundred and fifty pounds at stake. If the estate was valued at ten quid, I bet he'd demand his five. And there was a chance we'd find something valuable amongst his dad's possessions too, coupled with the above-market-price offer Sienna Hearst promised for the Steps. He'd panic at the thought he might miss out. But the fact remains, Bernard was killed before he could change the will back.'

John nodded. 'Right. Now, maybe we should do some actual valuing.'

'There's a novel thought.' Bella gave the room a once-over for any high-value items, then started to work systematically through the contents. 'I like these candlesticks, but that clock's nice too.' She nodded at the mid-1800s timepiece with its rich, rosewood case. 'If it's in good condition, it might fetch a few thousand.' Everything would add up.

'I'll have a look.' John stepped round a coffee table and made for the mantelpiece on which it sat.

A second later, he had the clock in his hands and his mouth fell open. 'Bella. Look.'

He opened the glass door in the rear casing and there, just under the pendulum, was Althea's ruby necklace.

Bella's breath caught in her chest as she saw what John had found. Either Rory had hidden it there, or he'd never stolen it in the first place.

The more she thought about it, the more certain she was that the latter explanation was the answer. If he'd really stolen it, she was sure it would be long gone by now, sold to some contact in London or Birmingham. He'd want the money quickly.

She lowered her voice to a whisper. 'Rory must have been set up.'

John nodded slowly.

She closed her eyes for a moment. 'Gregory has to be a top candidate. He was fed up to the back teeth with his dad letting Rory off the hook. And he was livid when Althea refused to involve the police, which he would be, if his carefully planned ruse had come to nothing.'

John was still frowning. 'But why not sell the necklace himself? We know he needs money to pay a blackmailer and he's short of funds in general too. He could easily have smuggled it out of High Seat.'

It was a good point. 'Perhaps he was scared someone would talk if he tried to sell it immediately. It's a very special piece. And if he wanted to fetch anything like what it's worth, he'd want to find the right buyer. It hasn't been that long.'

'True...' John didn't sound convinced, and Bella wasn't entirely either.

She thought back to the Lammas Day feast. 'Well, it can't have been Althea or Bernard, much as I'm sure Althea would have loved to set Rory up. Neither of them left the field. But leaving Gregory aside for now, I didn't keep a constant eye on Paula or Hester.'

'Let's take Paula first,' John said. 'You'd already guessed she wanted to end Rory's influence to save her cottage. If he'd got his way, she'd have had to move back in with Althea and Bernard, at least until she saved enough for a rental deposit – not easy, and especially hard to take if Rory was to blame.'

Bella agreed. In Paula's shoes, she'd have been incandescent.

'Though she didn't show up on the neighbour's camera, I suppose,' John added.

'I wouldn't read too much into that. Anyone the family trusted might have a key to the deadlock as well as the Yale, meaning they could have sneaked round and gone in the front way. That might include Paula or Hester. It all sounds good on paper, but I can't see it being Paula.' She thought back to the shouting match she'd heard between her and Rory. 'She sounded completely convinced Rory was the thief when she challenged him. I don't think anyone could act fury that well.'

John sighed. 'What about Hester, then?'

'As with Paula, I could see her wanting to scupper Rory. In Hester's case, it would be to protect her parents, who live in one of the Powells' rentals too. She might have decided it was worth the risk if she was certain Rory wouldn't guess. I imagine she'd be cautious, though. He was in a position to damage her in revenge, by telling Bernard about their scam.'

'You don't think she did it?'

Bella sighed. 'When she broke down when I visited, I had a sense she'd got everything off her chest. She looked relieved at finally sharing her guilt.'

John frowned and rubbed his forehead and Bella sympathised. It felt as if they were getting nowhere. And how did Clemmie's death relate to the fake theft? Maybe someone suspected Rory had killed her, but couldn't prove it. They might have wanted him sent down for something else instead. Or had these momentous events happened in quick succession by coincidence? Bella couldn't believe it.

'I've got a question,' John said at last. 'Why would anyone hide the rubies inside a clock with a see-through glass back?'

That was an excellent point. 'They wouldn't. Not unless they weren't thinking straight or in a tearing hurry. Let's have a look. Better use a tissue, or Barry will moan about us meddling.' They'd need to let him know what had happened as soon as possible.

Gingerly, John removed the rubies from the clock, then Bella took them, tissue and all, to the window for better light. If Gregory suddenly appeared, she'd slip them under the cushion on the sofa she was standing behind. For a moment, thoughts of the murders and the faked theft fell away. The necklace's beauty was breathtaking, and all she could register. But then she pulled back, shaking her head.

As she switched focus, peering at the necklace for clues to its recent history, the anomaly of the hiding place started to make more sense.

'I don't think whoever took it from Althea put it in the clock to start with.' She showed John the jewels and he took off his glasses to peer at them more closely. 'See. Tiny bits of dirt. It looks like mud. Unless Althea was in the habit of playing rugby in them, then I'd say they got dirty when they were hidden, the night of the feast.'

'So who moved them to the clock, and why?'

A possible answer floated in Bella's head. 'Wait, what if it was Bernard?' As the idea took hold, the implications flooded her mind too. *Sweet Agnes!* She'd take John through it, and see if he came to the same conclusion as her.

'Just think how Bernard would have felt, John.' She pictured him finding the necklace somewhere muddy. The garden, most likely. 'Imagine his guilt. Deep down, I think he thought it *was* Rory who'd taken the rubies. He certainly went along with Althea's demands to cut him out of his will.'

'So he'd have been mortified,' John said.

Bella nodded. 'We know he was as weak as water where Rory was concerned. Rory was furious at being accused and Bernard hated the tension it caused. Then suddenly, he had evidence that Rory was innocent all along. What would he do?'

'Dash out of the house, intending to find Rory and put things right.'

'Exactly. And Gregory told Barry Dixon he saw him leave High Seat at speed. If you were Bernard, would you take the rubies with you?'

John sighed. 'I see what you're getting at. No, not when they were worth half a million. You think he used the clock as a short-term hiding place while he went out?'

Bella nodded. 'He'd have been trying to work out who'd framed Rory, and Gregory would be a top candidate. He wouldn't want to leave them lying around, in case Gregory saw them.'

'Makes sense. So he hid the necklace in the clock, then dashed out.'

'That's my guess. I think we can take it he never reached Rory's cottage. His body was nowhere near there. So what happened?'

John's eyes were bright. 'He bumped into someone and they killed him.'

'And if I'm right that Bernard had just found the rubies?'

'He'd have poured out the news, if it was anyone who knew the background – from guilt, and to set the record straight.' He looked excited now. 'You think that's *why* he was murdered?'

Bella thought it very likely.

A sound made her jump so violently she almost dropped the rubies. A second later, Althea's dog Eustace pottered into the room. 'Sweet Agnes.' Bella slumped on the sofa as the schnauzer came over for a fuss, after which he attempted to bite the necklace. 'Oh no you don't.' Bella lifted the precious jewels out of the way. 'They've been through enough already. What was I saying? Oh yes, I agree. I think Bernard was killed because of his discovery.'

'So who was it, and what made them kill?'

'Let's go through the possibles. If it was Gregory, Bernard might have guessed he'd faked the theft and challenged him. Gregory would have three potential motives for killing Bernard in response: to perpetuate the myth of Rory's guilt, to hide his involvement in faking the theft, and possibly for profit, if he'd planned to sell the necklace.

'When all this started, I wouldn't have said he was the sort. But I can imagine his frustration with Althea, his dad and Rory building to boiling point. And we know he has secrets, which Clemmie had discovered. And Althea and Bernard's killings could both have been impromptu, done in the heat of the moment.'

'But why wouldn't he have moved the necklace somewhere safer, where it definitely wouldn't be found?' John said. 'Even if he only stole it to frame Rory, you'd think he'd have done that.'

He was right.

'And would he go to such terrible lengths to keep Rory looking guilty?' John went on. 'It's not as though the disappearance of the rubies affected him that badly in the end. Bernard was about to write him back into his will, after all.'

'True.' Bella thought furiously. 'Maybe Gregory knew about that, thanks to his job at the solicitors. Then Bernard confronted him about faking the theft and threatened to leave everything to Rory instead.'

'That would be an excellent motive, but I still don't get why Gregory wouldn't have sold the necklace to pay off his blackmailer. Your argument about him delaying to find the right buyer doesn't quite fit.' He looked at her nervously. 'Surely he'd be in a hurry?'

Bella suppressed a sigh. It was a strong argument. 'Let's put Gregory on the back burner for now and consider Paula. If Bernard was killed for blurting out the truth about the rubies, I believe it rules her out.'

John raised a questioning eyebrow.

'The necklace would have come to her anyway, as Althea's heir, so she wouldn't need to kill to get her hands on it. And if she knew she'd inherit after all, I doubt she'd care about Bernard forgiving Rory. She could just take the jewellery and wash her hands of the Powells entirely – rent somewhere else or buy her own place.

'And the more I think about it, the less I can see Hester Harper killing him. It's such a brutal, gory method and I really think she'd got fond of him. But what about Rory?'

John nodded slowly. 'After being blamed for stealing the rubies, he might have decided he was owed.'

'I agree. And I'm sure he'd be heartless enough. He could have banked on Bernard leaving the rubies somewhere obvious.' She visualised him searching and failing to find them. How angry he'd have been. 'And since he probably knew the cottages, the Steps and High Seat are mortgaged to the hilt, he'd be far better off swiping the necklace for a guaranteed half million, than waiting for Bernard to change his will. His fury with his dad could have driven him on too. Rory's definitely back on the list as far as the murders are concerned. I'm still not sure what Clemmie might have had on him, but I can keep digging, and he could have killed Althea in revenge or if she'd discovered he was guilty of the first murder. Then, I'd say Gregory's most likely to have faked the theft. But proving all this is the problem, and if we can't, then we're in trouble.'

John frowned. 'What do you mean?'

'We'll give the rubies to the police, of course, and explain what happened. It might be key to solving Bernard's murder. But once word gets out that Rory was wronged, he might have a good case for challenging Bernard's will. He was only written out of it because of the theft, and he was innocent.'

John's shoulders slumped.

If his challenge was successful, the rental properties would be in danger once again. They might be heavily mortgaged, but the ridiculous offer Sienna Hearst had made on the Steps might still bring a profit.

31

GREGORY'S GAME

Gregory called upstairs to say he was leaving for work, but they should feel free to carry on. Would he be so relaxed if he knew the rubies were there? It was hard to believe. Then again, if he was innocent of murder, but had faked the theft, he might have no idea Bernard had discovered them and taken them from their original, muddy hiding place. It would still be curious that he hadn't moved them somewhere safer earlier though, or sold them to pay his debts.

Bella had to wait with the rubies until the police turned up, but she sent John to open Vintage Winter. Dixon would have to like it or lump it.

He lumped it, muttering about needing to speak to John too. 'Tell me everything again.'

She went through all the facts she had, as well as the thoughts she and John had aired. When she'd finished, she stood up. 'Right, I must go. Can I text Gregory to let him know I've found the necklace?' It felt odd to be doing all this behind his back.

'We'll let him know.' Barry looked grim. 'But I'll tell him we told you not to pass it on – that we wanted to speak to him first.'

That was actually rather thoughtful of him. At least Gregory would know it wasn't her fault. 'Thank you.'

'We spoke to him and Kevin Baker too.'

'That's good news.' He wouldn't tell her the result, but she could get that from Tony. He'd done it, that was the main thing. 'I'd recommend coleslaw, by the way.'

'What?'

'As a way to get your kids to eat cabbage. Failing that, give up and go for broccoli. I found it a lot more successful.' She walked to the door. 'You'll let Paula Richards know about the rubies too? And Rory, I suppose.' Though he didn't deserve to be let off the hook. Bella imagined him striking Bernard. She only hoped Barry was up to finding the truth.

He nodded. 'As soon as we can get to it.'

That could mean anything.

On the way back to Vintage Winter, Bella texted Tony to tell him about John's momentous find and ask for updates on Barry's interviews with Kevin Baker and Gregory. He promised to meet them at the Steps at lunchtime for a conflab.

She arrived back at the shop to find John hadn't yet passed on the news about the necklace to his family.

'It felt unfair to do it without you.' He was dusting the displays.

'Your loyalty is very touching. We should wait until Dixon's caught up with Gregory before we spread it around, anyway.'

When they closed for lunch, they decamped to the Steps for the meeting with Tony. He was there already, seated and digging into his refreshments enthusiastically. Before they'd even said hello, Leo demanded news, so they confided their story as they put in their orders. Bella swore him to secrecy until the relevant people had been told.

'It feels like progress,' Bella said.

'But the thought of Rory contesting the will and pushing to

sell this place is horrendous.' Leo looked gloomy. 'Why is it so hard to bring him down?'

'He's a slippery tyrant.' Bella took her coffee and sausage sandwich from him. 'I'm hoping Dixon will take my arguments about him killing Bernard and trying to get hold of the rubies seriously. I've got an appointment to see Rory's friend, Foxy – Evan Todd – after work now too. He might know something.' It felt like a long shot, but Bella was going for a 'no stone unturned' approach. It wasn't as though she lacked energy or enthusiasm.

Leo looked a little more hopeful as he returned to the counter and Bella and John made for Tony's table.

They went through the discovery of the rubies, then got onto his news.

'Barry's interviews with Gregory Powell and Kevin Baker were inconclusive,' he said, swigging his tea as Captain shifted at his feet. 'They both talked their way out of it.'

'But I sent Barry a photo.'

Tony shook his head. 'Very pixelated, and only showing the top of Gregory's head, preventing a positive ID. Baker said he'd popped in for a swift half and chatted to some bloke he'd never met before. Gregory backed him up. When Barry asked about the envelope which changed hands, Gregory said he'd found it on the floor and thought it might be Baker's. Baker denied all knowledge, though he backed up Gregory's account, when Barry put that to him. He said he'd forgotten about it, because it wasn't his. Claims he left it at the pub.'

'So whatever went on, it must be suspect. Why lie otherwise?'

Tony gave a low chuckle. 'It probably *was* suspect, but even if it wasn't, Baker's not the sort for cosy chats with the old bill. And if he'd got wind of the murder enquiry, he'd distance himself, sharpish.'

That figured.

'But it puts the spotlight on Gregory,' Tony went on. 'What anomalies have you got relating to him? Always worth paying attention to those.'

'The empty envelope he left at the Hanged Man has to count as one,' John said.

'And then the whole meet-up with this Arabella Neville woman.'

'What?' Leo was passing again.

Bella turned to her godfather. 'You can sum that up as well as I can, Tony.'

He nodded. 'Gregory Powell went to some overpriced excuse for a bar in London with terrible beer. Met a wealthy art-dealer heiress who was kidnapped as a child and bought her a two-hundred pound bottle of champagne.' He sounded personally offended. 'Paid her a flattering amount of attention as she talked about snipers on a route through Milan. A moment later, she was pointing out her heavies to Powell and Powell looked nervous. As she drove off, he was staring after her, tapping something into his phone.'

Leo paused a moment longer, open-mouthed, and Bella closed her eyes for a moment. Going through it all just made it more perplexing.

But Tony looked relaxed as he leaned back in his chair. 'What you want to do, is to take your assumptions out of it. Forget every conclusion you've drawn and look at the bare facts. Keep going with the anomalies too.'

Bella remembered her dad saying something similar.

Tony leaned forward. 'I've got one for you. Barry interviewed Kevin Baker, so Baker knows word got out about him and Powell meeting. If Powell had hired him for a job, he'd blame Powell for blabbing. Reckon he'd put the frighteners on him, good and proper. He didn't, so far as we can tell. So what does that tell you?'

Bella ate her sausage sandwich and considered. She found

herself loth to accept the idea that came to her, because it didn't fit with the picture she'd been building. Her dad would have said that was a cardinal sin. *Always keep an open mind.* 'The subject of their meeting can't have been as serious as we thought.'

Tony looked irritatingly pleased and indulgent. Patronising, that was the word. 'I'd say so.'

'Well, why didn't you say so earlier!' Bella hoped he wasn't treating this whole thing as a glorified training exercise for her.

'Didn't think of it,' Tony said mildly. 'I assumed Baker was getting soft in his old age, and that might still be true, but on consideration I'd say your suggestion's more likely.'

She counted to ten. 'Okay, so maybe that means Gregory wasn't trying to order a hit on someone, or even paying Baker to rough someone up. But he was paying him for something.'

'Granted.' Tony slurped the last of his tea. 'I think we should look again at the meeting with Arabella Neville too.'

Bella sighed. 'Yes. The biggest anomaly there is why they'd be talking about snipers and a route through Milan. I can't see how she could possibly be planning anything criminal with him. I don't imagine he'd have the skills, and why go to him anyway, with the entire London underworld on her doorstep?'

Tony nodded. 'Absolutely. Just as we said on the way home. And so?'

'It's not what we think. But there is an overlap with Kevin Baker. Gregory was paying them both, effectively — one with cash, the other with expensive drinks.'

Tony shuddered.

'Him covering his notebook at the solicitors was an anomaly too,' John said suddenly. 'I think he'd keep anything confidential and work-related on his computer, with its privacy screen. But if it wasn't work-related, why risk doing something serious and secret in the office? Surely he could have waited until he got home?'

Tony nodded approvingly. 'Good thought.' Bella wished she'd had it. 'Meaning?'

'Whatever he was up to, it would have looked bad if someone spotted it, but it probably wasn't criminal.'

Bella sighed. 'Can you please not beat me to it, John? You're in danger of losing your employee-of-the-month status.'

He gave a small smile.

'Settle down, children,' Tony said. 'John's observation's spot on, I reckon. So where does that leave us?'

'Wondering if the explanation I lit on isn't the right one.' Bella's mind was working in overdrive. 'Gregory went ahead with his meeting with Arabella Neville in the immediate aftermath of his dad's death, so it must have been important to him. I imagine it took a while to set it up, and it must relate to something he minds about. Or something that's making him anxious.'

At that moment, a woman took a Ruth Rendell up to Bernadette, who ran the new-and-used books section at the Steps, along with a dog-eared copy of *Wolf Hall*. It was that which made Bella click.

'Wait!'

John, Leo and Tony all looked at her.

'I wonder if...' But it was no good unless she could prove it. She got up. 'I need to speak to Gregory Powell.'

32

GREGORY SPILLS THE BEANS

When Bella announced her intention to go and see Gregory, Leo was desperate to come too.

'I'm sorry, but he'll be at work and he might clam up if we both go.' That, or fail to get a word in edgeways. 'You can't really leave Poppy anyway,' Bella whispered. 'She needs you.'

'I'm glad someone does.' He managed to look pathetically woeful.

John went back to open the shop and Tony left for Shrewsbury, but Bella went straight to Butler & Co. She asked to speak to Gregory the moment he was free. He looked deeply uncomfortable and caved when she'd only been in the waiting room for five minutes. He ushered her into a classically decorated meeting room with padded, button-backed chairs.

'What is it?'

'I'm sorry, but being at High Seat, I've seen a lot over the last weeks. I got worried about Clemmie and Althea's deaths and of course about your poor dad's too. I saw you doing a few things I simply couldn't explain, but I understand now. You're writing a book, aren't you?' Bella didn't break eye contact. It was seeing the customer at the Steps, with books of different sizes, that had made her see. Eighty k and a hundred k. Not pounds, she was betting, but words.

She could see from the look in his eye that she'd struck gold.

'Perhaps you've already had one published, under a pseudonym,' she went on, 'but I think you're fairly new at the job.' The request for twenty thousand more words had panicked him. 'In truth, someone told me about your conversation with Clemmie, the day she died. Either she found out, or more likely she simply realised you were getting some extra money from somewhere and managing to save. You were anxious she shouldn't tell. I totally get that. You were finally making something for yourself and you didn't want to sacrifice it to the family coffers. I wouldn't have either.'

Gregory looked at his hands, then up at Bella. 'It's true. It shouldn't even *be* a secret. I should have been able to say no to my father and my own brother. But Rory has this way of making me feel like I've wronged him. And' – he reddened – 'I couldn't bear the idea of everyone thinking how well-off I must be yet refusing to support Rory.' He was worried about appearances, just like his dad. Then again, who wasn't? 'Besides, it hasn't brought in much. Not yet. It's just a sideline. But people always assume writers make millions.'

That might be what had put Gregory onto it. 'I understand.'

'I thought if I could make enough, I could get my own place. Finally move out, like Rory has.' His fists were clenched, knuckles white. 'He told Dad he needed that cottage to entertain business visitors from overseas. He said High Seat was too run-down.' Gregory scoffed. 'Rory has never had any business visitors that I know of.'

Gregory must be so fed up with him. 'Someone I know found an envelope you'd left in the loos at the Hanged Man. What was that all about?'

Gregory went crimson. 'I'm writing a spy thriller. I wanted to know what it would feel like to slip into a place I'd never been before and drop something off somewhere secret. I know it sounds odd, but the Hanged Man always looks intimidating from the outside.' He blushed even deeper, until Bella was worried for his health. 'I knew I'd get that thrill of adrenaline from going inside. It meant I'd be better able to write about it afterwards.'

'Ahh...' That made so much sense and unearthing the truth gave Bella a huge buzz.

'I managed to interview a real-life kidnapping victim too,' Gregory said in a rush.

That had to be Arabella Neville. Bella was glad he'd brought it up. It would be far too awkward to admit she'd followed him to London, and too unbelievable to claim she'd heard it on the grapevine.

'Focusing on that meeting kept me going, to tell you the truth,' Gregory went on. 'It was a relief to talk to someone who didn't know I was bereaved. I could almost shut out reality for an hour.' He slumped in his chair.

In that light, him keeping the London appointment made sense. 'I heard gossip that you met with a man called Kevin "Crusher" Baker too.'

'That's right.' Gregory's hands were twisting. 'I know word got out about that. The police questioned me.'

'Really? Wow.' Bella tried to look innocent.

'I told them it was just a chance encounter. When Baker agreed to talk, I promised I'd never name him, not even in my acknowledgements. And I paid, obviously. I still have to be careful with money, but what I got from him was so authentic. It was an investment.' He bit his lip.

Sneakily writing some of his novel at work fitted far better with the behaviour John had seen than something criminal too. And all that talk about having to review some details and everything being 'an appalling mess'. First-draft woes, perhaps.

'By the way, I'm sorry you ended up hearing about the ruby

necklace from the police rather than me. They insisted I shouldn't call you.'

Gregory nodded. 'I understand. And it's all material for my books. What beats me is, who framed Rory for the theft? Dad and Althea never left the feast, and Paula was as upset and angry with Rory as I was. I'd swear she really thought he'd taken it.'

He sounded just as perplexed as she was.

Bella thanked Gregory for talking to her, then went back to Vintage Winter to fill John in.

John googled 'Arabella Neville' and 'Milan' while Bella served a customer.

When she was free, he looked up at her. 'There was a plot to kill her dad that was foiled in Milan. A sniper was arrested – a disgruntled ex-employee.' He showed her the Google results.

Bella did a facepalm. 'I never thought to combine those search terms. I thought they were talking about something in the future, not the past.'

John nodded. 'So, what's the upshot?'

'Gregory seems very unlikely as the killer now. Clemmie knew his secret, but it was nothing criminal and although he's not rolling in cash, he's got the promise of some ahead of him. Even if Bernard told him he'd found the rubies, I can't see him killing for them, not now we know he wasn't being blackmailed. He's fulfilling his dream with an exciting new career. I think he's out of it. It's Rory who's back in the frame. Just as well I've got this appointment with Evan "Foxy" Todd.'

33

———————

FOXY PLAYS A BLINDER

That evening, after Vintage Winter closed, Bella drove over the border into Herefordshire, through rolling countryside, her car windows down, the sweet-smelling summer air soft on her skin.

She found Evan Todd's bar and restaurant easily and Todd came to meet her the moment she announced herself. He took her to a pleasant terrace overlooking a river, reeds shifting in the slight breeze, and a waiter rushed up to their table as they sat down.

'What about something to drink? Some of our wine?'

Bella gave him a regretful smile. 'I've heard so many good things about it' – she hadn't – 'but I'm driving. Perhaps a mineral water?'

'Of course.' Todd put in the request. 'You wanted to talk to me about Rory Powell, my secretary said?'

He sounded curious but not baffled, thankfully. Bella was right about them knowing each other. She nodded. 'Sorry. She probably mentioned it was a bit sensitive.' She hadn't gone into detail. She didn't know how Todd felt about Rory. She needed him to show his hand before she jumped in. 'You and he are close?'

Todd laughed gently. 'I know him very well, if that's what you mean.'

Bella waited, to keep him on the hook.

'I wouldn't say we were bosom buddies,' he added at last.

'Right.' Bella went into acting mode. She'd once wanted to go on the stage, just like her second to youngest sister, Suki. It was fun exercising her skills. 'Well, that makes it easier. To be honest, I have a friend who's... well, romantically involved with Rory, but the vibes he gives off make me uneasy. I haven't liked to say anything. I might be wrong. But I've occasionally wondered if he's involved in something that's not quite... above board. Someone mentioned you knew him, and I figured I could ask you about him in confidence, rather than wading in and causing offence without good cause.'

Todd was frowning now, leaning forward. 'Is this friend Paula Richards? I met her at a party and I tried to warn her. If she's still seeing him, she must have ignored what I said, so it's possible you're fighting a losing battle. He's full of it, is Rory.'

'I see. And what did you say to Paula, if you don't mind me asking?'

'That he only cares about himself. And that he'll do anything for easy money. I gave her proof.' He took out his phone. 'He came to see me a few months back about a business proposal. It felt too rude to put him off, but I'd never have said yes. He was all about minimum effort and I wasn't sure where he'd get the money to invest. We met at my home, in the garden, and I was sure he'd kick off when I turned him down. I ought to have been suspicious when he didn't. He asked if he could use the bathroom before he drove home.' Todd's eyes were on the river. 'All well and good, but the look he cast over his shoulder as he walked inside put me on my guard. I waited until he was out of sight, then followed him. And look what he was doing.'

Todd put his phone on the table between them, turning it so she could see.

He'd caught Rory holding a beautiful George V cigarette case. 'It's rare,' Todd said. 'Stunning enamel interior. Worth around three thousand pounds, so I'm told, though I inherited it from my grandfather, so there was sentimental value as well.'

Bella could believe it. It was gorgeous.

Todd scrolled to a second photo, where Rory was slipping the case into his trouser pocket.

She gasped, though she shouldn't be surprised. It was just so brazen.

'I know.' Todd met her gaze. 'Unbelievable. I think pinching things is second nature to him. I'd forgotten the case was even in that room. It was probably half hidden somewhere and if it had been gathering dust, I expect he guessed it would be months before anyone noticed it had gone. Canny of him.'

'You decided not to report him?'

Todd looked ashamed. 'I was planning to. I took my photos and let him walk off with the case. It was a sacrifice, but I thought it would be worth it if I could show everyone what he was like. But we *were* at school together.' He shook his head. 'I confided in a mutual friend, and he was shocked that I hadn't stopped Rory, "saved him from himself", as he put it. The truth is, I wanted him to pay. I was furious.'

Bella sipped her water. 'I would have been too.'

He sighed softly. 'That makes me feel a little better. But at the time, I convinced myself I'd acted dishonourably. Wanting revenge isn't pretty. So I never went to the police. I kept the photos, though, which is probably bad, because it fuels my anger.' He took a deep breath. 'I saw his dad had been killed and I wondered for a moment if Rory could have done it – to keep his thieving secret, perhaps, if Bernard had just found out. But in the end, I guessed he probably knew long ago. Rory was so casual about it.'

Bella lowered her voice. She wanted Todd to think she was confessing her worst fears in confidence, not playing detective.

'I wasn't going to say anything. It sounds so far-fetched. But I wondered how far Rory might have gone too. It made me even more scared for my friend. The thing is, I think he had another motive for murder. Might he have killed his dad for something very valuable, which only Bernard knew about?'

Todd's eyes opened wide. 'How valuable are we talking?'

'Half a million.'

He leaned forward. 'Seriously? Up until now, I'd have said he was too lazy and cowardly. He likes easy money. But faced with a prize like that, I'm not so sure.'

Bella thought of Althea. 'What about running someone off the road if he was furious with them?'

He put his drink down with a thud. 'We're talking about Rory's stepmother? I thought that was an accident. Why might he have been involved?'

Bella no longer believed he'd have killed her to ensure he wasn't disinherited. Yes, he'd been desperate to be reinstated in the will, but Bella still put that down to a determination not to lose out in even the smallest way to Gregory. Committing murder over it was another thing entirely. If Rory knew about the remortgaging, the financial benefit wouldn't justify the risk. No, it was white-hot fury that would have driven him.

'Althea had just made Bernard cut Rory out of his will and the family circle, as well as forcing him to give up his girlfriend. She'd humiliated him utterly.'

The shock was still there on Todd's pale face. 'I'm not sure he'd do it, if he ever hoped to re-enter the family fold. Bernard seemed to dote on Althea, on the occasions I met them. Discovering Rory had killed her might be the one thing that would make Bernard banish him forever.'

Bella finished her drink. 'Thank you for sharing your thoughts with me. At some stage, there might be compelling reasons to get Rory convicted as a thief, and not just for my friend's sake. Other people are getting hurt, too. If I can convince you it's a good idea, would you be willing to show the police your photos and explain what happened?'

At last Todd nodded. 'All right. You let me know.'

As Bella drove home, she felt the future of the Steps was a little more secure again. If Rory challenged Bernard's will because he was innocent of stealing the rubies, then Bella could prove he was still a thief, with Todd's help. It might persuade a court to keep Gregory as Bernard's sole heir.

As for the murders, Rory was a top candidate for Bernard's, and Todd's argument against him killing Althea hadn't convinced her. He hadn't heard the hatred in his voice as he'd vowed revenge. And she could easily see him killing Clemmie too – that had been a simple act. He'd never have imagined anyone would find out.

34

———————

A CULPRIT UNMASKED

Bella was back at High Seat before work on Saturday morning, the sun drifting in through the sash windows, dust motes shifting in the warm air. The hours she was taking to do the valuations were mounting up, but keeping her access to the house was invaluable. Besides, Vintage Winter would do well out of it. There was lots to sell, and her percentage would add up nicely.

She'd found a nest of correspondence in a box under a leather-topped Victorian desk – everything from ancient-looking letters, to postcards, dance cards and decorative stationery, dating back to the 1800s. Even that little lot would fetch something, but it wasn't a priority. She could offer to browse through them later, when the real work was over.

She ploughed on, but kept pausing to think about the case. Rory made a convincing killer, but who had faked the theft of the rubies? She couldn't believe it was Gregory. He'd sounded genuinely mystified. And Paula didn't fit either. She'd been convinced Rory was the thief. Althea and Bernard were out of it: they'd never left the feast. She couldn't imagine why Rory would fake it himself. He wouldn't have welcomed the fallout, including being disinherited. Of the key players, that left Hester. She might have wanted to discredit Rory to stop him selling the rental properties, including her parents' place, but somehow it didn't sit right. When Hester had broken down, Bella was convinced she'd made a clean breast of things. But who else was there? Perhaps it had to be her.

Bella was back in Althea's dressing room, going through her chest of drawers. It felt so personal and she had to swallow back emotion. Eustace had joined her, looking lost, as though he still expected his mistress to appear. She bent to make a fuss of him and muttered some soothing words.

A short while later, she found a citrine necklace hidden in a drawerful of scarves. It was very pretty, dating back to the 1870s, and might be worth a thousand or so, if Paula wanted to sell it, though it was a far cry from the rubies.

Eustace was showing far too much interest in it. 'Silly animal. If you want something to chew, you need to find that horrible ball I saw you with.' She gave him a pat. 'Why don't you go and play outside or something?' She stood up to stare out of the sash window at the garden below. There was the lush viburnum hedge, with the Powells' neighbour Sue's old red-brick cottage just beyond. Of course, Sue's place was one of the family rental properties. If she had a spare key to High Seat, she'd have a motive for discrediting Rory. But how likely was it really? How could she have made sure Rory climbed through the window in such an incriminating way? It was still quite possible he'd gone in, hoping to steal the rubies. If he'd over-heard Althea mention them, Bella doubted he'd have been able to resist.

Eustace was jumping up again and Bella put the citrines back in the drawer.

And it was then that she had the thought. It sent goose-bumps rising up her arms. She took off the vintage costume jewellery necklace she was wearing with only the tiniest trace of reluctance. It would survive. A moment later, she tucked it behind the valance of the dressing table, just where Althea had left the ruby necklace, and waited.

Eustace leaped towards the pretty curtain excitedly, nosed his way underneath it and took her necklace in his mouth. He gave her a proud look and dashed off, leaving her to leap up and rush after him.

Down the stairs he went, causing Gregory, who was taking his cereal bowl to the kitchen, to look up in surprise. 'Is everything—'

Bella overtook him as Eustace dashed out of the cat-cum-dog flap she'd seen him use before. 'Excuse me!'

Bella turned the back door key and shot outside. She and Gregory were both hard on Eustace's heels as he dashed towards a compact rhododendron. He went underneath and when he emerged, Bella's necklace was gone.

After that, he dashed to another bush, looked under that one too, then whined.

Bella found her necklace lying beneath a loose mound of earth under the first bush, and wiped it, then went to investigate the second one. She found tiny traces of what looked like a dog treat there, and a square mark in the earth.

'What's going on?' Gregory looked totally confused.

'I know how Rory was framed.' Bella was still reeling. 'Althea did it. She trained Eustace to fetch the jewellery she'd left under her dressing room table and hide it.' She should have realised sooner. Eustace had twice tried to take jewellery from her hand, but she'd thought he was just playing. 'She must have drilled him to bury it under the rhododendron, in return for a reward. The moment he got rid of my necklace, he went to a second bush. You saw?'

Gregory nodded slowly, his eyes wide.

'I'm guessing she put dog treats there – you can still see some crumbs. She probably used one of those timed pet-feeding bowls to dispense them, so he couldn't cheat and take them right away.' He'd probably learned quickly, knowing he'd get something delicious in return for his efforts. 'I think Rory really did climb in through the window, hoping to steal the rubies, but Eustace got there first.'

After Bella had finished hashing the whole thing over with Gregory, she called Barry Dixon. It had to be relevant. It took ages to get him to understand. He kept having to break off to talk to people who wanted his attention.

With that sorted, she returned to Vintage Winter and dragged John to the Blue Boar for lunch. She felt as though she'd earned it and she wanted to explain everything. She had to persuade him to leave his bulgur wheat salad in the fridge for the following day.

They ordered their food at the bar – flatbreads, with hummus and roast vegetables for John and chorizo, rocket and sun-blushed tomatoes for her – then took seats outside.

It was Jeannie who arrived with their food, which wasn't unexpected. She pulled up a chair as Bella related her news.

She was only partway through when she and John began bombarding her with questions.

'How did Eustace get back to High Seat from the neighbour's place?' John's gaze was intent.

'Through the hedge. I noticed it when we left for the Lammas Day feast, but it didn't seem relevant at the time. The rest of Sue's garden is fenced in, but the hedge must be pretty permeable if you're a miniature schnauzer. As we left the house, Althea was muttering about how she hoped Sue remembered to let him out "or there'd be a mess". She said she'd reminded her. But it wasn't a mess she was worried about – it was Eustace managing to fetch the necklace.'

'The timing must have been crucial.' John was cutting up

his flatbread very precisely. 'She'd have known that if Rory took the bait and climbed through the window, he might get the necklace first.'

Bella took a large mouthful of her food, savoured the flavour for a second, then all but swallowed it whole so she could carry on talking. 'It explains why Althea kept him so busy at the feast initially, insisting that he tend the hog roast. She followed him around, giving him jobs.'

'So she did.' John still looked amazed. 'I'd forgotten.'

'What a consummate operator.' Jeannie was trying to sound shocked, but Bella detected admiration and slight jealousy in her tone.

'You said it. I imagine she made sure Rory heard her talk about the rubies and the arrangements with the deadlock before we left the house. She must have guessed he'd organise it so he could still get in. I'll bet he was the one who left the window open a crack.' She kept thinking of the details Althea must have covered and feeling fresh waves of awe. 'She was so clever – showing me the rubies. I was the witness she needed. And she must have predicted I'd suggest she hide them before we left the house. It looked as though she'd left them somewhere random, but in fact, she must have trained Eustace to look behind the valance of the dressing table. I'm sure she left them exactly where she'd planned. Now I think about it, I remember her having to snap her fingers to get Eustace to leave the room. If she hadn't, he'd probably have fetched them immediately.'

'No wonder she didn't want to report it to the police,' John said. 'She knew they'd never find proof. But she still got what she wanted.'

'Quite incredible!' Jeannie's tone hadn't changed. 'Never did I think that the thief might be a dog.'

'Althea still had the rubies of course,' Bella went on, 'ready to pass on to Paula, just as she'd planned. I expect she'd have smuggled them back into the house as soon as she could, but in under twenty-four hours, she was dead.' It explained why they hadn't been moved. It was intensely satisfying to have that mystery solved.

They were silent for a moment.

'All that business about hiring a private investigator must have been for my benefit,' Bella said at last. 'She knew I was finding it hard to believe she'd just leave it.' Her satisfaction was replaced by annoyance at being duped. She needed to up her game.

'So Rory was left to guess whether it was a genuine theft, or if someone had set out to frame him,' John said. 'But I wonder if he decided Althea must be responsible, even if she hadn't removed the rubies herself. It was so convenient for her.'

'I could imagine it,' Bella replied. 'When he thought back, he probably realised it was out of character for her to let him overhear our conversation. She was shrewd. He'd have been absolutely livid.'

35

BAGS AND NAGS

Back at Vintage Winter after lunch, Bella was doing a deal on a beautiful turn-of-the-century hand-coloured lithograph when Hester Harper came in with Phoebe. As the woman who'd bought the picture left, John showed Phoebe around the shop and amused her with some rabbit bookends. Good old John. He was very convincing in the role of universal uncle.

Hester glanced at them, then moved closer to Bella. 'Tom Butler gave me the third degree when I said I wanted to refuse Bernard's bequest.'

Bella could imagine. There weren't many people who'd say no to the proceeds from High Seat House, even if a sizeable chunk of it was mortgaged.

'He pushed and pushed to get me to say why. I have a feeling Bernard confided about Phoebe, so he wanted me to accept the money for her. But in the end, he had to give in. I signed something called a deed of variation to say my share should go to Gregory too. I went to tell him straight afterwards. He wanted to understand the background, but I was too much of a coward to admit the truth. He probably thinks his dad was fixated with me or something.' She buried her face in her hands. 'I might write to him to explain. I don't want him to think Bernard was disloyal to Althea.' She heaved a great sigh. 'I'm afraid Rory could still throw a spanner in the works. Gregory says he's planning to contest the will.'

It was as Bella had feared. She'd need Evan Todd's evidence, then. She'd ring and ask for it, now she knew Rory was planning legal action.

Hester was shedding silent tears. 'It was right to give the money up, but I still feel terrible. I'm rejecting something that would have given Phoebe security. It goes against all my maternal instincts.'

Bella could imagine, but there'd been no way round it, whatever she felt. 'I'm sorry. But you're giving up less than you think. High Seat's mortgaged to the hilt and in need of repair.'

Hester looked worried. 'In that case, I can see Gregory having to sell everything, even if Rory doesn't get Bernard's will overturned. If he can't afford the upkeep, what choice will he have?'

'I'm sure he'll do his utmost to avoid it.' If only his writing career came good. The idea of Sienna taking over the Steps was too awful to bear.

'Tom Butler said I should at least use the tickets Bernard gave me and Phoebe to visit France,' Hester went on, wiping her eyes. 'I'm going to take his advice, though it feels wrong.'

Bella wasn't sure how she could square it with herself. But then they'd only go to waste if she didn't. And Hester hadn't lied for selfish reasons. She'd been worried about Phoebe and her parents. And ironically, her deception had probably given Bernard a great deal of pleasure. It sounded as though he'd doted on Phoebe. 'When are you off to France?'

'The day after tomorrow. The police have given their permission.' She looked at her feet. 'I'll be glad to get away. And then I'll be job hunting.' She sighed. 'Althea hated France, because her dad died there when she was tiny. I hope it's not a bad omen.'

John brought Phoebe back to where Bella and Hester were standing, and Bella escorted them to the door, then waved them off through the front window as they crossed St Giles's Close.

'Barry Dixon must be convinced Hester's innocent,' John said, his eyes on the pair.

'True. It's what I thought too, but something she said is nagging at me. I just can't quite work out what it is… No, wait. I can.'

John blinked at her.

'We've been told that Althea had hated France since she was a child.' She should have written it down. In fact, maybe she had. She checked and felt a surge of satisfaction. 'Here it is: Bernard said her father was killed in a car crash in Paris when she was six and she never went back.'

'So?'

'So why did she deliver Clemmie's worry beads in a bag from a Paris boutique?'

'You remember that?'

'It was stylish and I happen to think style's my thing. But why a bag from Paris, if she never went there when she was old enough to go shopping?'

John was frowning now. 'I don't know. Maybe she just had it in her general bag supply.'

'I don't think so. It was one of those posh, thick paper ones – not the sort you can fold down small, or crush to store.'

'Someone could have given her a present in it then. Or maybe the bag came from Clemmie's place.'

The first idea was possible, but Bella rejected John's second suggestion. 'If someone had asked me to collect something for them, I'd take my own bag, not rely on rootling around someone else's house to find one.'

'Clemmie must have told her where to find the beads. She could have said they were in a bag already.'

'That would fit. But who keeps worry beads in a posh French bag? Would you?'

He gave her a look. 'I don't happen to own any. D'you think it's relevant?'

She could tell he didn't. But Tony had said they should look out for anomalies. 'I can't decide unless I look into it.'

It probably wasn't, but as time wore on, the thought kept coming back to her. The boutique's name had been on the side of the bag, but Bella hadn't written it down. It had been before Clemmie died. La Boutique something... that wasn't very helpful. La Boutique Lagarde? La Boutique Lavergne? Then suddenly, she had it. La Boutique Lafayette.

Moments later, Bella was googling the store as John shook his head and went to help a customer.

The results surprised her. La Boutique Lafayette had closed down in 1971, yet the bag had looked new. It must have sat in a cupboard somewhere, unused for decades. What were the beads doing in such an old bag, and why hadn't Clemmie put them away somewhere? Her cottage was small, and the bag had been a full-sized carrier.

Then Bella remembered Clemmie's panicky reaction when she'd offered to pass her the beads. The weird mix of fear and agitation.

She couldn't think what it meant, but it bothered her, and circled in her mind as customers came and went.

In a quiet moment that afternoon, Bella called Evan Todd and explained that Rory was contesting his father's will.

'If he's reinstated, he'll want to evict a series of tenants to sell the cottages they're living in. I think there's a chance you might stop him if you take your photos to the police.'

There was a long pause. '*Count me in,*' Todd said at last. '*I should have reported him in the first place.*'

It was a huge relief. 'Thank you!' Though she wouldn't rejoice just yet. She couldn't be sure it would affect the lawyers' decision.

A moment later, Gregory called her.

'*I couldn't get my head around Althea framing Rory. I feel so guilty now about yelling at her for not going to the police. She wanted what I wanted: to end his influence. Though the way she went about it...*' She heard him blow out a puff of air. '*I still can't believe it! Anyway, I think you're right, right down to the way she managed to give Eustace a treat for performing to order. When I went searching, I found one of those timed pet-feeder things in the back of a cupboard. I'd never seen it before, so I called the pet shop on Market Street and they remembered selling it to Althea a couple of weeks before she died. I thought you'd like to know.*'

Bella thanked him and rang off. It was good to have some evidence, albeit circumstantial. She wondered if Barry Dixon had taken any notice of her theory. But he probably viewed the whole thing as a private matter.

As Bella left Vintage Winter that evening, thoughts of the day's developments swirled in her head. She extended her walk home to help her think and bought a halloumi kebab from Narin's for supper. Her server wrapped it in plenty of paper so it would stay hot as she took the Cliff Steps to reach Low Town.

Passing cottages clinging to the hillside, the smell of roses high in the air, she gave her mind over to the murders, from Clemmie who'd died anxious and worried, to Bernard who'd been killed with such violence. Her chest felt tight with pent-up energy; she sensed a breakthrough was coming. Various details nagged at her, including the French boutique bag and the worry beads, but when frustration hit, she consoled herself with Evan Todd's evidence. It didn't solve the murders, but it might make a difference to Leo and the other Powell tenants.

She paused, gazing out over the river. Its flow was lazy today, in keeping with the warm evening.

And then suddenly, a memory came back to her. Something important, but amongst the other developments she hadn't grasped it: Evan Todd had shown Paula his photos. He said he'd used them when he'd been warning her off Rory.

She dropped onto a nearby ironwork bench and stared absently at the river. Paula had had proof that he was a thief from that moment on! Yet when she'd broken up with him, she'd claimed she'd only wanted to tag along on his trip to Long Marston racecourse to prove he was stealing. Now Bella reviewed the facts, that made no sense.

Paula had had proof already. Whichever way you looked at it, she'd lied. She could have decided to search for her own evidence, of course, since Evan hadn't gone to the police. But surely she'd have tried to get him to come forward, if that was her plan? He'd been easily persuadable when Bella had made her appeal and Paula knew how badly Rory was behaving. She could have used that to push Evan to act.

It was another anomaly. So where did it leave things?

If Paula had already had evidence that Rory was a thief, she'd probably been tailing him for another reason. But why? She'd wanted to know about the person Rory met, Bella remembered. Whether they were male or female, and what they'd wanted. She'd tried to follow him to see the interaction too, but not to prove he was dishonest, seemingly...

She imagined talking it over with her dad as she got up to continue her walk. He'd tell her to look for connections. Anything she might not have spotted.

As the thought sank in, the hairs on the back of her neck rose. Rory's client was from the horse-racing world. The mother of a trainer with majority shares in the stables he ran. And

Paula had once been a jockey. Another coincidence? But what if it wasn't?

Paula had been booted out of her job at the Mansel Stud after Althea reported her. Althea had known she was risking her safety by taking drugs, so she'd told the management and they'd let her go. To Bella's mind it had been essential. Paula or others could have been killed. But that wouldn't stop Paula regretting it ever since. You only had to look at her on Rufus Hartford's horse to see it was what she was made for. Watching her lack of fear and her oneness with the animal had moved Bella.

She pored over every scrap of information she had. The management at the Mansel Stud appeared to have hushed up the reason for Paula's sacking, so her official record would be intact. She could look to renew her jockey's licence, without fear they'd give her away, because they'd been dishonest too, to protect their reputation. But Bella bet rumours would have gone round. She doubted any trainer would risk requesting her for a race. So how could she persuade them to give her another chance? Finding some leverage might do it...

Perhaps that was it! What if she'd wanted to blackmail Margot Teller, the woman Rory was selling stolen goods to? Margot's behaviour had made it clear she knew she was buying dodgy antiques. And she was mayoress of Long Marston – a pillar of society, with a racehorse-trainer son. Paula could have planned to pressure her into giving her a chance – just one – to show she was back in the game. And she'd probably have proved herself too. Bella was convinced she was clean now.

She paused as a snag struck her. If Paula had never managed to see Margot Teller, how did she know how valuable Rory's contact might be to her?

But then she remembered what Jeannie had said about Rory. 'I suspect him of gambling on the horses too. He's always sneaking over to the racecourse. He even had the nerve to offer my customers tips.' It would only take Paula to spot the same thing, and see him sneaking off with something from High Seat to sell, for her to put two and two together. It would explain her cosying up to Rory. She wanted to know who his contact was. And Rory would have been keen to woo her too, to irk Althea. If Bella was right, it was no wonder Paula had been desperate to find out more.

Then extra thoughts rushed in. Had Paula really been looking at Rory's satnav to see if he'd been on the Brynway the night Althea died, or was she still trying to track down his racing-connected client? Bella had overheard Rory tell her he'd visited them a second time, and on that occasion it had been at home.

After Paula got out of Rory's car, she and Bella had talked about their efforts to prove Rory was dishonest, and Bella had mentioned Bernard claiming he'd given permission for his stolen photo frame to be sold. She remembered how upset Paula had been – unable to speak for a moment. It must have been the first she'd heard of it.

She might have got Margot Teller's address from the satnav, but the blackmail plan was dead in the water. Margot had nothing to fear, thanks to Bernard's cowardly determination not to cross his son.

Bella wandered along the river, wondering if she was right. The blackmail theory certainly fitted with Paula dumping Rory the moment he let slip his dealings with that particular client were over. He was no longer any use to her. And now Bella thought about it, Paula having some kind of plan to re-enter her former profession seemed like a no-brainer. You could see her passion when she was in the saddle. It must have been devastating to have her future snatched away.

If Bella was on the right track, Paula would have altered her plans on realising her blackmail idea was no good.

She'd have been frustrated and disappointed. Angry even.

And Bernard would have been the cause, by protecting Rory. But Bella couldn't see Paula killing him over that, or why she'd kill Clemmie either. Even if Bella's theory was right, she doubted Clemmie would have seen enough to guess about the blackmail, and Paula had never got that far anyway. *No.* It was another bit of puzzle solved, but just round the edge. The centre of the jigsaw was still a jumble of pieces that wouldn't fit together.

36

IT'S ALL ABOUT TIMING

The weather was so balmy that Bella decided to sit on another bench by the river to eat her kebab. The halloumi was sumptuous. Mentally, she switched away from links that drew facts together to anomalies that pushed them wide open. She'd been focused on the French carrier bag, of all things, but as her mind ran over everything she'd learned, it settled on another query.

Originally, she'd decided that it was unlikely that Althea would have framed Rory, even if she'd been able to slip away from the feast, because the timing was odd. If Althea had had the ability to fix Rory like that, why hadn't she done it long ago? It was possible that the idea had only just come to her, but she'd been sharp and inventive, and he'd been bleeding the family dry for years.

Her planning had certainly been recent. Gregory said the pet shop had only sold the timed feeder to Althea a couple of weeks ago. Not long after Clemmie's death, then.

She took her phone from her pocket and looked absently at the photo of Althea, wearing the ruby necklace. The picture looked relatively recent – taken just last year, probably. Although...

A tiny sliver of doubt darted into Bella's mind as she considered the composition. The Christmas decorations. Althea in her smart winter coat. And the candles, on the mantelpiece, but also *decorating the grate*. In the middle of winter.

That wasn't right. She was cold suddenly, despite the evening sun.

She messaged Gregory to ask about the family's habits but his reply only confirmed what she'd been thinking. The fire in that room was lit every day in winter. It was a draughty old house and the extra heat was essential. She got up from the bench for a moment to put her kebab wrapper in the nearest bin, her insides feeling shivery at what she was starting to suspect.

What if that photo hadn't really been taken last Christmas at all? But in a room that Althea had carefully styled to make it look that way? There was only one conclusion to draw: that it was vitally important to Althea that everyone believed she'd owned the necklace back then.

Which could mean, in reality, that she hadn't. The lie and the photo suggested the truth was secret and that didn't look good. No wonder Bernard had said he didn't remember it. Althea had handled it beautifully, sounding irritated, claiming to have worn it on their silver wedding anniversary. She hadn't missed a beat.

Bella had been taken in totally, too. *Very annoying...*

Okay, okay... So Althea had come by the necklace dishonestly. She wouldn't have stolen it just so she could frame Rory, though. It had to be something else. And where would she have got it?

Bella thought of the necklace – not the blurry photo of Althea wearing it but of the real thing John had found inside the clock. An exquisitely beautiful antique French cluster necklace with Burmese rubies.

French.

It made her think of the French bag again. And she felt France had cropped up somewhere else too, if only she could remember. She texted John.

Thinking of the French connection again. French bag, French rubies, tickets to France for Hester but that's probably irrelevant. Any other French links?

John texted back a couple of minutes later.

Probably also irrelevant, but Myra, Clemmie's half-sister and guardian, had a new very wealthy French lover, just before she died. Let me know if you make any headway.

A creeping sensation snaked its way up Bella's back. John had jogged her memory, and she remembered how he'd described the lover when he'd first filled her in on Clemmie's history. A wealthy playboy, who'd showered Myra with gifts.

Had the bag from La Boutique Lafayette come from him? The dates would fit. Myra had died in 1969, when the shop was still operating. Bella couldn't imagine the lover giving Myra worry beads, though. It wouldn't be very romantic. So how had they ended up in there, and what kind of gift had he given Myra instead? A French cluster necklace, with Burmese rubies?

She felt panicky. Everything must be connected, but how and why? And how could she piece it all together?

New thoughts emerged. Why had Althea left the bag on Clemmie's locker, out of reach? Because she hadn't wanted her to look inside? And why had Clemmie looked so frightened when Bella had offered to pass it to her? Because she hadn't wanted Bella to see inside either?

If so, if so... then it looked as though Althea hadn't wanted Clemmie to know the bag contained worry beads. Perhaps Clemmie had thought the bag contained something else and

Althea had made a switch. The ruby necklace? If so, Clemmie hadn't wanted Bella to see it.

And Clemmie had been expecting a visit from Adam Davies, CID's latest recruit. Bella went hot and cold all over. What if Clemmie hadn't been intending to report someone at all? What if she'd wanted to make a confession, because the ruby necklace wasn't rightfully hers, either?

From what everyone said, there was no way Myra would have left something so valuable to her.

But then her musings made a fresh leap. Clemmie couldn't have stolen the necklace when Myra was alive. Her half-sister would have noticed and all hell would have let loose. Yet taking it in the immediate aftermath of her death didn't fit either. Her childminder's kids said she hadn't left her room for days. *Oh, Sweet Agnes.* But Althea could have taken it for her. She'd been such a champion of the underdog. John had called her Hope Eaton's answer to Robin Hood, stealing from the rich to give to the poor... Althea had seen Clemmie suffer at Myra's hands – she knew how unhappy she'd been. She probably hated Myra for it – felt that Clemmie was owed. Bella remembered Althea's words when she'd visited her shortly after Clemmie's death. 'It was so unjust. Myra had done nothing to earn her fortune.' Bella was starting to believe she'd decided to do something about it, as soon as she'd heard Myra was dead.

She thought back to the phone call she'd overheard between Clemmie and Althea, the morning of Clemmie's death. Before Althea had known she was listening, she'd said: 'My dear Clemmie! I wish I'd never persuaded you to have it. It's only ever made you feel awful.' When she'd noticed Bella, she'd claimed she'd been talking about Clemmie's tonic – how it hadn't been agreeing with her. But that looked like an excuse now. Bella was willing to bet she'd been referring to the necklace.

It fitted with the note from Clemmie that Bella had found amongst Althea's memorabilia too. It had been dated 30

December 1969 – immediately after Myra died. *What you've given me is far too much. I feel terrible accepting it but you're a true friend.*

It would make total sense if Althea had stolen the necklace for her. Clemmie might never have known how much it was worth, but Bella bet the theft had made her deeply uneasy. It looked as though she'd kept it in the same bag all those years, never thinking of selling it. Too guilty to even look at it, perhaps. Bella wasn't surprised she hadn't told anyone, though, or insisted Althea take it back. That would have been too much responsibility. She'd only been fourteen, and in a state of shock. She'd just let it sit there, a weight on her conscience.

Until the end drew near, at least. At that point, Bella guessed she'd decided she needed to let someone know she had it. Because it should have gone to the Powells, of course, along with the rest of Myra's belongings. Bella was convinced it was personal guilt that Clemmie had felt. She'd hung on to the thing for decades. She was certain she'd never have told Adam Davies that it was Althea who'd stolen it. It would have been wholly out of character, and she'd admired Althea. Her words about her friend, the day she died, were confirmation if it were needed. 'She was brave when I was weak, daring when I toed the line. She's been willing to risk everything for me, even when I wished she wouldn't.'

But even if Clemmie had kept Althea out of it, Bella imagined there was proof Clemmie couldn't have stolen the necklace. By the time she'd left her childminder's house, Myra's place would have been in the hands of her executors, and out of her reach. If Bella had worked that out, others could too. And if Bella was right, the fallout would be unthinkable from Althea's point of view. Any influence she'd had over her husband and the family would be smashed to smithereens when she was revealed as a thief who'd done them out of a valuable necklace. She'd no longer be able to keep a roof over

Paula's head, or protect the other tenants, including Leo and Carys.

But there'd been a way out for Althea, if she chose to take it. It was all so unthinkable, but Bella made herself think it.

She guessed Althea had fetched the rubies from Clemmie's house, taken them to the hospice, then given Clemmie a doctored drink. She'd probably introduced the idea of trying a new tonic on the back of the excuse she'd made to Bella, to avoid any awkward questions. Paula had known about the suggestion after all. But Bella guessed Clemmie had trusted Althea implicitly anyway. It made the situation even more achingly sad.

Then at some point, when Clemmie had nodded off or wasn't looking, she must have put the bag out of her reach and swapped the rubies for the worry beads. Clemmie had panicked when Bella offered to pass the bag over. She'd been determined to confess, but she was probably also ashamed. She'd have wanted to tell the story privately to Adam Davies, not to Bella and John. And while their visit took place, Althea must have been sabotaging Adam's bike tyres.

It had involved planning and calculation, yet Bella was sure Althea's affection for Clemmie had been genuine. Perhaps she'd told herself she was saving her friend from the drawn-out pain of dying. She'd said it was like having her heart ripped out, each time she went to see Clemmie. But the time of her passing should never have been Althea's decision.

Bella imagined she'd been consumed with guilt afterwards. She'd protected herself, by committing murder, but instinct told Bella that hadn't been her motive. She guessed it had been to protect the Powell tenants by maintaining her influence in the family. She probably hadn't known the necklace would be valuable enough to make a real difference, if the Powells finally got it. She'd have assumed debts, repairs and Rory's 'living costs' would have swallowed the proceeds. Which meant only she could protect the tenants, long term.

Bella didn't want it to be true, but it all fitted; Althea had bought the timed pet feeder just after Clemmie's death.

Bella got up to head home. She needed proof. She could ask Gregory if there was any mention of Myra's French lover amongst her papers. It was a long shot, but if they could contact him, he might remember giving Myra the necklace.

In the meantime, there was more work to do. If Bella was right, and Althea had decided she must kill her beloved friend, then who had killed Althea and Bernard?

37

A HORRIBLE THOUGHT

Bella was approaching Southwell Hall and her flat, and barely two seconds into her musings, when she realised the conclusions she'd drawn changed everything. She'd decided Paula must be innocent of Bernard's murder. It wasn't a problem for her if news of the rediscovered necklace came out, and she had no reason to try to steal it. It would come to her anyway.

Except it wouldn't have, of course. Not if anyone worked out the rubies had belonged to Myra and should have gone to the Powells.

And that was a definite danger. Paula would have known the level of gossip the necklace's discovery would create. Several townsfolk were convinced that Rory had stolen it; realising he'd been framed would set every tongue in Hope Eaton wagging. The rubies would be the centre of attention. The police might want to examine them, and perhaps Bernard would realise he really didn't remember them. Eventually, someone would follow the trail, just as Bella had, and work out the truth.

As Bella unlocked the door to Southwell Hall, she didn't like the thoughts she was having. Allowing Bernard to spread the news might have lost Paula her inheritance. And money equalled power.

If Bella was right, Paula's plans to blackmail her way back into racing had fallen flat, but what could she have done with half a million pounds? Renewed her jockey's licence? Bought a racehorse and hired a trainer? Got back into the game? She googled and found an owner-rider who'd done well in the Grand National, riding as an amateur. Paula wouldn't have to find someone who'd pay her to ride. She could prove herself independently, and if she managed it, surely offers of work would follow. Trainers and owners would see she was a winner, not a risk.

She might have fantasised about using the proceeds from the rubies, if only Rory hadn't stolen them. Bella imagined her bumping into Bernard and hearing that they'd been found. He'd be sure to tell her. She'd been Rory's girlfriend, so he'd want to set the record straight.

His grovelling outburst and the news that Rory would be forgiven all over again would have angered her. And at the same time, she'd have seen her chance. She could use the necklace after all! But only if it came to her, and if she knew it was stolen, she'd have realised her opportunity to reboot her career was hanging by a thread.

And Bella bet Paula had known. She'd spent a lot of time with her aunt. She must surely have been suspicious, if she'd never clapped eyes on the rubies. And then, just after Althea died, Bella had given her that photo of Althea wearing the necklace. Paula would have looked at it with a critical eye, wondering about the truth. And she'd know they had fires at High Seat in winter. The fake photo would have confirmed her suspicions, if she'd been in any doubt.

Bella could imagine her killing Bernard, set on taking the necklace with no one any the wiser. Her determination would have been spurred on by fury at his leniency with Rory.

But she hadn't found the rubies.

Perhaps Bernard had told her he'd discovered the necklace under a bush in the garden and she'd struck him before he'd got any further. She'd have sneaked in to look, then been filled with despair.

As she stood there in the foyer of the hall, Bella's thoughts turned to Althea. She'd been Paula's aunt, a stand-in mum, but because Althea had minded about Paula desperately, she'd felt she had to put paid to her career to keep her safe. Paula would probably have been angry, even if that was unreasonable. And just before Althea's death, it would have seemed to Paula that her aunt had robbed her of her blackmail opportunity, scuppering her career all over again. By demanding Rory stop seeing her, she'd prevented Paula from going on his next visit to Margot Teller. Paula had probably been furious. She'd cleaned up her act, yet Althea still hadn't trusted her to make her own decisions.

Absently, Bella picked up her post from her pigeonhole. Paula must have been especially angry at Althea's heavy-handedness, because in reality, she hadn't been taken in by Rory at all.

Suddenly, Paula's words came to her. 'Althea ruins everything for me. I push doors open and she shuts each one in my face.'

Bella could see it now: her driving over the Brynway to have it out with Althea at that private view she was attending. Perhaps she'd thought Althea would be more likely to give in and lift the relationship ban if she threatened to make a public scene. Bella guessed she'd been desperate to pursue the blackmail plot.

But Althea left the private view early. Paula could have met her on the road and driven at her in a sudden fit of pure, unthinking anger. She'd have been sleep deprived, just like everyone else, and primed to act irrationally. Another person might have met the onslaught by steering towards Paula and crashing into her, to avoid sliding into the ravine. But, despite what Paula might have thought, Althea had loved her deeply. Bella guessed her overriding instinct would have been to protect her. She'd veered away to avoid the collision and plummeted to her death.

It fitted with Paula's devastation afterwards.

Bella turned the key in her own front door. It was terrible, but the more she thought about it, the better it fitted. If Althea had come face to face with Rory in the road, surely she'd have put up more of a fight – risked a collision rather than a probably fatal descent into the valley?

Bella shut her front door. The worst of it was, she had no way of proving any of it, and she didn't see how she ever could. If only—

But she was pulled from her thoughts as she walked from her hall into her sitting room. Every day she'd been coming home and rushing around the flat to open the windows. It was so stifling and stuffy at the moment. But today it was different. Even with the front door closed, there was movement in the air.

38

DEEP TROUBLE

Bella froze. The windows in the sitting room were closed, but there must be one open somewhere. Hairs rose on the back of her neck. She'd never have forgotten to close one herself. She'd collected antiques over the years – nothing very valuable, but a thief might not know that, and they meant everything to her. She was careful about security.

She made for the nearest sitting-room window. If she'd had burglars, they might still be inside. Her immediate thought was to call the police, but she needed to get out first, and that route avoided re-crossing the hall. It was a lot closer than her front door.

But as she fiddled with the catch, a voice came from behind her.

'I'm damned if I'll let you go!'

Bella jerked her head round to see Paula standing close, the poker from the fireplace clutched tight in her hand. Her eyes were frightening. Full of fury and hatred.

She swung the weapon and Bella ducked to one side. She'd only missed her by half an inch, and now Bella was further from the window.

'What are you doing?' Bella looked around desperately for something to use to protect herself.

'Getting rid of you while I still can. I was with Gregory when you messaged about the fires at High Seat in winter. I knew it must be Althea's fake photo which had triggered the question. If you haven't worked out the truth already, you very soon will. Why the hell couldn't you leave things be?' She struck out again and Bella's mouth went dry as she dived behind the sofa.

Bella needed to think fast but her mind was blank with fear. Paula had rational reasons for wanting her dead, but she was clearly out of control too. Driven by rage and disappointment. Bella was a sitting duck on which to take her revenge.

'Paula, wait! Wait! You might lose the rubies, but no one can prove you killed Althea and Bernard. You get a second chance.'

'You think?' Paula spat the words at her. 'I've been fighting to overcome the position Althea put me in ever since she got me sacked. When I finally got close, she put another roadblock in my way.' Tears streamed down her face. 'I loved her, but I hated her too. She saw things in black and white, never doubting she was right. I didn't mean to kill her – I just lost control. But from then on, I knew there was no going back. You didn't have to interfere. Your death's on you.'

She was creeping around the sofa, poker in hand, and Bella backed away once more. 'You're wrong. You're responsible. And by killing me, you'll ensure you get done for murder.'

Paula shook her head. 'I'll take your antiques with me. They might not be enough to buy myself back into the racing world, but they'll convince the police this was a burglary gone wrong.'

Bella could see her getting away with it. This was horrific. She couldn't get hold of anything to use against her. Once, in extremis, she'd used her shoes, but she was wearing flat pumps today, not stilettos.

But then Bella spotted something so common in her life that she almost laughed. It was a possible lifeline. She took off one of her flats and hurled it, not at Paula, but at the teal armchair behind her.

There was a tremendous yowl, and Matt's cat Cuthbert shot across the room.

Paula jumped and turned suddenly towards the noise, knocking Bella's treasured 1960s floor lamp to the floor.

It landed near Bella's feet and she pulled and lifted it just in time for the flex to trip Paula up. She was on her knees now, but still holding the poker.

Bella rushed behind her and seized her by the ankles before she could get to her feet. Yet still she didn't drop the weapon. Bella's grip was loosening fast as Paula flailed.

And then there was a knock at the door. When Bella shouted for help, the knocking got louder.

For heaven's sake! 'I can't let you in!' Bella had to let go of one of Paula's ankles so she could grip the other with both hands. Paula was kicking and turning, trying to swipe Bella with the poker. 'There's a window open. Climb in!' She was yelling. Surely the person at the door could hear her?

Bella was just doubting she could hold on any longer, when Robert Mead appeared in the room, carrying his large umbrella. He always took one with him, even when it was obviously set fair. She found it slightly annoying.

He was pointing at Paula's flailing form, as though he could shoot her with it or cast a spell. Bella felt a surge of hysteria. 'What about hitting her with it?'

He looked horrified and gave Paula the merest tap, but in a second, Bella had seized it from him and landed a blow on the hand that held the poker. At last, she dropped it.

Robert picked it up gingerly and waved it in Paula's general direction as Bella called the police.

39

JUST DESERTS

After Paula had been arrested and removed from Bella's beloved flat, Barry Dixon arrived. He looked at the destruction, closed his eyes for a moment and took a deep breath. 'I suppose you know why Paula Richards attacked you?'

Bella nodded. 'I can't prove any of it, though. It'll be my word against hers.'

He groaned. 'Right. You'd better tell me everything.'

When Bella had finished explaining, Barry looked slightly shell-shocked.

'If you're right, why wouldn't Clemmie Crowe have spoken up sooner about the rubies? It was a long time to keep all that guilt to herself.'

'When Althea gave them to her, she was only fourteen. Too young to work out how to handle the situation, I'd guess, and too overwhelmed after her half-sister's death. I can imagine years going by before she looked at the situation with adult eyes, and by then it must have seemed too late. The secret had grown in enormity. I suspect she tried to close her mind to what had happened, until she knew she was terminally ill. She obviously never wanted the necklace – she could have sold it and had a comfortable life.' It seemed tragic, really, that something Myra had perhaps taken for granted could have been so life-altering for poor Clemmie.

Dixon looked disgruntled. 'Althea Powell could have confessed too. If the Powells had got the necklace sooner, their finances would have been a lot more secure.'

Bella sighed. Barry could be very unrealistic sometimes. 'I doubt either Althea or Clemmie realised how very valuable the necklace was. Althea might have imagined it was worth twenty or thirty thousand, say, not five hundred. Enough to make keeping quiet about it an unforgivably hurtful crime in her husband's eyes, but not enough to really help. Bernard could have frittered away any amount of cash subbing Rory and Althea knew that. I think she guessed any benefit from the necklace would be short-lived, whereas keeping her influence would protect the Powell tenants. It made hiding what she'd done essential. After she'd taken the terrible step of killing poor Clemmie, perhaps she thought she must make the act count by using the ruby necklace to banish Rory too. She might have imagined Clemmie approving. She'd cut him out of her will, after all. Because of the way he got her to relinquish her rights to her cottage, I imagine.' Bella was deeply disappointed that Rory wasn't the killer.

'Of course,' Dixon said, 'Myra Powell could have given the necklace to Clemmie Crowe before she died. Then Clemmie could have passed it on to Althea, to frame Rory.'

Why wouldn't he just give up? Was it all the paperwork involved? 'I can find several people who'll swear Myra would never have given Clemmie that kind of gift. As for Clemmie giving it to Althea to plot Rory's downfall, I'm afraid she was far too ill to come up with that sort of plan. And besides, why was she so frightened when I offered to move the boutique bag if she knew it only contained worry beads? And why had she asked

Adam Davies to visit?' She could tell Dixon was tiring. He'd admit defeat eventually.

'Or Althea Powell could have stolen the necklace back then, without ever giving it to Clemmie Crowe. There's no firm evidence she did.'

Bella counted to ten. 'True, but that also doesn't fit with Clemmie's fear when I offered to move the bag. And if Althea had had it all that time, why fake a Christmas photo of her wearing it? I'm sure there'll be supporting evidence out there. I hope Gregory can find the French lover's contact details.'

'All right,' he said at last. 'We'll examine that photo and see what else we can find. Meantime, we're checking the necklace for dog saliva and analysing the mud you found on it.' He tapped his phone to dismiss a notification.

'This'll make a difference to the accusations against Daisy Birdwell, I hope,' Bella said. They'd all be pleased about that.

Dixon sighed. 'Probably. If it all checks out. Shame we haven't identified the hospice thief.'

Bella regretted that too. She would put it on her to-do list.

Once Bella had given her version of events to the police, and Robert Mead had added his, they sat awkwardly in her kitchen as scene-of-crime officers bustled about.

Bella still couldn't believe she'd forgotten she was due to see Robert that night. She dimly remembered dismissing the reminder she'd set earlier in the day, when her mind was on the case. It was so awkward. He sat there looking ruffled and crumpled.

'Promise me you'll never get involved in anything like this again,' he said at last.

She had to take a deep breath before replying. His request annoyed her on principle. Robert wasn't her keeper. And if she got the chance to solve another crime, she had no intention of turning it down. She secretly felt her dad and Tony were right: she would have made a decent copper. And she enjoyed detecting. The roller-coaster ride followed by success was as addictive as making a sale. She looked at Robert. 'I'm sorry. This – us – it's not really working, is it?'

For just a second, Robert looked sad, but then he blinked and relief seemed to take over. Rather insulting really, though it did make things simpler. 'No,' he said at last. 'Maybe we should just be friends.'

She'd liked him very much before they'd started going out. 'That sounds perfect.'

It was three days later that Bella met John, Tony, Jeannie, Leo and Carys in the Blue Boar for an update. She'd already told them the basics, of course, in the immediate aftermath of her run-in with Paula.

Jeannie had sat there making a noise like a turkey, goggling over what Bella reckoned Althea had done. But it had been Leo who'd been most upset. 'Poor, poor Clemmie,' he'd said, looking aghast. 'Althea killed her to save us all. Including us, so we could keep the Steps going.'

'You can't feel any responsibility,' Bella had told him. 'It was Althea's decision alone. And she was fighting to keep a roof over the head of her own niece too, don't forget.'

Carys had put a hand on Leo's shoulder and said that Bella had a point.

Bella had gathered on the grapevine that Rory had been advised not to contest his father's will. The police had proof he was a thief now, and a decent lawyer would probably argue that he'd climbed into High Seat with the intention of taking the necklace, even though Eustace had got there first. And if his case failed, it could all prove very expensive. Instead, he was waiting to be tried for theft and the threat from him was over.

Everyone was patting everyone else on the back as they took seats in the Blue Room.

'Nice work, team,' Tony said. His gaze came to rest on Bella and she couldn't help feeling pleased, even if he was patronising.

She gave him an eye-roll all the same. 'What news, Tony?'

'All positive. Gregory Powell came up trumps with a contact for Myra's lover. Pierre somebody.' He frowned as he tried and failed to find the right place in his notes. 'I seem to remember his details were in an old address book of Myra's. Number didn't work any more, as you'd expect, but Adam Davies traced him to an old folks' home just outside Paris. Mind's still clear as a bell, and he remembers giving Myra the necklace. I think he'd assumed it went to Clemmie when she died. Either way, he never raised it with anyone, so no one would have realised it was missing. There's no proof that Althea stole it for Clemmie, but the cops have searched High Seat as well as Clemmie's place and found some evidence to back up your theory.' He turned the pages of his notebook again. 'A note from Clemmie to Althea: *I know you meant well, but I can't help wishing you hadn't taken it. I feel so guilty.* Undated, but a handwriting expert reckons it was written around the same time as the thank-you note you found, Bella.'

Jeannie was shaking her head. 'What a sad state of affairs.'

'There's more,' Tony said, after a tactful pause. 'The police went through Clemmie Crowe's personal effects again, with your theory in mind, Bella. There was a note from Althea saying: *Stop fretting, you were owed,* dated the January after Myra's fatal accident. They verified the purchase of the timed pet feeder too, just after Clemmie's death.'

Bella nodded. 'That must be when Althea hatched the plan and started training Eustace to play fetch.'

Tony sat back in his seat. 'Beyond that, Gregory Powell managed to find a photo of Althea and Bernard's silver wedding celebrations, and she wasn't wearing the necklace, so she lied about that. He says he has no memory of it. And they've found the jpeg file for the photo of Althea supposedly taken at Christmas. It was created the same day Althea bought the timed pet feeder.'

Jeannie sighed.

'Most importantly,' Tony went on, 'they discovered traces of the right brand of sleeping tablets in the bottom of Althea's handbag. Reckon some must have got transferred after she crushed them. So, although Althea's dead, and the evidence is piecemeal, the police have dropped the case against Daisy Birdwell. She's still got this slight cloud hanging over her because of the hospice thefts, but it's a job well done. And Gregory Powell will get the rubies. They ought to cover some of his debt, at least.' He reached to pat Bella on the arm.

She felt just like Captain. She wondered if Tony would offer her a dog treat next. 'Gregory's told me he's going to sell High Seat but he's got no intention of letting the rental properties go. I've updated Sienna.' She'd asked if John would like to come with her, but he'd declined. He was far too noble. Bella was still enjoying the memory of the sour fury on her face. She wished she'd taken a photo. 'What about Paula Richards, Tony?'

'She's finally talking. I told Barry she probably would if he pressed the right buttons, after what you said. He went on about how saintly and caring Althea had been, until Paula finally cracked and said she'd ruined her life. She started off raging, but then broke down and said how much she missed her.'

A complicated mix of anger, family ties and guilt. It was the impression Bella had got too.

'Once she'd cracked over Althea,' Tony went on, 'she confessed to Bernard's murder too. Said she'd acted in an instant and how could it make things any worse when she'd already killed her own aunt?'

It was so awful: depressing, sad and shocking. 'I'm glad she's not going to fight it, at least.' Paula had been charged with attempted assault after breaking into her flat too.

Bella was distracted by Jeannie, who was looking through one of the Blue Room's internal windows. Her face had softened and she was beaming.

They all looked round and saw Matt striding towards the snug, looking relaxed in his black jeans and T-shirt.

Carys lowered her voice and whispered to Bella: 'I haven't seen him in here for years. Not since his fiancée ran off. Jeannie kept trying to fix him up with people, so he made himself scarce.'

Jeannie had rushed to the snug door, and pulled Matt into an embrace. Despite what Carys had said, he didn't pull away but put an arm round his mother and gave her a squeeze. Bella could see how fond he was of her really, even if he did avoid her counselling sessions.

He came in and perched on the end of one of the sofas as Jeannie retook her seat. 'I just bumped into Fred from Fox Hollow Farm and he had a bit of gossip you might be interested in. His mother-in-law works at the hospice, and they've solved the mystery of the thefts.'

They all leaned forward.

'It was Gilbert Rowntree's grandson.'

'What? Seriously?' Bella pictured the small boy, focused on his trainset. But then she remembered his *Bluey* rucksack, which Gilbert said he took everywhere. And the way he'd kept putting things into it – from a train to a bit of shortbread.

Matt grinned at her. 'Yup. Gilbert often takes him to the hospice, because he cheers the residents up.'

Of course. He'd told Bella *that* too.

'Fred says Gilbert found his grandson sitting in his bedroom, gazing at himself in the powder-compact mirror, then waving it around to catch the light.'

'Good heavens!' said Jeannie.

But of course, it made perfect sense. Thieves stole desirable things, but the triggers for that desire could be many and varied. A small child *would* home in on something shiny and reflective.

'The rest of the missing items were stuffed under his bed at home,' Matt went on. 'I gather Gilbert's quite embarrassed.'

'I'll bet. It'll be one bit of tittle-tattle he won't want spread.' Perhaps being on the receiving end would make him think twice about gossiping again. Though it was probably unlikely.

'Poppy's sister will be relieved,' said Leo. 'And perhaps normal Poppy service will be resumed. Not that that's anything to write home about.'

'The hospice has given Daisy a restaurant voucher and some paid leave,' Matt said. 'Fred thinks she'll stay on, despite the upset. Oh, and Bella, let me know when you want to cook me dinner.'

Bella rallied her mental resources. 'What?'

'I assumed you'd want to say thank you after my cat saved your life.'

'Seriously?'

Matt just laughed and went on his way.

No, of course not seriously.

That evening at home, Bella ignored the thought of Matt next door and put her feet up on her velvet sofa, sinking into the blissfully comfy cushions. She'd got an iced drink beside her, the glass running with condensation, and the box of postcards, letters and dance cards from High Seat next to it. Nothing in the box would be worth much, but she loved delving into the past. There'd been an element of self-interest when she'd offered to look, now all her other valuations for Gregory were complete.

She avoided touching her glass before picking through the box's contents. She didn't want to get the papers damp. But half an hour later, she put the whole lot down, sat up straight, and caught her breath. And then she took a large swig of her drink.

She couldn't believe it. In fact, she wouldn't. It wasn't feasible. But then she put her glass down again, dried her hands, and re-examined the ancient letter she'd found halfway down the box.

On its envelope was a Penny Red stamp. That was nothing unusual. Of the many millions issued between the 1840s and 1870s, hundreds of thousands had survived. But still, the stamp sent the hairs on Bella's neck rising. Because she was sure this was a Plate 77 Red Penny. A single sheet of 240 stamps had been printed before someone realised the plate was faulty. It was thought that 9 of those 240 stamps had survived, including one said to have been lost in the 1906 San Francisco earthquake. But here, inexplicably, was one of those very rare stamps. Collectors went wild for them.

Bella paced her living room in the dying sun. *Sweet Agnes!* All that time she'd spent at High Seat looking for something to save the Powells' bacon, the stamp had been sitting there, modest and unnoticed. Someone like Rory would never have seen its value, but different things mattered to different people. It was one of the things about antiques that Bella loved most.

Within the hour, she'd called an expert friend to verify her conclusion. And after that she rang Gregory. A very rare £650,000 stamp to add to his nest egg. After everything that had gone on, imagining his face as she delivered the news was the greatest pleasure of all.

A LETTER FROM CLARE

Thank you so much for reading *The Antique Store Detective and the Deadly Inheritance*. I do hope you had fun sorting the clues from the red herrings! If you'd like to keep up to date with all my latest releases, you can sign up at the following link. Your email address will never be shared, and you can unsubscribe at any time. You'll also receive an exclusive short story, 'Mystery at Monty's Teashop'. I hope you enjoy it!

www.bookouture.com/clare-chase

The idea for *The Antique Store Detective and the Deadly Inheritance* came to me after reading an article about a priceless ruby necklace. I liked the idea of incorporating something similar in a Bella mystery, so I started thinking of unusual ways to do it.

If you have time, I'd love it if you were able to write a review of *The Antique Store Detective and the Deadly Inheritance*. Feedback is really valuable, and it also makes a huge difference in helping new readers discover my books. Alternatively, if you'd like to connect with me direct, you can find me on Facebook, Bluesky, Instagram or via my website. It's always great to hear from readers.

Again, thank you so much for spending some time reading *The Antique Store Detective and the Deadly Inheritance*. I'm looking forward to sharing my next book with you very soon.

With all best wishes,

Clare x

www.clarechase.com

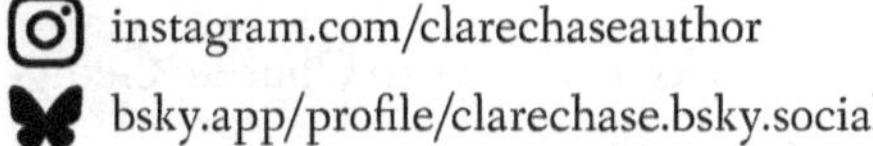

facebook.com/ClareChaseAuthor
instagram.com/clarechaseauthor
bsky.app/profile/clarechase.bsky.social

ACKNOWLEDGMENTS

Much love and thanks as always to Charlie, George and Ros for the feedback and cheerleading!

And as ever, I'm grateful beyond measure to my fantastic editor Ruth Tross for her wonderful insight, clever ideas and support.

I'm also indebted to the entire Bookouture team who work on my novels. You can see what a fantastic group effort it is by looking at the following page, where everyone involved is mentioned by name. They are the most wonderful, skilled and friendly group of professionals and it's an honour to work with both them and Ruth.

Love and thanks also to Mum and Dad, Phil and Jenny, David and Pat, Warty, Andrea, Jen, the Westfield gang, Margaret, Shelly, Mark, my Andrewes relations and a whole bunch of family and friends.

Thanks also to the lovely Bookouture authors and other writers for their friendship and support. And a truly heartfelt thank you to the generous book bloggers and reviewers who pass on their thoughts about my work, including some who have been with me right from the start. Their support is wonderful and it's also a joy when newcomers join in.

And finally, but crucially, thanks to you, the reader, for buying or borrowing this book!

PUBLISHING TEAM

Turning a manuscript into a book requires the efforts of many people. The publishing team at Bookouture would like to acknowledge everyone who contributed to this publication.

Audio
Alba Proko
Melissa Tran
Sinead O'Connor

Commercial
Lauren Morrissette
Hannah Richmond
Imogen Allport

Cover design
Debbie Clement

Data and analysis
Mark Alder
Mohamed Bussuri

Editorial
Ruth Tross
Sinead O'Connor

Copyeditor
Fraser Crichton

Proofreader
Liz Hatherell

Marketing
Alex Crow
Melanie Price
Occy Carr
Cíara Rosney
Martyna Młynarska

Operations and distribution
Marina Valles
Stephanie Straub
Joe Morris

Production
Hannah Snetsinger
Mandy Kullar
Ria Clare
Nadia Michael

Publicity
Kim Nash
Noelle Holten
Jess Readett
Sarah Hardy

Rights and contracts
Peta Nightingale
Richard King
Saidah Graham

Dear Reader,

We'd love your attention for one more page to tell you about the crisis in children's reading, and what we can all do.

Studies have shown that reading for fun is the **single biggest predictor of a child's future success** – more than family circumstance, parents' educational background or income. It improves academic results, mental health, wealth, communication skills, and ambition.

The number of children reading for fun is in rapid decline. Young people have a lot of competition for their time, and a worryingly high number do not have a single book at home.

Our business works extensively with schools, libraries and literacy charities, but here are some ways we can all raise more readers:

- Reading to children for just 10 minutes a day makes a difference
- Don't give up if children aren't regular readers – there will be books for them!

- Visit bookshops and libraries to get recommendations
- Encourage them to listen to audiobooks
- Support school libraries
- Give books as gifts

Thank you for reading: there's a lot more information about how to encourage children to read on our website.

www.JoinRaisingReaders.com